THIS THING CALLED LOVE

DEBBIE HOWELLS

B

Boldwood

First published in Great Britain in 2025 by Boldwood Books Ltd.

Copyright © Debbie Howells, 2025

Cover Design by Alexandra Allden

Cover Images: Shutterstock

A CIP catalogue record for this book is available from the British Library.

Paperback ISBN 978-1-80415-051-1

Large Print ISBN 978-1-80415-052-8

Hardback ISBN 978-1-80415-050-4

Ebook ISBN 978-1-80415-053-5

Kindle ISBN 978-1-80415-054-2

Audio CD ISBN 978-1-80415-045-0

MP3 CD ISBN 978-1-80415-046-7

Digital audio download ISBN 978-1-80415-049-8

This book is printed on certified sustainable paper. Boldwood Books is dedicated to putting sustainability at the heart of our business. For more information please visit https://www.boldwoodbooks.com/about-us/sustainability/

Boldwood Books Ltd, 23 Bowerdean Street, London, SW6 3TN

www.boldwoodbooks.com

In memory of my parents.
Forever in our hearts.

DEAR UNIVERSE

I hope you don't mind me writing to you but I don't know what else to do. You see, I don't believe in God. If he existed, he wouldn't have let my mum die.

The reason I'm writing is my dad. These days, it's just him and me. And don't tell him I said this, but he's miserable. All the freaking time. He misses my mum. And I think he's lonely.

My dad never used to be like this when my mum was around. He played his guitar and painted the house. He used to laugh, too. But then she died and it all stopped.

My mum was really special. She made everyone else feel special, too. I miss her every day. Augusta says it's good I think about her. Augusta's our neighbour. She lives in a tiny house and keeps goats and chickens. She's sad, too, but she says we have to think about the future, which is why I'm writing to you.

Please... Do you think you could find my dad a girlfriend? She'll have to be really patient. And she'd have to like him a whole lot because he isn't very tidy. But if it worked out, maybe he'd be happy again. And maybe in time, I could have a sister.

I know it's a big ask. But life's supposed to be about being happy, isn't it?

Thank you in advance.

Mackenzie Friday (aged 9 years and 2 months)

P.S. If a girlfriend is too much to ask, I think the next best thing would be a piano.

1

BEE

It's a beautiful autumn morning, the sun rising above a fine layer of mist, the leaves vibrant shades of copper and gold. It doesn't get much better, I tell myself as I arrive at work. Living in this corner of England, the flat in Brighton I share with my friend Saskia; this thing I'm having with Phil that's not too serious, which suits me fine. It's as it should be, I tell myself. I mean I'm young. Life's about fun, having a good time.

Having parked, I get out and survey the view towards the English Channel. The mist has settled in the valleys, the hilltops like little islands bathed in early morning sunlight. Feeling the chill in the air, I pull my jacket around me. It's new, from Zara, with a nipped-in waist in a rich shade of plum – not that anyone around here will notice. They're too busy thinking about trees.

But that's what I love about this place. Going into the office, I wave a hand towards Cindy. 'Morning,' I call out to her. In dungarees and a faded sweatshirt, she's worked here as an arborist for ten years and knows everyone and everything in this place.

As I knew it wouldn't, my jacket doesn't receive so much as a passing glance. 'Morning, Bee. Come and see me when you get a moment.' She looks happy. But we all are here, in this beautiful oasis on the edge of the South Downs, employed in jobs we love.

It sounds too good to be true – especially when I'd always had the vaguest sense of not fitting in anywhere in life – until I started working here at the arboretum as a receptionist. At least, that's my official title. As well as being the face our visitors see, I'm also in charge of press releases; and I liaise with the media about publicity, which we rely on because – as we're all too aware – funds are limited.

I never imagined somewhere devoted to researching and nurturing rare trees would be the most satisfying way to spend my working life. But I love it here, among the eclectic crowd of scientists and horticulturalists, even if they don't appreciate my fashion sense.

After checking my emails, I leave my desk for five minutes and go to the arboretum's coffee shop to pick up an Americano. While I'm waiting for it, my phone buzzes with a notification about a dress I've ordered online that's due to be delivered, just in time for a party this weekend.

I click on it to take another look. It's loose fitting yet body-skimming, in black. Expensive, but hopefully worth it. Imagining Phil's approving glance, I pick up my coffee, still looking at my phone as I head towards the door, and collide with someone.

'Shit.' I look down at my jacket, now splattered with coffee. 'Bollocks.' I look up at the guy I barged into, who I assume is a visitor. Taller than me, with brown hair, he's wearing jeans and a well-worn jacket.

'I'm so sorry.' He looks mortified. 'Your jacket... Can I help you clean it up?'

'Don't worry.' I shake my head. 'It was my fault.' I'd been too busy staring at my phone. And now, my lovely new jacket's ruined.

'Can I at least buy you another coffee?' he says.

Our eyes meet for a moment. They're kind eyes, I realise, holding his gaze. Brown, with dark lashes. 'Thanks.' I tear myself away. 'I'm supposed to be at work. I should go.' Gathering myself together, I head for the staffroom to clean myself up, filled with regret that it has to be now that I bump into a good-looking stranger. Just as I finish mopping my jacket, Phil comes in. Forgetting about the guy, my heart skips a beat. Phil's an Aussie, studying for his master's in arboriculture. Tall and dark, he's drop dead gorgeous – did I mention that? I should probably also say that he and I have been having a bit of a thing since he arrived six months ago.

'Hi.' I go over to him. 'I've had a great start to the day. Some guy just spilled coffee on my jacket.' I reach up to kiss him.

But when he doesn't kiss me back, I know instantly something bad is going to happen.

* * *

'He's broken it off with me,' I sob to Cindy. In the solitude of one of the poly tunnels, I let out feelings I didn't know I had. 'His dad needs him back in Sydney – something to do with the family business.'

'Oh, Bee,' she says sympathetically. 'That's really tough.' She pauses. 'But he was never going to stay, was he?'

'I know,' I say tearfully. 'I'm really going to miss him, though.' But as I speak, I've no idea where the words are coming from.

She looks surprised. 'I had no idea you were so emotionally involved.'

I blink away my tears, frowning. 'Nor had I.' Phil's stay here was always going to be time limited. But the thought of him leaving triggers a surge of sadness inside me. 'I have to get on,' I say miserably. The arboretum depends on people knowing about us, meaning social media is key, another responsibility that has come to rest on me.

I love my work, but after Phil's bombshell, today, my heart isn't in it. I start with LinkedIn, then as I try to focus on posting the carefully curated photos I've taken with suitably captivating wording, I'm thinking of what Cindy said. She's right. Until Phil told me he was leaving, I hadn't felt emotionally invested in our relationship – not beyond the most casual level, that is. It's only now that he's going that out of nowhere, overwhelming emotion has hit me.

But if that isn't enough, as I go about my day, things are about to get a whole lot worse, when just before lunch, I'm summoned into my boss's, Geneva's, office.

To my mind, her office is just about the perfect space. There are rough wooden shelves on which an array of unusual plants are arranged; botanical pictures gracing the exposed stone walls, while a large window looks out across the grounds towards the South Downs.

'Have a seat, Bee,' Geneva says gently. Her shoulder-length hair is hooked behind her ears and she's wearing perfectly fitting jeans and an immaculate white blouse, accessorised somewhat incongruously by her glasses hung around her neck on what looks like a piece of string.

'Sure.' Smoothing my jeans – also new, from Mango this time – I sit down. 'Is there a problem?'

'I suppose there is.' She sighs. 'There's no point me dressing this up. We've all noticed that there have been fewer visitors this year. But it isn't just that. The corporate days are fifty per cent down on previous years, ditto school visits. It means our funds have taken a substantial hit.' She pauses. 'You must know how much it hurts me to say this, Bee. But I'm going to have to let you go.'

I gasp in shock, suddenly numb. Then my mind goes into overdrive as a million thoughts race through my head. 'Please, Geneva. We can do something about this. I'll come up with something. I'll work for nothing,' I beg, desperation taking over me.

'Oh, Bee...' She shakes her head. Then, as she looks at me, her eyes are troubled. 'The problem is, it isn't just that.'

I gaze at her, puzzled. 'What do you mean?'

'It's your social media posts. Look, I know how passionate you are – about trees and the environment, but...' She hesitates. 'Let's just say there's been a bit of a backlash. In fact, more than a bit.' She goes on, explaining to me that one of our main benefactors has taken offence at a rant I put out, quite obviously directed at the petroleum industry. 'You do know he's the CEO of an energy giant?'

I gasp again. 'I had no idea. But it shouldn't matter, Geneva. I haven't posted anything that isn't true. All I've done is write about the importance of preserving forests and woodlands.' OK, so there was this one post where I got carried away, but it was about deforestation in the Amazon, for frick's sake. It matters, on a global scale. 'If people don't like it, that's their problem. It's obvious, isn't it?' I pause, looking at her. 'He's only giving us money to make himself look good. We both know he doesn't care.'

Her eyes meet mine. 'Outside this office, I'd agree with you. But I have to think about the survival of the arboretum. Bee...' she hesitates '...getting angry and ranting at people just doesn't get them onside. We need to engage them, so that we can educate them. If they're dismissing us as activists...'

'Activists?' I blink at her. 'Is that what they think we are?'

'That was the word that was used. They were going to withdraw their funding. I've managed to talk him out of it... But as he pointed out, this isn't the first time it's happened. Now...' she pauses '...I just can't risk it happening again. You do understand, don't you?'

As the reality sinks in, it's like the breath has been knocked out of me. Sitting there, I stare at her. Then I turn my gaze to the window, taking in the rolling grounds of the arboretum. I've given heart and soul to my work here. But the fact is I've screwed up. More than that, I'm dispensable. And just like that, the three glorious years I've spent here are over for me.

As it slowly sinks in what this means, I make it through the rest of the day – just about. The only person I tell is Cindy.

She stares at me, a look of shock on her face. 'That's so unfair. You write from the heart. We need you, Bee.'

Which goes some way to making me feel the tiniest fraction better, but in reality, changes nothing.

On my way out, Phil catches me.

'No hard feelings, right?' He grins at me.

I look at him, for a brief second wondering what he's talking about. 'I've had a terrible day, Phil.'

He looks confused. 'Hey. We were fun, but it was never serious between us.'

'This isn't just about you.' My voice wavers. 'I've lost my job.'

'Wow. That sucks,' he says. 'How about we go for a drink tonight? Make the most of the time I have?'

'Didn't you hear me? I've lost my job, Phil.' Unwanted tears fill my eyes.

'Yeah, but you'll get another one. You need cheering up,' he says brightly. 'Let's hit Brighton for a last night out – my flight doesn't leave until Sunday.'

I shake my head, suddenly realising, Phil has zero sensitivity to how I'm feeling.

He goes on. 'What do you say?'

'There's no point.' I'm not interested in going out, just for a laugh, and getting drunk with him. But more than that, Phil leaving is no longer of earth-shattering significance to me. 'I just want to be alone, OK?'

'You don't mean that,' he says, not getting the message.

'Go away, Phil,' I say, blinking away tears.

'Really?' He looks astonished.

I stare at him for a moment. He clearly has no idea how terrible this is; that my entire life is literally crumbling around me. Feeling my temper flare again, I turn to face him. 'Don't you understand?' I say tearfully. 'You're going back to Sydney. And I need to sort my life out.'

He gets the message after that, leaving me to walk out to my car alone. After getting in, I drive away from the arboretum, more tears starting to fall, as it hits me it's one of the last few times I'll ever do this.

I don't go straight home. After everything that's happened, I don't want to speak to anyone I know. I need time for it to sink in. So I drive into Brighton, doing battle with the rush hour traffic, until eventually reaching the seafront, I find somewhere to park.

It's high tide when I reach the beach; quiet, apart from a few kite surfers and dog walkers. I walk along the shingle, listening to the sound of the waves breaking as I go over the events of the day, trying to make sense of why everything has to happen all at once.

In the end, I reach the only conclusion I can: that I was right when I said my job was too good to be true. Naive to believe that it would last; that the arboretum was where I would spend the rest of my working days, when only one thing is certain in life – and that's change.

Tears fill my eyes as I think of Phil. Tears that are unexpected, because if I'm brutally honest with myself, our relationship was purely physical; the emotions I feel are disproportionate. But I've never been good at dealing with loss.

Sitting on the shingle, I gaze out across the English Channel and give myself a pep talk. I have my home, I tell myself – well, the flat Saskia owns that I rent a room in. With two months' money, and this year's leave to take, I have time.

It's getting dark by the time I get back to the flat. No closer to finding a solution, I'm still mulling it over as I let myself in. It's quiet, from which I assume that Saskia's already gone out. Standing there for a moment, I take in the generous-sized rooms, the large sash windows, the huge comfy sofa and the contemporary artwork Saskia loves, not at all sure how much longer I'll be able to afford to stay here.

It's a problem to which the solution currently evades me, as I change into running clothes. Running is the answer to most things, I find. Sure enough, as I pound along the streets for forty minutes, my worries fade and my positivity is back. OK, so it's sad, but it's hardly the end of the world. People lose their jobs all the time. I have enough money to pay the rent. I just need to get my shit together and get over this.

Meanwhile, I'll have more time to run. And to go to my favourite place in Brighton – the Lanes. Until I started seeing Phil, I used to go there most weekends, wandering the narrow streets in search of retro clothes or accessories. Things I won't be able to afford any more, I remind myself.

It occurs to me that maybe I should try to find a job there. For a moment, I imagine myself styling shopfronts, or working in a funky café, or doing social media for someone. I'm not fussy – there has to be something there for me.

Reaching the tree at the end of our road, I slow to a walk. The tree marks the end of my route; it's a rare and beautiful elm. I've learned a little about trees since I started working at the arboretum. For example, I know how calming they are and, stopping, I lean my back against it, almost immediately feeling my mind quieten.

Even so, I'm hot, my face still red by the time I get back to the flat. After showering and changing into slouchy, super-comfy jogging bottoms and a cropped top, I'm in the kitchen putting the kettle on when I hear the door click open, then closed, before Saskia appears.

'Hey! I wasn't expecting to see you. I thought you'd be out with Phil.'

I shrug. 'Turns out Phil has other plans.'

Studying me, she frowns slightly. 'Are you OK?'

'Not really.' As the euphoria of running wears off, the reality is back and my shoulders slump. 'Would you like some tea?'

She ignores my question. 'What's happened?'

I gaze at her for a moment. Her hair is newly coloured and I recognise her clothes from a recent revamp of her wardrobe. She looks bright, cool, in charge of her life; an impression I try to emulate, albeit in slightly more subtle colours. But there's no way of covering up what's happened today. 'Phil dumped me,' I mutter.

'No shit.' Her eyes widen. 'Why? What did he say?'

'He has to go back to Sydney,' I say miserably. 'Something to do with his dad's business, he said.'

'I'm sorry,' Saskia says sympathetically. 'But you two were never serious, right?'

'It doesn't stop me feeling rubbish.' My bottom lip wobbles. 'But it isn't just that.' I hesitate. 'I've also lost my job.'

'Fuck.' Saskia stares at me.

'The arboretum is cost-cutting.' A wave of misery sweeps over me, the lie tripping off my tongue. 'Plus one of our investors apparently doesn't like my approach to social media.'

'Shit.' Saskia frowns. 'What exactly don't they like?'

'I suppose I get a bit carried away sometimes.' As I speak, I can't meet her eyes. 'Recently I posted about the destruction of the Amazon rainforest. I did it because I care, and because social media is the only way I can reach people.' I pause. 'It just so happens the investor works for an energy giant.'

Getting out her phone, Saskia brings up Instagram and finds the arboretum's profile. Scrolling down the posts, she frowns. 'I can't see anything wrong with your posts.'

'They've probably taken it down. Geneva gets it,' I say quickly, defensively. 'But she needs her investors. She can't risk losing him. We have fewer visitors these days. I suppose I'm a victim of the times – things haven't got back to normal since Covid struck.' The 'we' is automatic; from my first day there, I've always felt a part of the place.

But far from being sympathetic, Saskia is no-nonsense about it. 'What will you do?'

I shrug. 'Get another job. I need to work out my notice – I have a couple of months to find something else. Don't worry. I can still afford the rent.' At least, for now.

She looks as though she's about to say something, but thinks better of it. 'You need something stronger than tea.' Going to one of the cupboards, she gets out her bottle of Grey Goose vodka. After fiddling around for a few minutes, she produces two Bloody Marys.

'Screw Phil,' she says. 'It'll be OK, Bee. Maybe it will lead you to something better. Things have the strangest way of working out. But...' She hesitates. 'When it comes to social media, I know you mean well, but have you thought you maybe need to rein it in a bit? Not everyone wants a lecture.' Pausing, she chinks her glass against mine. 'Anyway, here's to your next chapter. May it be the best one yet.' But there's a lack of conviction in her voice, in the way her eyes don't meet mine.

'Thank you,' I say gratefully. 'For being such a good friend.' I take a gulp of the Bloody Mary, for some reason thinking of the guy I collided with earlier.

'I mean it,' she says, still not meeting my eyes. 'You'll be OK.'

Half an hour later, she shoots out again to meet her boyfriend Jaspar, promising to be home early and telling me to help myself to her vodka. It's times like this, you find out who your friends are, I tell myself, as I make another Bloody Mary, simultaneously scrolling through social media and settling in to watch a movie.

You also find out who they're not, as I'm about to discover the following morning. When I go into the kitchen, Saskia is sitting there.

'Bee?' She hesitates. 'I need to tell you something.'

Under the pretext of saying she needs her spare room back because her mum's coming to stay, Saskia effectively renders me homeless. And it might sound melodramatic, but that's how it feels. For the rest of the day, I refuse to speak to her.

'I'm sorry the timing is bad,' Saskia says. 'I was planning to tell you yesterday – but after the day you'd had, it didn't seem right.'

But as I gaze at her, she doesn't look sorry at all. 'Do you really think anything's changed since yesterday?' I shake my head at her, dumbfounded. 'I've lost my job and my boyfriend. And now you're telling me I have to move out.'

'Phil wasn't really your boyfriend,' she says. 'You were just shagging. And honestly, I really am sorry about your job, but you have to admit, you didn't do yourself any favours. Can't you move back to your mum's for a bit? You might enjoy being in London.' She hesitates. 'I have to think about me, too, Bee. I can't put my life on hold just because yours is going through a tough phase.'

I stare at her in disbelief. 'You can't be serious.' I wrap my arms around myself. 'What am I going to do?' It's as though the entire world is set against me. 'If it was me watching your life fall apart around you, I like to think I'd try and support you. I wouldn't do something like this.' I shake my head, numb. 'Friends are supposed to be there for each other. Aren't they?'

She opens her mouth, but before she can get a word in, I go on. 'Please, Saskia. Don't. There's no point.' Suddenly I realise what this is about. 'Why can't you just be straight with me? This has nothing to do with your mum. You want Jaspar to move in – and three's a crowd.' Jaspar's her boyfriend of all of about twenty-four hours. I pause. 'That's what this is really about, isn't it?'

Her eyes grow very round. 'How did you know that?'

'It didn't take much working out.' I shake my head. 'Don't worry. As soon as I find somewhere, I'll be out of here.'

* * *

After Phil flies back to Australia, three painful weeks follow as I work out my notice at the arboretum. My last day comes too soon and I walk around the grounds, take a few moments with some of my favourite trees before one of the happiest eras of my life comes to what feels like an erroneous and premature end.

As I walk out that last time, my heart is heavy; any hope I had that a miracle would happen, gone for good as I drive away.

It seems there are no bespoke jobs waiting for me in the Lanes, so I fill out numerous job applications I don't even get a reply to, enquire after flats I haven't a hope of getting because at this rate, come the end of the month, I'm not going to have an income. Meanwhile, the realisation is creeping up on me that I have only one option left. My most unwanted one.

'I suppose you could have one of the spare rooms,' my mother says a little reluctantly. 'Just for the short term. I mean, the house isn't very big. We wouldn't want to get on top of each other.' Even though she's my mother and her house is a three-bedroomed semi with a sizeable garden in which she has her home office, where she works as a legal secretary. Even though her daughter is potentially homeless.

'Thank you.' I force myself to sound grateful, still hoping I won't have to take her up on it.

'Hopefully you'll find a job soon.' My mother sounds less than optimistic.

At home, I go out of my way to avoid Saskia, aware that the day is fast looming when I'll have to move out. Between extra-long runs, I drink too much tea; hiding out in my bedroom, ruthlessly sort through my possessions, packing what little remains.

Nice one, Bee. Just look at your life. Jobless. Boyfriend-less. About to move home to live with your mother. And don't go asking yourself why. You're a failure, a small voice whispers to me. *Face it. Things like this don't happen to people like Saskia. You're the only person you can blame for this.*

2

ALEX

My life is in many ways a very ordinary one. Home is a terraced house in Brighton on a quiet street, with a narrow garden at the back. I work online: outside, under the shelter of an ancient apple tree when the weather allows me to. Otherwise, in the small room with a curtain instead of a door, which I call my den.

I live here with my mother – by choice. Though not for reasons you might imagine. You see, before, I used to live in London – a very different kind of ordinary life, albeit one more fitting to a twenty-something single guy, where I went on occasional dates; frequented galleries and museums, classical music concerts and the occasional rock gig.

Now, however, my outings amount to the occasional visit to an arboretum in the heart of the Downs, as much people-watching as immersing myself in the sense of visiting a whole other world. Working as a climate researcher, I want to learn more about trees. But what I'm not expecting is how they make me feel.

It's a little known fact about me that I'm a tree-hugger – a truth I like to keep to myself. On this particular morning, I don't have long – a window of a couple of hours while my mother's having her hair done.

Walking among the trees, a rare sense of peace filters into me – until I head for the coffee shop. As I step inside, I collide with someone.

'Shit.' There's a look of despair on her face as she stares at her jacket. 'Bollocks.'

I stand there, utterly mortified, taking in her long fair hair, her pale jeans; the phone she's holding. 'I'm so sorry,' I say. 'Your jacket... Can I help you clean it up?'

She shakes her head. 'It was my fault.'

Which is true enough. But something in me wants to keep her here. 'Can I at least buy you another coffee?' I say. Our eyes meet for a moment; hers are blue, fringed with long lashes.

'Thanks. But I have to go,' she says. Then turning, she hurries away.

I'll admit I'm disappointed. But maybe I'll see her again, I ponder, during one of those rare and entirely unpredictable hours I get to myself. Because these days, my life revolves around caring for my mother.

Before I moved back here, I'd already been noticing slight changes in my mother's behaviour. At first, I told myself they were more obvious because I saw her less often; put them down to her getting older. But as time went on, I couldn't deny my suspicion that it was about more than that.

My mother is in her late fifties. Not old, by any stretch. But it became clear life was getting more challenging for her. There were the middle-of-the-night phone calls when she couldn't find her phone. That's right. The same one she was calling me from. The lack of groceries in the cupboard, the odd combinations of clothes she started wearing. The times she locked herself out, laughing it off until a neighbour called me to ask for a spare key – it was happening more often than my mother was letting on.

With a sinking heart, I acknowledged that for whatever reason, there was clearly a trend – one she denied. But a few months ago, I did the only thing I could; packed up my London flat and moved home. I had no idea what lay ahead. Nor had I counted on her resistance to the idea, because of course, she continued to deny there was anything to worry about. Even now, she tells people, 'Alex is only here until he finds a new place to live.'

After the lengthy GP appointments I've accompanied her to, she also refuses to talk about her test results. Meanwhile, things aren't getting any easier. Once or twice she's asked where my father is, which would be fine if my father hadn't died six years ago, an event that dramatically altered both our lives and the upshot of which is that now, she relies on me.

Since moving back here, it's been a learning curve; an exponential one. When you find yourself looking after someone who can't take care of themselves, you learn to expect the unexpected. Who am I to tell the woman who raised me that it probably isn't best to put ketchup on her ice cream – or because her hands are shaky, it isn't safe for her to make a cup of tea? In her mind, both are completely normal – and it isn't my place to tell her otherwise.

* * *

Driving away from the arboretum, I head into Brighton to collect my mother from her hairdresser's. She looks glam, her eyes bright, her hair newly highlighted and coiffed.

'You look lovely,' I say. 'Ready to go?'

Looking at her, you wouldn't imagine anything had changed. But when we get home, despite my many attempts to persuade her it isn't a good idea, she insists on making a cup of tea.

'We've run out of tea bags, Mum.' Hoping she doesn't check, I steer her away from the kettle. 'Let's have orange juice. Why don't you pour us both a glass?'

I still have my work as a climate change researcher, though these days my hours are less. But my overheads are considerably reduced, meaning I dedicate much of my day to my mother. It amounts to walks on sunny days to the park nearby, or sometimes as far as the coast. Trips to garden centres for the garishly coloured plants that have replaced the subtle palette she used to fill the garden with. Outings for lunches that she moans about.

Out of the corner of my eye, I watch my mother go upstairs. It's one of our realities that, more and more, I need to watch her – hopefully without undermining what independence she has. I also try not to look too far ahead; to live in the eternal moment as my mother increasingly does. But now and then, I can't help thinking about what this means for my life. I mean, now that I'm back here, I can't imagine not being here. Maybe this is my destiny, I've thought more than once. To be single; my mother's carer for the rest of her days.

I don't begrudge it. On the whole, my outlook tends to be a philosophical one. I also have a theory that sometimes the Universe puts people our way, while generally, I like to think there's a reason for the way things work out – or not, which makes me think of the girl I spilled coffee over this morning, my ears pricking up as I hear my mother come down the stairs. Instead of strong and steady as they used to be, these days, her footsteps are lighter, irregular. I go out to the hallway. 'You OK, Mum?'

She frowns at me. 'Of course I am. I wish you'd stop asking.'

She's changed into pale pink trousers and faded ballet pumps, her outfit topped by one of my well-worn hoodies and an old beanie hat my father used to wear, the same red lipstick she's always worn less than perfectly applied. 'Are you ready?'

I look at her, nonplussed. 'For what?'

'You said we were going for a walk this afternoon,' she says impatiently. 'Are we, or aren't we?'

I've no recollection of mentioning a walk. But exercise is good for her – and me. 'I'll just get a fleece.' I pull on my trainers, then hurry upstairs and grab the fleece from my chair. In a hurry, yes, because I can't count on my mother remembering either what we're about to do, or that she shouldn't go out without me.

Sure enough, I reach the bottom of the stairs just as she clicks the front door open and steps outside. Catching her up and taking her arm in one seamless motion, I simultaneously close the door behind us.

In my experience, October can go either way. But it's a really lovely day, the early morning mist long gone and the sun is warm, the blue sky scattered with fair-weather clouds.

My mother gazes around. 'We should go to the beach. You love the beach, don't you, Alex?'

'I agree.' I place one of my hands over hers. 'But it's quite a long walk. Sure you're warm enough?'

'Of course I am. Stop fussing.' But she says it half-heartedly.

The walk usually takes about half an hour – that's without stopping to talk to the random dogs and cats along the way, or to admire a late season rose in full bloom in one of the gardens we pass. I have to hand it to my mother. She knows how to appreciate the simple things in life.

Eventually we cross the road onto the beach. The tide is

midway, the grey-blue sea fading towards the horizon until it's impossible to tell where the water ends, the sky begins.

'It's a good thing you're a strong swimmer. You used to scare the life out of me,' she says out of the blue. 'Diving under the water... You used to hold your breath for such a long time. Once or twice, I thought you'd disappeared.'

I feel a pang of something. It's increasingly rare that we remember things the same way. 'I was always trying to beat my own record.' I remember the blood pounding in my ears, my lungs almost bursting as I pushed myself and counted three more seconds. How surfacing, I'd gasp for air. As my mother carries on talking, her words go over my head. Instead, I'm frowning. Staring at the girl sitting on the shingle. The girl from the arboretum. The one I spilled coffee over – so what's she doing here?

But then I realise it isn't so odd. The arboretum isn't that far away. She probably lives around here.

'You're not listening to a word I say,' my mother says crossly. Then she follows my gaze. 'Who's that?'

For a moment, I entertain the ludicrous idea of going over to her. Assuring her I have no coffee to spill over her – and to ask her if she's OK, because from where I'm standing, I'd say she's anything other than that. I watch her wipe her eyes, then replace her sunglasses.

'You should go and talk to her,' my mother whispers none too quietly. 'It's about time you had a girlfriend.'

'It looks to me like she'd rather be alone,' I say quietly. 'No offence, but you really should mind your own business, Mum.'

'Rubbish,' she says, adding in a moment of lucidity, 'I've learned not to let things pass me by, that's all.'

'That may be,' I say quickly. 'But I'm not you.' Sensing her disagreement, I grip her arm firmly as we carry on walking, steering her away from the girl – these days, I'd put nothing past my mother. Nevertheless, I can't help but glance back, just for long enough to see the look of despair on her face.

I find myself pulled towards her. But I don't know her. And it's a fact of life that we all have ups and downs to deal with. If I were her, I wouldn't want some random almost stranger who spilled coffee on me stopping to ask me what was wrong.

My thoughts are interrupted as my mother stumbles, then clutches at my arm.

'Are you OK, Mum?' But as the colour visibly leaches from her face, it's clear she isn't.

'It's my ankle. This dammed shingle.'

'I'll help you up to the road and we'll get a taxi home,' I say gently. 'Hold on to me.' Her grip is tight as we inch our way back up towards the road, as out of the corner of my eye I notice the girl, still sitting there, her fair hair caught in the breeze as she stares towards the horizon.

* * *

After struggling into the house on what appears to be no more than a twisted ankle, that evening my mother goes to bed early. Putting my feet up, I find a film on the TV. But as I sit there, it goes over my head. Instead, work fills my thoughts. Abandoning the movie, I get my laptop and start on the series of reports that need analysing, from which I'm mapping changing temperatures in our oceans. Climate change is urgent – a global issue. I don't give it enough time. But these days, there simply isn't enough time; I have more pressing concerns closer to home.

I pause for a moment, thinking of my mother. Of the sassy girl who used to be a singer in a band called The Rhythm Sheds, a band I have an unquenched fascination with; someone for whom middle age should have been a breeze. About how through sheer bad luck, her mind isn't what it used to be so that now even the smallest, most everyday action can represent a risk.

But at least for now, I'm able to help her. Life goes on, I remind myself. Just not always the way you'd imagined it would.

3

BEE

This isn't my life, I find myself thinking. Somewhere along the way, I've side-slipped; in the passing of just a few days, everything I've always relied on has been taken away.

But if there's one thing experience has taught me, it's to only rely on myself. A couple of weeks into my enforced unemployment, I have to face the facts. I can leave Saskia's now, with most of my money still intact, or stay and wait until it runs out, a thought that fills me with fear and galvanises me into action. And I'm totally done with watching Saskia and Jaspar barely able to keep their hands off each other.

I start to pack my stuff to move it to my mother's house. As I think of living with my mother, it feels like a massive backward step. But when the day comes, I'm resigned, so that not even Saskia's apparent regret has any impact on me.

'Please don't go.' She wipes away the tears streaming down her face. 'Not like this.'

When until now, she's been unemotional about me leaving, I shake my head at what I'm not at all sure aren't crocodile tears. She's made it perfectly clear she wants her flat to herself; it's too late. In any case, to my mind, she's pushed the limits of our friendship to the point where we've crossed a line. 'Jaspar's moved in already. It's obvious there isn't room for three of us.' I fold the last of my clothes and put them in my suitcase.

'I mean not today.' Her voice wavers. 'Please stay, Bee. At least another night. I was going to cook us one last meal.'

A last supper. That's really appealing. As if that's going to change anything other than the guilt she feels. I zip up my suitcase and slide it onto the floor. 'You need your space. I don't want to be in the way.'

It's classic Saskia, throwing me a curve ball designed to make me feel I'm the bad guy. I know from the way she's bragged, she's done this before.

Coming over, she hugs me, tightly, cocooning me in her familiar perfume, then gazes at me with watery eyes. Make-up still perfectly intact, I can't help noticing.

'We are still friends, aren't we?' she says.

I wriggle out of her arms and wheel my case to the door, grateful for the most ruthless of clear-outs that means I don't have much stuff. I go back for my bags, one of which holds my beautiful new dress, as yet unworn; find a spark of self-esteem. After all, there are limits, even for mostly conflict-averse people-pleasers such as I am. 'I won't tell anyone you've evicted me and I have nowhere else to go.' Except to my mother's, which as Saskia knows only too well, is my least desirable option. 'As for friends...' I pause. 'Let's see, shall we?' I reach into my pocket. Taking out my door key, I place it on the shelf just inside the front door. Then I open the door and take my bags outside. 'I hope it works out with Jaspar.'

I'm aware of Saskia standing there, wiping her face as she watches me. 'I'll miss you so much,' she sobs.

Not that much, I can't help thinking. Otherwise I wouldn't be leaving. 'You'll be fine. You have Jaspar, remember?' I say calmly. Sodding Jaspar who's the reason I'm moving out. But I keep it to myself. Life experience means I'm good at bravado. There's no point banging on about events you have no control over. It doesn't mean that underneath, I don't feel. And leaving the flat that was my home for three years, all kinds of emotions are churning inside me. But there's no way Saskia will ever think about that. She's too selfish; will be too loved up, living her best life with Jaspar, to give more than a passing thought to how I'm feeling.

* * *

Two hours later, I park in the street outside my mother's house in Isleworth, contemplating I'm about to enter my next chapter, one I hope will be an impressively short one. At best, a few days. At worst, anything longer than that.

There's no hello. Only the briefest hug. 'Lovely and thin, aren't you?' After glancing over my red and black lumberjack shirt over a cropped top and stretchy leggings, my mother's eyes fix on the middle of me.

It isn't lovely; my face is gaunt, my body starting to look bony. In the last two weeks, thanks to a mixture of unhappiness and stress, too much weight has fallen off me. 'Try having your life fall apart and living on next to nothing for a while,' I say, thinking of my diet of baked beans on toast; my addiction to running to make the blues go away. 'Beggars can't be choosers.'

I follow her into the kitchen. Her make-up is immaculate, her hair newly coloured, her skinny jeans showing off her curvy figure, an array of bracelets decorating one of her wrists. My mother and I are chalk and cheese. So much so, it remains a mystery that she gave birth to me. But there is more than one mystery around the subject of my birth.

'So what are your plans?' Instead of offering to make a cup of tea, she busies herself wiping down the already immaculate worktops.

'I'm not sure.' I watch her leaf through a couple of letters; anything, it seems, to avoid looking at me. 'This has only just happened. I'm job hunting. I just haven't found anything yet.'

'Have you thought about doing something different?' She stops cleaning and looks up at me. 'Working at the arboretum, well, it was quite an unusual choice of career I've always thought.'

I stare at her. 'My job was really interesting.' I'd counted on at least a day before she'd start trying to redesign my life. In any case, I loved my old job. Not only are they beautiful, but as I now fully appreciate, trees are the lifeblood of this planet. 'If they hadn't been cost-cutting, I'd still be there.' As I always do, I drip-feed her information on a need-to-know basis. Anyway, she never reads my posts and I haven't told her about the social media side of things. 'I'm experienced. I'll find a job. I just need time.' Bold words that mask the uncertainty I feel.

She casts her eyes over my clothes again. 'Wouldn't you rather work somewhere a little more...' she hesitates '...glamorous?' Then she frowns. 'When did you last have a haircut?'

'I have perfectly nice clothes. This is running gear,' I point out. 'And I cut my own hair.' I know I sound defensive. But my hair is long and straightish; I've never enjoyed sitting in a salon, staring at my reflection while I'm snipped and curled into someone else's version of me.

She's silent for a moment. 'Bethany, I've been thinking.'

I roll my eyes. She's the only person in the world who doesn't call me Bee. Plus this is a phrase I've heard enough times to know I'm not going to like what comes next.

An expression of annoyance wrinkles her perfect foundation. 'Don't look at me like that. I'm trying to help. I was about to say there's a job going at...'

I'm already starting to panic. 'No.' I don't let her finish. My mother has no idea about my life. Come to that, she has no idea about me.

She looks annoyed. 'You might at least hear me out. You're hardly in a position to be picky.'

I sigh inwardly, listening resignedly as she tells me how her grand plan is for me to work for her friend, Moira. Moira runs a cleaning business in south London and is always looking for staff. 'Of course I don't mind you staying here,' she says. 'Just until you get yourself sorted again. It shouldn't be for long. Moira also knows someone who will be looking for a housemate – in a month or so.' She frowns at me. 'Aren't you at least going to say "thank you"?' She pats my arm. 'Think about it. I need to get on with work.' She heads outside to her office.

I've known for a long time she doesn't want me here. I tell myself I should be grateful. But I'm not. I like to dress up for work. To be someone who chats to people. Is customer facing. But even though it's the antithesis of my old job, and I'll be living with someone I've never met before, maybe working for Moira is better than staying here?

Or is it...? But I already know the answer, by the way my heart sinks.

* * *

As I lie in bed that night, I'm unable to sleep. Already, it feels as though the life I had in Brighton no longer exists. I think back over the years I spent working at the arboretum. The rare trees that have been nurtured over that time: the black poplars and large-leafed limes, the glorious bird cherry, none of which I would have been able to name before.

Such happy years, with people I liked, when I learned how it felt to be in tune with the natural world. Then going home to the flat, to long runs, shopping before nights out, the parties Saskia and I used to go to.

I try to imagine working for Moira. Don't get me wrong. There's nothing wrong with suburban life – or with working as a cleaner. And before I worked at the arboretum, I was very much a city girl. But over my years there, things have changed; the realisation comes to me that big city life is no longer for me. Yes, of course I like dipping in and out of it, but constantly crowded spaces, being surrounded by too many people, no longer appeals to me. In and amongst it all, I have a need for clean air, for space.

Right now, however, my choices are limited. I have a sudden sensation of clouds gathering overhead, of a weight settling over me. Rolling over, I pull the duvet over my ears, imagining the arboretum again; the rare plants and trees, the mist-filled valleys, my last thoughts before I drift off to sleep.

* * *

It isn't exactly the loveliest of autumn mornings as I set off on a route specifically designed to end near Kew Gardens, my worries hanging over me as I run along the streets.

Even the greyness of the sky seems sympathetic to how I'm feeling and I try to clear my mind, to take in the neat front gardens I pass. The kids on their way to school, the waggy-tailed dogs who don't have a care in the world. To figure out a way of dealing with my mother's unwanted interference in my life.

Stop being so ungrateful, I reprimand myself. *At least you have a mother – even though she's never been motherly. But she has a spare room, and right now, you need that.*

I'm still trying to focus on the positives in my life when I reach Kew Gardens. Stopping outside the ticket office, I stare at the prices, a feeling of dismay coming over me. Without a job, there's no way I can justify the cost of this.

Going back out to the road, I carry on, then make my way down the steps to the river. As I walk, my eyes fill with tears, a feeling of self-pity taking me over; it seems so unfair that this is happening to me.

Reaching a bench, I sit at one end of it. Watching the water flow past, a sigh comes from me. The truth is, I know I should feel more grateful to my mother. Some people don't have anyone in their lives. She brought me up, single-handed; made sure I've never wanted for anything.

Staring at the water, I find myself thinking about my sister. How she'd be someone to share times like this with – and of course, happier times. But she isn't here any more, nor do my mother and I ever talk about her. Instead, there's this emotional void between us, the gaps in my past like pieces missing from a jigsaw, the biggest of which is not knowing who my father is.

A sigh comes from me. I've no idea what kind of person he is. But it's at times like this, I miss the idea of him. There have been no birthday cards or fleeting childhood visits over the years. There's no record of him on my birth certificate and whenever I've asked, my mother refuses to talk about him. Quite simply, I've no way of tracing him.

It's left me with a deep sense I'm missing something, which

I've often thought is akin to grief; not sure if it's possible to grieve for someone I've never known.

But it preys on my mind and that afternoon, when my mother comes in from her office, I try to talk to her about it again.

'Why is it so important?' she demands. 'I'm the one who's been there for you. He's never been part of your life.' Turning away, she lights a cigarette.

When she's so obsessive about cleaning the house, when she knows how much I dislike it, I can't help wondering if she's smoking to annoy me. 'Can you imagine if you were in my shoes?' I plead. 'Wouldn't you want to know who your father was?'

'Honestly?' Exhaling, her eyes fix on mine. 'I don't see what the fuss is about. Parenting isn't about blood. It's about putting food on the table and providing a roof over your head.' Not once does she mention love. She sweeps out of the kitchen, pausing in the doorway. 'If I were you, I'd give Moira a call. Plenty of other people are after that job. If you leave it too long, you'll miss the boat.' She pauses. 'Have you thought there might be a reason things are as they are? It doesn't do to go stirring up the past.'

It's about the most profound thing I've ever heard her say. Standing there, I'm frowning as she stubs out her cigarette and disappears upstairs, leaving me wondering exactly what it was she meant.

That evening, when she goes out, she doesn't tell me where she's going, and I can't help wondering if there's something – or someone – she's keeping from me. Then curiosity takes me over, followed by annoyance at my mother's silence, because I've every right to know who my father is.

I get up and go over to the cupboard behind the sofa, where I know she keeps old photos. Trawling through a box of them, there are familiar snaps of my mother in her younger, more hip days; of me as a child, and as I leaf through them, memories of my childhood come back. Birthdays, Christmases, of the times we moved house, I started at different schools... Life never stood still; my mother was constantly onto the next thing.

I look for more photos, from way back. But she must have moved them somewhere else. My mother censors everything in her life; she removes anything that reminds her of sad times. And I happen to know there have been sad times. Times that she's buried, as if they've never happened. Times that to this day remain unspoken of.

After putting the photos back, I go to my mother's desk and open it. It's something I've never done before, that I shouldn't be doing now. But when so much is uncertain in my life, I reach for her old diaries, unable to stop myself.

* * *

It's late when my mother comes in. But determined to stay awake, I'm still lying on the sofa, waiting as she closes the door behind her, then comes in and puts her keys on the table.

'I know who my father is.'

She freezes momentarily, then turns to look at me. 'What do you mean?'

'His name is Luke Friday. Don't try and make out it isn't.' My voice is shaking. 'But what I really want to know is why you wouldn't tell me.'

'He was in the past,' she says tightly. 'I was very young at the time. I don't want to live in the past, Bethany. Can't you understand that?'

'He wasn't that far in the past when I was born,' I say stubbornly.

'But he was in my past.' Sighing, she comes and sits at the other end of the sofa. 'Luke and I...' She pauses. 'We were never meant to be together.'

I shake my head. 'It doesn't give you the right not to tell me about him.'

'Perhaps the implications were too damaging for my life,' she says.

'Damaging?' My eyes widen. 'Was he a serial killer or something? And what about me? I was a child who grew up without her father, because that was what you wanted. You weren't thinking of me. Only of yourself.'

'It wasn't like that,' she says shortly. Then she frowns. 'Just how did you find this out?' But as she speaks, a look of anger spreads across her face. 'Oh, Bethany. How dare you.' Her eyes glint furiously. 'You should be ashamed of yourself.'

'I am so ashamed.' Hanging my head, I blink away my tears. 'But his name isn't on my birth certificate. It was the only way I was ever going to know.' I wipe my eyes. 'You should have talked to me. If you had, this wouldn't have happened.' I pause, looking at her. 'But we don't talk, do we? Not about anything important.'

* * *

That night, as I lie in bed, I'm unable to sleep. I am deeply ashamed of looking in my mother's desk. But after finding a diary from the year before I was born, I couldn't stop myself from looking in it.

However wrong what I've done is, I at least have a name. Switching on my bedside lamp, I get up and fetch my laptop. Then getting back into bed, I lean back against the pillows. Resting my laptop on my knees, I enter 'Luke Friday' in the search bar, finding him a few pages in, my mouth dropping open as I read.

* * *

When I get up in the morning, from the cigarette butts in the ashtray, my mother has been sitting in the kitchen for some while.

'I owe you an apology,' she says stiffly. 'I should have been honest with you. But it doesn't give you the right to go through my things.'

'I know,' I say. 'I'm sorry, too. I shouldn't have done it.' I'm about to ask her about Luke, when she gets up.

'I think it would be best for both of us if you leave.'

I gasp. 'I don't have anywhere to go.'

She's silent for a moment. 'I'll do a deal with you. Call Moira and tell her you want the cleaning job. If she offers it to you, you can stay here temporarily until some accommodation works out – on one condition. You don't go through my personal things.'

And if it doesn't? Sensing I'm trapped, I start to panic. But just as quickly, I realise unless I do something else, I don't really have a choice. That, as it always has been, it's my mother who calls the shots. It was one of the reasons I didn't want to come back here. Fighting back the resentment I feel, I nod. 'OK.'

'I'll send you Moira's number,' she says, slightly less angrily.

Taking my phone, I go upstairs. A WhatsApp message comes through with Moira's contact details. Staring at it, I'm about to open it. But then as I sit on my bed, a much better idea comes to me.

4

ALEX

However challenging it is at times, I've also found that caring for someone brings out the best in people – not least, in myself. It also brings out the love. And it's amazing the extraordinary lengths love can drive us to, the way it immerses us in someone else's world – however different to ours it may seem.

Generally I work in my den, a tiny room that's more of a cupboard, leaving the curtain pulled back so that I can keep track of what my mother's doing. I'm used to interruptions, but on this particular day, as I'm working, a thud comes from the sitting room. Dropping everything, I run in to find my mother lying on the floor. Trying not to panic, I crouch down next to her. 'Mum... Are you OK?'

She winces as she tries to move. 'I was standing on the chair. I wanted to change the light bulb. It's been flickering,' she says, slightly accusingly.

It doesn't matter that there is no chair, no flickering light. In her mind, all of it's real. 'I would have done it, Mum.'

As she tries to get up again, she cries out in pain. 'Stay where you are, Mum. I'm calling an ambulance.'

'I don't want an ambulance,' she protests, albeit weakly.

She may be my mother but there are times when increasingly, for all the right reasons, I have to overrule her wishes. I get my phone and call the emergency services. After giving them her details, I pick up a cushion and crouch down next to her again, placing it gently under her head. 'Try not to move, Mum. The ambulance is on its way.' Her hand is tiny, delicate, as I take it in mine. But her grip is iron-like.

A look of pain flickers across her face. 'This really won't do. I need to get up. Alex will be home from school soon. I can't have him seeing me like this.'

It gets me every time when she slips into the past. Reaching for the blanket neatly folded over the back of the sofa, I gently drape it over her. 'It's OK, Mum. He'll be a little while yet – and anyway, I can look after him. Let's just wait for the paramedics to check you over.' But as I look at her, I swallow the lump in my throat.

While we wait, she's back in the present again, flitting from one subject to the next. 'You should find yourself another job, Alex. It's no good someone your age sitting around the house all day.'

'I work from home, Mum,' I remind her.

She pulls a face. 'You know perfectly well I'm talking about a proper job. In an office. With people.'

'It isn't unusual, you know. A lot of people work from home now.' There's no point explaining that my job is no less valid because I don't go into an office every day. But she forgets how much has changed. Her mind has for the most part blanked out the nineties and noughties, transporting her back to the seventies and eighties. We've watched rerun after rerun of all the old sitcoms. Played hours and hours of music of that era, which is great, but much to my frustration, by everyone other than the band she used to play in – a band I'd love to know more about. I look up just as a flashing blue light comes to a stop outside the house. 'Stay there, Mum. I'll be back in half a minute. I'm just going to let them in.' I get up and open the front door to find two paramedics making their way up the steps. 'Hi,' I call out. 'Thanks for coming so quickly. She's in here.'

They follow me into the sitting room, where my mother is lying where I left her.

'Hello, Mrs Bloom. Can I call you Rachel?' One of the paramedics, a woman, squats down next to her. 'Can you tell me what happened?'

My mother looks blank. 'To be honest, I can't remember.'

I watch as they gently check her over, before one of them turns to me. 'I think we should take her in and keep her under observation. We can't rule out that she hasn't hit her head.'

'It's probably a good idea. I wasn't in here when it happened.' But I should have been; she's vulnerable. I shouldn't have left her. The age-old guilt that comes with being a carer is never far away. 'I heard a crash... Then I came in and found her lying where she is.'

'I'm perfectly all right.' My mother's voice is faint.

'Don't worry, Rachel. We'll look after you.' The paramedic's voice is filled with kindness.

'You should probably know.' I hesitate before saying quietly, 'But she's been diagnosed with early-onset dementia.'

'I'm not going in a bloody ambulance,' my mother says obstinately.

* * *

In a sense, I understand why my mother is in denial about her illness. Her dementia comes in waves – is like the flattest, most benign sea, until a breaker sweeps in and completely disrupts it. Fortunately, today, by the time we reach the hospital, it's mill-pond smooth again.

'I really am so sorry to have caused all this fuss.' Sitting up on her bed, she looks impatient. 'Alex? Take me home, please.'

'They want to check you over, Mum. Just in case you hit your head.'

She starts feeling around her skull. 'There's nothing wrong with my head.'

'They need to check, Mum. I'm sure it won't take long.'

A stony look settles on her face. She doesn't like it when things are taken out of her hands. But when it comes to it, most of us don't. She turns away just as a man is wheeled in on a stretcher. A similar age to my mother, he's dressed in what looks like a rather expensive suit that's got somewhat crumpled along the way.

'Bloody hell,' he snaps. 'You can't just leave me here.'

The paramedics with him take no notice of his outburst. 'Let's get you onto the bed, sir.'

'Ow. STOP,' the man cries out, as they shift him onto the bed next to my mother's. 'This really is not...'

'Mr Carlisle?' The doctor appears. 'It is Mr Carlisle, isn't it?'

He glares at her. 'Yes. It is. Are you a doctor? I'd like to make a complaint about the way I was just... manhandled...' he blusters.

'May I look at your ankle?' The doctor gently raises the bottom of his trouser leg to examine him. 'We're going to need to get you out of these before we take you for an X-ray. Someone will be with you shortly to take you over there.' She pauses. 'If you can't take them off, I'll ask someone to bring some scissors.'

The man looks outraged. 'You'll do no such thing. I'll have you know these are part of my most expensive suit.' Lying back, he unfastens his belt and does his undignified best to wriggle out of them.

I glance at my mother. Her eyes are wide, a quizzical look on her face as she stares at the man.

'Kevin?'

Still half wearing his trousers, the man barely looks at her. 'What?' he says rudely.

'Good God. It is you.' My mother's face creases into a smile. 'I'm Rachel, Kevin. Rachel Bloom. You probably remember me as Roxy.'

And there it is, just like that. One of those random examples of past and present colliding in the most unexpected of places. You see, Roxy was my mother's stage name when she was the singer in The Rhythm Sheds. As for Kevin...

'Kevin played drums.' She beams at me. 'Didn't you?' Turning to him, she reaches out one of her hands. 'Oh, Kevin. I've missed those days. I've even missed you.'

He looks like the air has been knocked out of him. 'Roxy?' he says with disbelief.

This time, I don't question her memory. I already know Kevin Carlisle was the drummer in the band. By all accounts, a very good one. Just so you know, my interest in the band borders on obsession.

But my mother has always refused to talk about those days – until now, it seems. Suddenly, this rather odd day grows even odder. 'I'll never forget the last time we played.' Her voice sounds distant. 'Saved the best till last, didn't we?'

'Um, did we?' He looks flummoxed. Then his face clears. 'If you're talking about that gig at the festival, I suppose we did.'

'I'm Alex.' Going over to his bed, I hold out my hand. 'I'm Rachel's – Roxy's – son. Good to meet you.'

Looking utterly perplexed, he shakes my hand. Then he leans back on his bed. 'Good God,' he mutters.

'How are you, Kevin?' my mother asks.

'Apart from this ankle, I'm very good, thank you.' He sounds dazed. 'How are you? Only I suppose that's a rather stupid question given that you're in here, too.'

'I'm not really sure what I'm doing here,' my mother says vaguely. 'I'm fine. I'll be out of here any minute.'

I decide to intervene. After all, this is my perfect opportunity to talk to the elusive drummer I've been longing to track down since my mother was diagnosed. You see, I've read about music and dementia. How it can help reduce anxiety and maintain speech; evoke memories of happier times. Surely the most relatable music to my mother is what she used to sing with her band? The only problem being, she has no tapes or recordings and I'm hoping one of the others might. But thanks to her unhelpfulness, so far I've failed to track down any of them. It means I can't let it pass. 'Could I take your phone number, Kevin? Er, Mr Carlisle?'

'May I ask why?' he says sharply.

Given he clearly isn't in the friendliest frame of mind, I find myself hedging. 'Well, it isn't often that you bump into friends from the past. It might be nice for you and my mother to reconnect – in, er, slightly different circumstances.'

He opens his mouth and closes it again, which makes me think that what he's actually about to say isn't at all what he wants to say; that he's attempting to be what he perceives as polite. 'I suppose so. Do you have your phone to hand?'

I type in the number he dictates, as out of nowhere I'm struck by a flash of inspiration. I have an idea – and for once, it's a truly great one.

I glance at Kevin, trying to imagine him behind a drum kit

and failing. There are the other band members to find, too. But also maybe Kevin could help with that? I feel a thrill of excitement. Perhaps between us, before my mother's illness truly claims her, we could get the band back together, one last time.

'You couldn't find a nurse, could you?' Kevin sounds irritable.

'Of course.' My mind is still in overdrive as I go off in search of the nurses' station. Behind the huge, semicircular desk, two are scrutinising computer screens, while a third is working her way through a huge pile of typed pages. 'Excuse me? Mr Carlisle asked me if someone could come and see him.'

'Can I help?'

I turn to see an older woman standing next to me. In her navy-blue uniform, her grey hair is tinged with a hint of pink, her twinkling eyes belying her slightly ferocious demeanour. 'Mr Carlisle was asking if he could talk to one of you.'

'Mr Carlisle, hey?' His reputation clearly precedes him. 'Tell him I'll be with him shortly,' she says briskly.

I obediently wander back to find my mother pulling faces in Kevin's general direction. *He's not very happy*, she mouths, spiralling one of her fingers at the side of his head.

'Someone's on their way,' I tell him, just as the nurse I spoke to appears behind me.

'Mr Carlisle?'

'At last,' he says sarcastically. 'Only I'm supposed to be somewhere. In court, as it happens. I'm a defence lawyer and my client will be wondering where I am.'

She doesn't bat an eyelid. 'I'm not sure you'll be going anywhere until that ankle of yours has been seen to.'

'I'm afraid you don't understand,' he says firmly. 'It's imperative I get there. I'm the only person capable of carrying this off.'

She shoots him a look. 'I suggest you make a phone call and

ask someone else to take your place. No one is that indispensable, Mr Carlisle.' Then she glances at the trousers, still somewhere around his knees. 'Would you like me to help you take your trousers off?'

'Absolutely not.' His face contorts with pain as he swings his legs over the side of the bed, before reaching for his trousers. 'All I need is a crutch,' he says authoritatively. 'If you wouldn't mind?'

The nurse shakes her head. 'If your ankle is broken, Mr Carlisle, it will need a plaster cast. Today,' she adds firmly, preempting his next question.

'I think that's my choice,' he says bullishly. 'Now be a good girl and get me some crutches.'

She gives him a look – the closest she can professionally get to tearing him off a strip for being patronising and misogynistic. 'In the nick of time,' she says crisply as a porter comes in. 'I'd consider yourself lucky, Mr Carlisle,' she mutters. 'And I'd think twice about how you talk to the staff around here.'

I watch Kevin's mouth drop open. He mutters something about crutches again as he's transferred into a wheelchair and efficiently despatched in the direction of the X-ray department.

'He always was an awkward bugger,' my mother says.

'Was he?' Turning to look at her, I take in the paleness of her skin. 'How are you feeling?'

'For goodness' sake, Alex. Stop fussing over me.' Frowning slightly, she raises one of her hands towards her head. 'Actually, I don't feel so good.' Her hand falls. Then her eyes close and her head rolls sideways.

* * *

Three hours later, I open the front door and let myself in. After closing it, I go through to the kitchen, pour myself a very large drink. It isn't something I'd normally do, but nothing about today has been normal.

I take it over to the sofa. Just as I sit down, my mobile rings. It's Auntie Lorna, my mother's sister.

'Hi.' I lean back. 'I was just about to call you.'

'Your mother phoned me from the hospital.' Lorna sounds distressed. 'She wasn't making a lot of sense. Is she OK?'

'I think so. She had a fall this afternoon. They took her in as precaution. Then she passed out. They did tests. They think it was low blood sugar. She's on a drip – and if all goes well, she'll probably be home tomorrow.'

'Thank goodness for that.' Lorna sounds relieved. 'How about you, Alex? Are you coping?'

'Yeah.' There's no point telling her I'm beyond exhausted. It's simply how things are. I have to deal with it.

'I'm worried about you. Can't you have a break?' she says.

'Not exactly.' But Lorna doesn't know what my mother's demands are. 'Someone has to be here. I can't leave her alone.'

'I suppose not,' she says vaguely. 'Isn't there a respite carer who could move in?'

I sigh inwardly. 'Can you imagine how that would go? Mum would tell them she doesn't need them and kick them out.'

Lorna's silent for a moment. 'She could come here.' She follows it up hurriedly with, 'It would only be for a week or so, wouldn't it?'

'It's lovely of you to offer,' I say, not at all sure how Lorna would cope. 'But we're fine. We really are. Today was a blip – it isn't usually like this.' It's true – for now. But I have enough of an understanding of dementia to know that the blips become more common; that normal is ever shifting.

'As long as you're sure.' She pauses. 'I know my sister isn't easy, Alex. She's far too obstinate. She always has been. But if it gets too much, please call me.'

Promising I will, I end the call, switching my phone to silent before putting it down. Closing my eyes, I take a deep breath. Lorna's right. It isn't always easy. But this is my mum we're talking about. She raised me; those hands that are now shaky, cooking meals, washing my clothes, keeping me safe. Now that she needs help, it's me who should take care of her. It's the natural order of things.

But I can't help sighing. It doesn't matter how much I love my mother. The fact is that sometimes it's really hard.

5

BEE

After discovering a reference to Luke playing at a music gig, somehow I manage to find the name of the village where he lives. Picking up my phone and finding it dead, I scribble it on a piece of paper, making a note to self to add it to my phone when it's charged again. The way my life is panning out – or not, as it seems right now, I have pretty much zero to lose by trying to find him.

Yes, I'm taking a risk. But it beats working for Moira – and if I don't go, I'll never know. But the next morning, when I explain my plans to my mother, she tells me in no uncertain terms that I'm off my head to even consider doing this.

'For starters, you have no idea what this man is like,' she says. 'He's probably a clapped-out wrinkly rocker by now. And a womaniser. Girls flocked after him back then. I don't suppose anything's changed.'

I stare at her. 'You don't know any of that,' I say. 'In any case, whether he's still playing music or not, it's irrelevant.'

She shakes her head. 'I'll tell you what I do know – and that is, leopards don't change their spots. Don't get your hopes up.

And don't assume you can move back in here yet again when it doesn't work out.' Her words sting. When I've been independent for years, I can't understand why she's so harsh towards me. Then she asks more casually, 'Have you found out where he lives?'

'Yes,' I say. 'Majorca.'

'Majorca?' Her eyes widen. 'You're going all the way there on a whim?' There's disapproval in her voice.

'It's hardly a whim – but yes, I am going,' I say shortly. I go over to the kettle. I'm silent as I fill it and switch it on, then get out a couple of mugs and make tea. Right now, there are no certainties. Nor have I any idea what he'll say if I turn up on his doorstep. But there's one thing I do know and it doesn't seem unreasonable. He's my father. I want to find him.

I take the mugs over to the table as my mother's phone buzzes with a text. After reading it, she looks up at me. 'Moira's going to offer the job to someone else. But she says to let her know when you're back and she'll see what she can do.'

'You've already told her?' I look at her incredulously, realising she must have done it while I was making the tea. I shake my head. 'Never mind. But there is one thing you can tell me.' I pause, looking at her. 'I just don't understand why you're being so negative about this. You've said nothing nice about Luke. In fact, quite the opposite – and there must have been a time you liked him.'

'I was young and stupid.' She stubs out her cigarette, then, after taking a gulp of tea, she turns the subject onto my finances. 'Can you really afford this?'

'As it happens, I can.' I haven't told her about my redundancy package. And she still hasn't answered my question. 'Look, you couldn't make it any clearer you're against me going. All you've done is make assumptions about his character – not very pleasant ones. And you haven't actually told me why.'

She and I are like this. But that she actually stops in her tracks for a moment means she knows that, for once, I have a point. Giving me the silent treatment, however, isn't good enough.

I watch her reach for another cigarette. After lighting it, she inhales deeply then breathes out smoke at me. 'Would it make any difference?' she says. Then, 'If you're dead set on going, I can't stop you. You're an adult, Bethany. Even if, at times, you don't behave like one.'

Coughing, I fan away the smoke with one of my hands. 'You know how much I hate that.'

'Touché,' she says sharply.

* * *

Her unjustified antagonism only makes me more determined. Alone in my bedroom, I sit at my laptop and book a flight to Majorca, which, being at the end of the season, is mercifully cheap. She says no more about it, but her silence leaves me in no doubt that she's no intention of giving me the smallest amount of encouragement.

Her negativity leaves me unsettled, a dark cloud that seems to follow me. For the next few days, I go on long runs which temporarily lift my mood, in between scouring the internet for more information about Luke, finding some old footage of him playing with his band. I scrutinise photos for the vaguest resemblance between us as I wonder if he still plays – my brief flicker of excitement replaced almost immediately by trepidation, because I've no idea how he'll react to me.

In so many ways, it would be easier not to be doing this; to stay here and get a job. Find a boyfriend with kind eyes, like that guy who spilled coffee over me. But the reality is I am surrounded by less than appealing options. When I think of Moira's cleaning job, of staying with my mother, I quickly come to the conclusion it wouldn't be any easier for me to stay.

It's a time I could really do with my mother's support rather than her antagonism. Somehow we manage to stay out of each other's way. Then the big day, 15 October, is finally here. Of course, being my mother, she has no interest in coming to the airport with me, or in how long I'll be away. All she knows is I have a one-way ticket and where my destination is.

'Aren't you even going to ask when I'm coming back?' I ask.

She lights a cigarette. 'Do you know?'

I stare at her. I haven't decided. But that isn't the point. She's my mother. She should at least take an interest. I go over to the window and open it, gulping in the relatively fresh air.

'Just let me know, OK?' She pauses. 'Be careful, won't you? You've no idea how he'll react.' Then before I can respond, she says quietly, 'I've booked you a taxi.'

It's her way of calling a truce. Even so, as I sling my rucksack over my shoulder and go out to where the taxi is waiting in the street, I'm irritated. It's her stubbornness, her intransigence, her inability to imagine things from my point of view until I force the issue. And I'm anxious, too, because she's right about one thing. I've no idea how Luke will react.

'Going somewhere nice?' the taxi driver asks as he pulls away.

'No.' Not in the mood for inconsequential chat, I pointedly turn to gaze outside.

As I watch the streets of London flash past, my mood starts to dissipate. It isn't the driver's fault I'm mad at my mother. *You are being so frigging mean*, Bee, I reprimand myself. *And you know what happens to mean people. They meet more mean people and live unhappily ever after in a cycle of perpetual meanness.*

Whatever's going on in my life, I do not want to be that person. When he drops me at the airport, still feeling guilty, I give him an overly generous tip. Then I head into the terminal and make my way through security.

As I join the slow-moving queue, I imagine arriving in Majorca. The warmth of the sun, the glorious sunsets I've read about. The miles of hills swathed in trees. Being welcomed by Luke and... My eyes widen. I've no way of knowing what his life is like, just as I haven't considered he might have a family.

Uncertainty washes over me. But there's no going back. In the departure lounge, I go to the bar and order a beer. I take it over to a table by the window and sit watching the aircraft taking off. Then as I contemplate the magnitude of what I'm about to do, any bravado I had goes up in smoke.

Instead of boldly stepping towards my future, this feels like a long-winded detour via a past swathed in uncertainty. But that's why I'm here, I remind myself. To answer the questions I have – so that I can move on. I'm a firm believer that there are times in our lives when we have to stop procrastinating and just do things. After all, we are put on this earth not to fester quietly, but to live. Today is one such day, I remind myself. A day I've been longing for most of my life, yet now it's here...

Seeing the boarding gate flash up on the screen, my head feels fuzzy. Suddenly nervous again, I give myself another pep talk.

It's your life, Bee my girl. You've got this.

6

ALEX

The house is oddly quiet when I awake the following morning. Early – out of habit, as I instantly leap out of bed to check on my mother, before remembering the hospital kept her in; that just for today, there is no urgency.

I take a more leisurely shower than usual, linger over my breakfast. And grateful as I am not to have to worry about her for a few hours, there's no denying I miss her.

It's been the hardest thing to watch my previously vibrant mother slowly ravaged by a devastating and irreversible illness. But if there are positives to be found, it has brought us closer, such that I am now privy to things that most sons would not be – her innermost, previously unvoiced opinions; her unfiltered comments. Her favourite socks as well as the ones she can't stand. And however stubborn and proud she is, she's coming around to the idea that she relies on me.

But she still has the ability to surprise me and when I go to the hospital in the afternoon, she isn't alone. More astonishingly than that, she's deep in conversation with Kevin Carlisle.

As I stand there holding the roses I've brought her, the

carrier bag of grapes and the chocolate she loves, neither of them appears to notice me. I clear my throat. 'Afternoon.'

'Alex.' Seeing me, my mum's face lights up. 'Kevin and I were having a good old catch-up.'

'Yes.' Kevin stands up rather awkwardly and I notice the plaster cast on one of his feet. 'Apologies if I was, er... a little standoffish yesterday. It wasn't a good day.'

'No worries.' I shake the hand he holds out. 'How's your foot?'

'It's been better.' He sinks back into his wheelchair. 'I had an adverse reaction to the anaesthetic they gave me when they set it. So they kept me in.'

For the first time I notice he's still wearing a hospital gown.

He goes on. 'Rather inconvenient. As I was just telling your mother, it's given me some enforced time off, which is something I'm not very good at.' His eyes flicker towards her. 'Rather annoying, actually.'

'There's no one at home to look after him. Kevin's wife left him years ago,' my mother says calmly. 'It's turned you into a miserable old git, hasn't it, darling?'

I can never decide if it's a curse or a blessing that dementia is eroding her inhibitions. 'Mum. You really shouldn't say things like that.' I turn to Kevin. 'I'm so sorry. Sometimes she forgets what she's saying.'

My mother looks annoyed. 'I know exactly what I'm saying.'

'Don't worry. Quite refreshing, actually.' Kevin's cheeks tinge with pink. 'There's also the fact it happens to be true of course – about my wife leaving, that is.' He frowns. 'The other... It's the curse of getting older, I always think. Not being as happy as you used to be, I mean.'

I stand there, thinking of all the older people I know who are grateful, happy with their lot, not sure what to say. 'I'll go and find a vase for the flowers.'

My mother suddenly registers them. 'They're lovely, Alex. But you shouldn't have. We'll be going home shortly.' Looking past me, she frowns. 'I know that man.'

'Who?' As Kevin turns, he frowns. 'It's Leo. What the devil's he doing here?'

In the midst of my quiet, dementia-based life; when these days, I rarely leave the house I grew up in, this is getting weirder by the second. 'Who is Leo?'

'He used to be our roadie.' My mother frowns. 'Are you sure that's him?'

'Of course I'm sure,' Kevin says irritably.

'He looks a bit old,' my mother says doubtfully.

'I suppose he is showing his age. But we're all getting older,' Kevin adds magnanimously.

'Speak for yourself. I don't look any different,' my mother says. Before I can stop her, she waves her arms in his direction. 'Leo?' she calls out. 'Is that you?'

The man freezes. Then as he turns and sees my mother, a look of surprise registers on his face. He comes over, his pleasure at seeing her obvious.

'It is you, Leo! How wonderful. Do you remember me? Roxy – from the band?' My mother sounds delighted. 'How long's it been? Twenty years? Do you remember Kevin?'

'Coming up for thirty,' Kevin mutters.

'"Course I do.' Leo glances at the plaster cast on Kevin's foot. 'So what's happened to you?'

'Broke the damned thing. Feels like bloody concrete,' Kevin says as a nurse comes hurrying over.

'Mr Carlisle, you really should be resting.' She adjusts the blanket that's fallen off Kevin's legs. 'I will come and check on you in half an hour.' She pauses. 'Please. Do the sensible thing and stay where you are.'

'Nothing changes,' Leo chuckles, glancing at me. 'Always did what he wanted. No regard for anyone else.'

Still holding the flowers, I study Leo more closely. He's slightly built, with little hair and his complexion has a grey tinge. But his eyes hold a light.

'It isn't funny,' Kevin says through gritted teeth. 'I'm missing the second day of an important court case.'

'Really?' Leo raises his eyebrows. 'Like a murder trial, or something?'

Kevin musters an air of dignity as best he can given he's in a wheelchair wearing a hospital gown. 'Not this time.'

'There you go. They'll manage without you. They're going to have to,' Leo says kindly.

I catch my mother's eye as Kevin gazes up at the ceiling. 'It can't be easy being a lawyer, darling,' my mother says to him. 'Especially when you're such an important one.'

'It pays the bills,' Kevin says stiffly.

'I'm Alex,' I interrupt, seeing as no one's going to introduce me.

My mother glances at me, unabashed. 'I'm sorry, darling. Leo, Alex is my son.'

'Nice to meet you, Alex.' Leo's face crinkles into a smile. 'Can you sing like your mother? Has the voice of an angel, she does.'

'He can't sing a note,' my mother says matter-of-factly. It has always been a disappointment to her that much as I love listening to music, when it comes to playing, I am not musical in the slightest.

'So what brings you here?' I ask Leo.

'Routine check-up,' he says briefly. 'Good timing, though. I can give you a lift if it helps.' He glances at Kevin. 'It's not like you have anyone else, do you, mate?' He says it half-jokingly.

'Goodness.' My mother looks taken aback. 'Haven't you ever married, darling?' Completely forgetting she already knows.

'I've already told you, I was married and she left me. I haven't seen her for four years,' Kevin says sharply.

But despite his irritation, my mother seems unabashed.

'Bad luck, wasn't it?' Leo sounds genuine for once. 'Have to say, I never understood what she saw in you!' His face splits into a smile and he roars with laughter again.

Kevin's face is mutinous. 'Me neither,' he says drily. 'Bit of a mistake all round. Would have been easier for everyone if we'd never met.'

My mother makes an unsubtle attempt to move the focus onto Leo. 'So how about you, Leo? Married, single, divorced?'

The question has the desired effect and he instantly stops smiling. 'I met the love of my life a long time ago, Rox. Remember Dora? I'd have done anything for her. Only before I got my shit together, she went and married someone else. Haven't seen her for years...' He sounds wistful. 'But I never met anyone else worth giving up my precious independence for. And now...' He shrugs. 'Past it, aren't I? Let's be honest.'

'Pair of sad gits, aren't we?' Kevin says as the nurse comes back.

'Fucking sad gits,' Leo chuckles, reaching out one of his hands towards the nurse. 'Hey, gorgeous. Have you come to boot these two out?'

'Only this one.' She nods towards Kevin, before looking at Leo. 'The doctor wants to see you.'

'It shouldn't take long,' Leo says. 'Why don't you get dressed? Then I'll take you home.'

'Thank God,' Kevin says with feeling. 'Right. It's been good seeing you all. But the sooner I'm out of here, the better.'

'See you, darling.' My mother gives him a regal wave. 'Don't forget. We're going out for a drink.'

'Yes. Right.' Kevin turns to Leo. 'You should join us. Give Rachel – Roxy – your number.' Feeling into the non-existent pockets of his hospital gown, he looks slightly mystified. 'Don't seem to be able to find my bloody phone.'

* * *

With Kevin discharged into the capable hands of Leo, at last I'm alone with my mother. 'I brought you these.' I hand her the bag containing the grapes and chocolates, then sit down on the chair next to her bed.

'It's been rather fun.' There's a light in her eyes I haven't seen before. 'Seeing those two again, after all these years...' She leans towards me conspiratorially. 'Though between you and me, Kevin's turned into a right miserable old sod. Shame. He never used to be like that.'

I try to get her to focus. 'So what has the doctor said about you?'

She frowns. 'Something about... She said that I... You know...' She looks frustrated.

'Don't worry, Mum. I'll have a word with her.' But I'm worried. This struggle for words has been happening more and more. 'Auntie Lorna called me last night. She wanted to know how you are.'

'Did she indeed,' my mother says. 'I should imagine she was more worried about you, to be honest.' Pausing, she turns to look at me. 'I've been thinking about this, Alex. I think I might go away – just for a week or two.'

I'm taken aback. 'To Auntie Lorna's?'

'God, no.' My mother looks horrified. 'She'd drive me mad. And I'd drive her mad.' She shakes her head. 'I was thinking more along the lines of a nice hotel.'

'You need a bit of help, Mum,' I remind her.

'You keep saying this, but I really don't,' she says crossly.

I take a deep breath. I don't keep saying anything of the sort. But there's no way she'd cope on her own. 'We could look together.' My eyes linger on a brochure on the table next to her bed. I pick it up. 'What's this?'

'One of the nurses gave it to me.' She looks at it disdainfully. 'It's for a nursing home. Absolutely no good for me, of course.'

And this is the impossible I am faced with daily. Dementia versus clarity; denial versus reality, as I've come to think of it. 'Why don't you go and stay with Lorna?' I say at last. 'I'll give her a call. She is your sister – and the change of scene will do you good.'

She looks disgruntled. 'I suppose so,' she says ungratefully.

* * *

So it is that the following day, after my mother is discharged, we set off for Lorna's house in the New Forest.

'I wish you'd take me home first,' my mother complains. 'You're sure to have forgotten something.'

I'd known when I packed her suitcase, it was bound to be wrong. But I also know if I take her home, I'll never get her out again. 'I've packed the clothes you wear most often. And your pyjamas,' I tell her. 'I'm sure Lorna will lend you anything I've forgotten.' I've packed her toiletries, too. I know which moisturiser she favours and what she considers a rip-off; the brand of deodorant she's worn since her teenage years.

She's silent for a moment, then she slams her hand on the dashboard. 'Oh goodness,' she says suddenly. 'Alex, I really do have to go home.'

'Why?'

'It's your father.' She shakes her head. 'You know what he's like. Utterly hopeless without me there.'

It's like I've been punched. It's true, my father depended on her. It's fair to say he would have been lost without her – if he was still with us. But he died very suddenly, six years ago. For the most part, I try not to let these things get to me, but today it does. Not wanting her to see, I blink away the tears that are suddenly in my eyes. 'Don't worry, Mum. I'll tell him you've gone to stay with Lorna. And I'll make sure he's OK.'

'You're a good boy,' she says in a completely different voice. 'You do so much for me, Alex. I know how lucky I am.'

And there it is, out of the blue as they often are; making my heart burst. One of those more lucid moments. Of love rarefied.

I reach to the side of me for her hand; swallow the lump in my throat. 'I'm the lucky one,' I say quietly.

More than ever now, I live in the moment. Living with my mother is a constant reminder that each day is a sequence of such moments. Some astonishing or rapidly forgotten; others remembered, albeit, at times, somewhat scrambled.

'We should stop for breakfast,' she says an hour into the drive. 'Aren't you hungry, Alex?'

'We stopped not that long ago.' I had smashed avo on sourdough; my mother had porridge. 'Are you hungry?'

'I'm starving,' she says impatiently. 'I know you young people don't do proper meals. But it isn't good for you.'

A few miles on, we pass a sign to a service station. 'Let's stop here,' I suggest.

She looks at me as if I'm mad. 'Are you hungry again already? It seems like five minutes ago you had breakfast.'

'What about you, Mum?'

Shrugging, she gazes out of the window. 'I've never been that fussed about breakfast.'

We manage a more everyday exchange about Lorna's son, my cousin Michael. 'He lives in New York,' my mother tells me. 'He and his girlfriend are getting married next year.'

It's years since I've seen Michael – and it all sounds perfectly plausible. 'How exciting. I bet Lorna's looking forward to it.' But it's the first I've heard of it; I've no way of knowing if it's true or if she's muddling him with someone else.

The New Forest landscape is steeped in the colours of autumn, of heather shades and golden leaves as we drive past grazing ponies along miles of quiet lanes. The village where Lorna lives is no less idyllic. Pulling up, I park outside her picture-postcard cottage, under the apple tree that overhangs the lane.

'Oh God.' My mother stares at the gate that leads into Lorna's garden. 'You really are leaving me here, aren't you?'

'Yes, Mum. We talked about it.' I pause. 'It's just for a week. Look, here's Lorna. I'll get your bags.'

'Alex is starving,' my mother says to Lorna as she gets out of the car. 'How are you? Garden looks pretty.' Brushing off her sister's hug, she crouches down to talk to Lorna's cat.

'Thanks for driving her. You'll stay for lunch, won't you?' Lorna looks slightly uncertain.

'Better not.' The fact is I'm torn. But the longer I stay, the smaller my chances of getting away alone. 'I have her medication. I've written a list.' I pass Lorna the bag, then turn to my mother. 'Bye, Mum. Have a lovely time.'

'Oh. You're going.' Standing up, she looks miffed.

'See you next week.' I kiss her on the cheek, then turn to Lorna. 'Thank you.'

'You're welcome. I'm sure we'll be fine.'

'You will.' I add more quietly, 'Call me if you need me.'

Getting in my car, I drive away. I toot once and wave my hand out of the window, glancing in the rear-view mirror, but my mother is looking the other way.

I feel the strangest wave of protectiveness as I leave her with Lorna; guess they're the same emotions she must have felt once, when I was a small child she was leaving at pre-school or at a friend's house. The same sense of responsibility, of handing your vulnerable loved one over to the care of someone else, even when that someone happens to be her sister.

And yes, in so many ways, my mother still thinks she's invincible. It's just that now and then, I know she has an awareness that things are changing. I see it in her face, in the way she turns away, changes the subject or talks about something random. Anything to detract from the painful reality that she knows her mind isn't what it used to be.

But she's with Lorna, I remind myself. And while they're very different people, Lorna's family, I know she'll look out for her. Nevertheless, as I drive, I can't stop thinking about her. In her lucid moments, she'll understand where she is. But when she doesn't... It's Lorna's turn, I tell myself firmly. And it's only for a week.

It's dark by the time I reach Brighton. The roads are awash from the earlier rain, the headlights of oncoming cars pixelated in the drizzle. Mercifully, our street is quiet and I park a few feet away from our house.

Sitting in the car, I gaze at it for a minute. It's my mother's house; the house I grew up in, a place of safety and refuge; of chaos, for sure, but also love, in abundance. It was where I came back to when I finished at uni and ended up staying longer than I'd planned to when my father died. I remember the day I left it for my flat in London as if it were yesterday. My excitement as I'd thought about the new life waiting for me, conflicting with guilt at leaving my mother alone, never imagining that only three years later, after more than a few unexplained incidents and a long call from her GP, I'd find myself moving back here.

I'd been aware for a while that the house had become even more chaotic, if that was possible. My mother's always had a penchant for clutter. But, it quickly became clear that she was struggling. Had been for some time, judging from the muddle the house was in.

The familiarity of her surroundings had masked the extent of her problems. And, as I soon found out, she was firmly in denial. Her diagnosis was greeted with derision; my offer to look after her finances firmly rebuffed. So I've learned to take things one step at a time, one bill at a time; dealing with things without unduly drawing attention to them.

I get out and lock the car. The house is in darkness and when I go inside, it feels oddly empty. More than that, I feel oddly empty. But the feeling is short lived. No sooner have I put my keys down, when my phone buzzes.

I pick it up. 'Hi, Mum.'

'Alex.' She sounds distressed. 'Where are you? You said you were coming back.'

'I am, Mum. In a week,' I try to reassure her.

'No,' she says, distraught. 'You said today. You said you were coming to take me home.'

'Mum...'

In the background, I hear Lorna's voice. Then she takes the phone. 'Alex, she's OK. She fell asleep. When she woke up, I think she thought she was still in the hospital. But you don't have to worry. She's calmer now.'

'Thanks.' But hearing my mother's voice has unsettled me. 'Call me if you need me, won't you? Any time.'

'I will. But don't worry,' she says again. 'We'll be fine.' She passes the phone back to my mother.

'I'm so sorry, Alex. I don't know what happened.' She breaks off. 'I think I must have dreamed you said that.'

'That's probably what it was,' I say gently.

'I must go. Lorna's just cut the most delicious cake,' she says in a completely different voice. 'Sorry to have bothered you. Night, night.'

'Night, Mum.' I switch my phone off. Then a sigh comes from me. It's hardly the best of starts. But only now that I'm alone, do I realise how weary I am; that in a way, this break is timely for both of us.

I go to the fridge and get a beer. Sitting down, with the prospect of a week to myself, the reality of caring for my mother fully catches up with me.

7

BEE

After making my way to the boarding gate, a few minutes later, we're herded down some steps onto a bus, that takes us out to our plane.

I may not know what awaits me in Majorca, but a sense of relief fills me at the prospect of leaving England. If it all goes horribly long with Luke, I'll figure out what to do next.

As I board the plane, I fantasise briefly about becoming cabin crew, spending my working days flying around Europe; mentally noting the idea for some point in the future. The first part of the flight goes quickly, mainly because I'm caught up in the magical view from my window of the patchwork of tiny fields and sprawling towns, then as we get further south, the vast expanses of snow-capped mountains; revelling in the very real sense of leaving my troubles behind. But two hours into the flight, with some eight hundred and seventy miles behind me, as the plane starts its descent, the reality of what I'm doing hits me full on and I start to panic.

Holy crap, I whisper to myself. *What made you think you could do this?*

It's only Majorca, I tell myself. It's hardly the other side of the world. Then we break through the finest layer of cloud and I forget about everything else, as I gaze with wonder at the rocky coastline, an impossibly clear turquoise sea.

* * *

Given it's October, the airport is busier than I expected. But in what seems like no time, I'm outside, where I find a taxi straight away. And then it all starts to go horribly wrong. As I scroll through my phone for the address I found online, I realise I forgot to type it in; that it's on a scrap of paper on the chest of drawers in my mother's spare room.

I try to remember the name of the village. 'It's near Pollensa. I think it's called…' I break off, unable to remember.

'You do not have the address?' He looks at me patiently. 'There are many villages in the north of the island.'

I start to panic again. 'Luke Friday lives there. Does that help?' I try to remember more information about him. 'Maybe you know him? He's a musician.'

But he shrugs. 'I do not know this Luke Friday.'

'Are you sure?' I say desperately. 'I mean, this is a tiny island. Surely everyone knows everyone else.'

'Senorita, this island is not so small. Almost a million people live here. I can assure you I do not know him.'

I stare at him, aghast. 'What am I going to do?' I remember how I found the name of the village. 'Can you give me a few minutes? I'll look it up online.'

'I cannot wait, senorita.' Shrugging, he gestures to someone behind me. After they climb into his taxi, he drives away.

Left standing there, tears fill my eyes. I've no idea what to do next. Needing to think, I drag my case towards an empty bench, when someone barges into me – or maybe it's me who barges into them. It doesn't even matter. What counts is we both stop and stare at each other.

'Sorry,' I say tearfully, looking up into a pair of dark eyes tinged with irritation that swiftly changes to concern.

'Are you OK?' he says.

'No.' Even through my tears, I can see this guy is gorgeous. 'I've just got here. And I've lost the name of the village where I'm supposed to be going. All I know is it's close to Pollensa.'

He looks hesitant. 'I'm sorry. I have a flight to catch. But I know someone who might be able to help. My aunt lives near Pollensa – she makes it her business to know everyone.' He turns, calling out, 'Aunt Augusta? Can you help?' He beckons towards someone. 'You'll be fine now. I have to run.' He pauses. 'Good luck.'

I turn to watch him disappear into the terminal, as a voice comes from behind me.

'Are you a friend of my nephew?'

I turn to see a woman of indeterminate age giving me the once-over. 'No,' I say miserably. 'We ran into each other. He only stopped because he saw I was upset.' I sigh. 'I can't believe it, but I forgot to bring the address of where I'm staying.'

'Well, that's easily solved,' she says. 'Call them.' She pauses. 'If you don't have a phone, you can use mine.'

'I can't.' I hesitate. 'I don't know his number – and he doesn't know I'm here.' My shoulders slump; this is hopeless. Then suddenly I imagine what she's thinking. 'It isn't a boyfriend,' I say hastily. 'It's family. Distant family.'

She frowns slightly. 'They don't know you're coming?'

I shake my head. 'It seemed like a good idea at the time. But now, I'm not so sure.' Suddenly I remember the name of the village. 'They live near Caimari.'

'Good heavens. Who is this mysterious family member?' she says. 'I live around there. I've lived here a very long time. There's the outside chance I might know him, or at least, know of him.'

I sigh. It's a long shot. But I have nothing to lose. 'His name is Luke. Luke Friday.'

'Why didn't you say?' she says briskly. 'I know Luke. Rather well, as it happens. Come on. I'll give you a lift.'

I hesitate. I've never met this woman before. She could be a psycho.

'Hurry up,' she calls over her shoulder. 'My dog's in the car. If I leave him too long, he chews the seat backs.'

OK, I tell myself. So I love dogs. And if she does too, even if they chew her car, I'm figuring she can't be an entirely bad person.

I follow her towards a small, dusty four-by-four. The dog turns out to be a rangy, somewhat elderly podenco reclined on the rear seat; the fact that he does indeed chew seat backs evidenced by both of them hanging off in tatters.

I put my rucksack into the back of her car, curious to know more about Luke. But as she drives off, I can't get a word in, as Augusta, as she reminds me her name is, can't stop talking about her dog.

'He was hit by a car driven by some arsehole of a tourist,' she says as she turns onto the main road. 'Poor chap wasn't much more than a puppy. Makes my blood boil to think of some feckless interloper hitting a dog and leaving it to die.'

'It's terrible,' I agree. 'How long have—' I start.

But she interrupts. 'It really was. He was in a dreadful state – poor old Cato.'

'Cato?' I frown.

'It's his name. It means wise. But you're fine now, aren't you, boy?' As she turns to stroke his head, the car drifts into the middle of the road.

'Shit.' I grab the steering wheel just in time, saving us from certain death as a car speeds around the corner towards us. Hooting furiously, the driver waves his fist.

Winding down the window, Augusta gives him the finger. 'Wanker,' she mutters.

In what seems the oddest sequence of coincidences, it turns out that after dropping her nephew at the airport, Augusta had been driving away when she'd noticed his passport lying in the footwell of the passenger seat. Having driven back to hand it over to him, he'd been hurrying into the airport when he and I had collided with each other. 'Quite fortuitous, really,' she says thoughtfully. 'The timing, I mean.'

'It really was. When you talk to him next, please tell him how grateful I am,' I say.

'I shall indeed. Though I doubt I'll see him for a while, now. He works all over the place. Heaven knows how his girlfriend puts up with him – he's totally unreliable. But he has a heart of gold.' She glances at me curiously. 'So, Bee, have you been to Majorca before?'

I shake my head. 'No.' After leaving the hustle of Palma behind, I can't take my eyes off the breathtaking views of rocky hills and tree-clad valleys in which villages are nestled; wider stretches of ploughed fields and isolated, white-painted houses. Now and then, a glimpse of a distant sea comes into sight.

'It's very lovely here,' she says. 'I moved here thirty years ago – or rather, I should say I came out here on holiday. I never left. Rather reckless of me, I suppose, looking back. But it was very different back in those days. And as I said, I know Luke. Rather well.' She pauses. 'You said he doesn't know you're on your way there.'

'No.' Suddenly I'm on my guard again.

'I have to say I'm curious. But it's none of my business.' For a moment she doesn't speak. 'However, there is something you should know about Luke's life. You see...' Her voice changes. 'He lost his wife – about two months ago.'

Shock hits me. 'Oh my goodness.' Suddenly my doubts are back, big time.

'Yes. Terribly sad...' She shakes her head. 'No one's seen much of him since the funeral. They were a wonderfully devoted couple. I can't imagine he's having an easy time of it. But maybe you'll be good for him.' She pauses. 'A word of advice, though. If you don't mind me saying, don't expect too much. He's grieving.'

Her words bring me up short; stop me thinking about myself. Until now, I haven't even thought about this from Luke's angle. In every sense my mother's daughter, I've been too busy thinking of myself. A tear rolls down my cheek as I turn to look at her. 'This is probably a really bad time to be doing this.'

'Not at all.' She considers what to say. 'Anyway, isn't it a little late, now that you're here?'

It turns out Augusta only lives a quarter of a mile away from Luke. 'You've chosen a lovely time of year to come here,' she says. 'Most of the tourists have gone. The island draws breath. And the weather is still wonderful in October.'

'It's just the way it turned out,' I say honestly. 'I've been thinking about it for a while, and then, I kind of had a lull in my life.'

'Oh?' She sounds interested.

'I lost my job.' I shrug. 'Then my flatmate asked me to move out, basically so that she could move her boyfriend in.'

'That was bad luck.' She looks curious. 'What was your job?'

'I was a receptionist – in an arboretum.' It occurs to me she might not know what an arboretum is. 'They have an amazing collection of rare trees. I handled publicity and press releases.' I deliberately leave out the social media side of things.

'In that case, I imagine you'll love it here,' she says crisply. 'We have some wonderful old woodlands and ancient trees on the island. Come to think of it, I have a few trees on my land I'd love you to take a look at – if you have time, of course.'

Before I worked at the arboretum, a tree was just a tree. But now, I'm always interested – and it's astonishing how many people suddenly have a tree they'd like me to look at. 'Of course,' I say politely. 'But I'm not an expert.'

'I'm sure you know more than most of us.' She turns off the main road and follows a narrow, uneven track. 'Gets a bit bumpy from here on, I'm afraid.'

She isn't joking. The car jolts and shudders for about half a mile until the track forks and Augusta stops.

'This is as far as I can take you.' She gets out and goes around to the back where she gets out my rucksack. 'Luke lives up there.' She points towards an even rougher stretch of track that slopes uphill, at the top of which there's a white house set amongst pine trees.

I stare at the track. 'Do you think he's going to mind me turning up like this?'

'No doubt he'll be surprised. But I'm sure he'll cope,' Augusta says, getting back in her car. 'Good luck, my dear. Luke's a decent man. And send my love to Mack.'

Mack? 'Thank you for the lift,' I call after her as she pulls away. Waving a hand out of the window, she drives off in a cloud of dust, leaving me standing there.

I start to struggle up the track. I'm reasonably fit, but the slope is steeper than it looks, the stones loose under my trainers so that more than once my feet slip. 'Fuck,' I mutter under my breath, jumping out of my skin as a lizard runs out in front of me.

But if there's a single blessing to being my mother's daughter, it's that I am not one to be easily defeated. At the top, the track levels out onto a stony parking area, beyond which is quite a decent stretch of lane that leads down the other side. I stare at it in disbelief, wondering why Augusta didn't use it.

'Who are you?'

I turn to see where the voice has come from, finding myself looking at a little girl with a tangle of long hair, her eyes hopeful as she looks at me.

'I'm Bee.' I pause. 'What's your name?'

'I'm Mackenzie. I'm usually called Mack.' She doesn't take her eyes off me. 'Did you get out of Augusta's car?'

'Yes. She offered me a—' I break off as a man appears behind her. In a shapeless black T-shirt that shows off his faded tan, I can't help noticing how sad he looks.

'Hi. Can I help you?'

I take a deep breath, then try to smile. 'Hello. I hope so.' I hesitate. 'Are you Luke Friday?'

He frowns at me. 'I am. Who are you?'

'I'm Bee.' My doubts are back as suddenly I'm regretting the foolish, impetuous optimism that's brought me here; the determination not to listen to my mother when just for once, I'm wishing I had. But it's too late. I'm here. And he's looking at me, without a clue as to this new reality I'm about to launch into his life.

'I'm... your daughter.'

Three things happen: as soon as the words are out, I regret them; Luke freezes, an expression of disbelief on his face. Then as I glance at the girl, she bursts into tears and runs away.

Suddenly I feel terrible. I'm guessing she's Luke's daughter, which means she's just lost her mother. Standing there watching as Luke hotfoots it after her, I've never felt so clumsy. Silently berating myself for not being more subtle, too late it's crystal clear that I should never have come here.

Or at least, not like this. My eyes fill with self-pitying tears as I take out my phone to call a taxi. Then I realise how hopeless this is; that I still don't know the address of this place. Picking up my rucksack, I head down the slope, then back down the track towards the road.

8

ALEX

My mother's absence leaves me slightly at a loose end. But wanting to make the most of this rare free time I have, the following morning, already the cogs of my mind are whirring. After calling Kevin, he invites me over that evening – somewhat reluctantly, and mostly because with his broken ankle, he's stuck there.

'I have this idea,' I say to Kevin as I perch on the edge of one his enormous sofas. His house is in Midhurst; large, detached and impressive, it's also totally devoid of homely touches. 'It's connected to Mum's dementia.' I pause. 'But actually, I think it's been percolating much longer than that.'

'God. I hope you're not planning to get the band back together,' he says disparagingly.

I look at him in disbelief. Kevin is so emotionally unaware, he's the last person I'd imagine to be a mind-reader. But by some fluke, he's bang on. 'As a matter of fact, that's exactly my idea.'

'Dear God.' He rolls his eyes.

I glare at him. 'Would you at least hear me out?'

'Sorry.' He looks slightly less arrogant. 'Go on.'

'Do you know music reaches people with dementia in ways speech often doesn't?' I tell him. 'I don't fully understand how, but it can help reduce anxiety and even remind them who they are. It can also bring back memories they've lost because of the illness.' I watch his face. It's true of much of what I'm trying to engage her with – old photos, friends, family holidays.

'Rachel didn't seem that bad to me,' he says unemotionally.

'I live with her.' I go on, telling him about the small things that would go unnoticed if no one was there to witness them. Her inability to keep track of time, her way of getting up at three o'clock in the morning and going downstairs for breakfast. Of going outside in her pyjamas. 'She can't manage her finances; she forgets she's eaten, and forgets when she hasn't.' I shrug. 'It's all these things put together. I agree. She does look great. But that's partly because I'm there to make sure she looks after herself.' I pause. 'And she's on medication – but I'm also trying to do what I can to slow the illness down.' To draw out these better days, put off the seemingly inevitable.

'Blimey.' Kevin looks flummoxed. 'I have to say I still think getting the band together again is a terrible idea.' He glances at my empty glass. 'Can I get you another beer?'

'I'll get them.' The sight of Kevin hobbling and sloshing beer all over the place is too uncomfortable to witness a second time.

His kitchen is on the same scale as the rest of the house – cavernous and minimalistic, ridiculously large for one lonely, divorced man. But the entire house reeks of loneliness. Kevin clearly has no idea of how to make a cosy, welcoming home, as evidenced by the Gestapo overhead lighting, the uncomfortable sofas in the living room.

I pass him his glass, then sit down. 'Don't you ever miss those days – with the band?'

'Not in the least. I've grown up, thank fuck.' He pauses,

looking at me. 'So, have you actually given up your life to look after your mother?'

I frown. 'I haven't given up my life, as you put it. I decided to move back – and we have a nice life. I work from home, when I can.' Though increasingly, my work time gets interrupted by my mother's demands. And I know as time goes on, it will get more so.

'Bloody hell. There's no way I could do that.'

From the little I've seen of Kevin, he's too selfish to accommodate anyone else's demands, let alone those of someone who has dementia. 'We muddle along.' From the outset, I decided the only way to do this was in a spirit of positivity. Plus, she's my mother. I love her. 'Don't you have parents?'

'Both dead,' he says briefly, as his brow knits in an unattractive frown. 'Doesn't it drive you mad? When she forgets things, or gets up in the middle of the night?'

I think about the last time it happened. It was 4 a.m. and in the end, I left her watching a film. At her insistence, I went back to bed. But I couldn't sleep. I was on edge, waiting for the sound of her clattering in the kitchen, or unbolting the front door. 'To her, it's just the way her world is,' I say simply. 'The fact that I see it differently doesn't make it any less valid than mine.'

'Fuck.' He looks uncomfortable. 'I don't mean to sound callous. But you've probably worked out I have absolutely no feelings. In my world, everything's governed by the law. It's black and white. It means you've put me in an impossible position, Alex.'

Completely lost, I wait for him to elaborate.

'If I'm totally honest with you, the last thing I want is some ghastly reunion with a load of people I haven't seen since our twenties. For the record, it isn't impossible some of them are dead.' He sits back. 'But hearing you talk about Rachel just now...'

'Would you at least help me try to find them?' I ask. 'They may feel the same as you – that's if we're able to track them down. But at least I will have tried.'

'Hmm.' He looks thoughtful. 'Does your mother still sing?'

I nod. 'Only when she thinks I'm not listening.' She sings along to the radio, or when she's alone in her bedroom. Her voice is beautiful.

'Well, Miles should be easy enough to find,' he says crisply. 'I heard him on the radio not that long ago. He was presenting a rather irreverent news show on Friday and Saturday nights. I'll send him an email.'

'Wow.' I'm taken aback by his change of heart. 'Thanks.'

'As for the others,' he goes on. 'There's Atlas – his actual name is Brian. He might be a bit tricky. He moved to Glasgow. After that, he pretty much disappeared. Then there's Luke. Luke Friday – there can't be too many of those. That's about it.' He glances towards the door. 'Couldn't get my laptop, could you? It's in my office – through the door opposite.'

Across the hallway, Kevin's office is the size of our living room. Spartan and organised, the desk is clear apart from his laptop. Picking it up, I take it to him.

'Thanks.' He types away for a minute, then pauses. 'Here we are. Miles Grant. There's an email address for his researchers.' He looks at me. 'What shall I say?'

'Shall I write it?'

Kevin looks put out. 'If you must.'

'Only because I want to explain about my mother.' I take his laptop and start typing an introduction, not wanting to put him off before we've started.

Dear Miles,

I'm contacting you about my mother, Rachel. She used to call herself Roxy, back in the days when you were all in The Rhythm Sheds together. I would really like to talk to you about any old music you might have from that time. My mother has dementia and I think it would help her.

Yours,

Alex

I pass it to Kevin. 'What do you think? It's only a starting point. But hopefully, he'll reply.'

'Hmm.' He's frowning again. 'If it's our old music you want, I can help you with that.'

I look at him, wondering why he hasn't mentioned it before. 'You can?'

'I had it all converted to CDs,' he says.

'You mean you recorded it?' It's the first I've heard of it.

'Leo made tape recordings. I had them digitally enhanced. A moment of untypical sentimentality, I'm sure you'll agree. But if you like, I can lend them to you.'

'I'd love that.' So will my mother, or at least, I'm hoping she will. I glance at his laptop. 'Can you send my email?'

'Oh, yes.' He presses send. 'I'll let you know if he replies. Meanwhile, what about the others? Any thoughts?'

'Not really.' I frown at him. 'Do you have time for this? Shouldn't you be working?'

'In the evenings? Not bloody likely – not unless there's some client dinner or something. In any case, I'm pretty much stuck here at the moment. Doctor tells me I have to rest the thing.' He stares balefully at his ankle.

'OK. So what was Brian's last name?'

'No idea. We only ever called him Atlas. But I wouldn't be

surprised if Leo knows. I'll call him in the morning and ask him.'

'That would be great.'

'Which leaves us with Luke.' Kevin shakes his head. 'Funny old sod. Women seemed to love him, but he was a disaster at relationships.' He looks at me. 'What's so amusing?'

'Sounds a bit like someone else I know.' I try not to smile. 'Can you find him?'

It's lost on Kevin as he types and scrolls for a few minutes, muttering to himself about checking Luke isn't dead first. Then he says, 'Oh.'

'What is it?'

'There's an obituary here for an Amanda Friday. Wife of Luke and mother of Mackenzie. She died two months ago.'

My heart sinks. 'It might not be the same one.'

'The funeral was held in somewhere called Pollensa.' He looks up. 'Good God. That's in Majorca, isn't it?'

'I've no idea.' Getting out my phone, I look it up. It is indeed in Majorca, in the north of the island. I try to think. 'If it is the same Luke Friday, if he's just lost his wife, it isn't going to be the best time to get in touch.'

'My dear boy, when you've been a lawyer as long as I have, you learn there is never a good time.' Kevin sounds impatient. 'It's better just to get on and do things.'

I look at him warily. 'What are you suggesting?'

'I'm suggesting we fly to Palma and hire a car,' he says crisply. 'I'll have to call my office and possibly send a few emails while we're away. But you're free this week, aren't you? I certainly can't do very much. But I can sit in a car, if you don't mind driving.'

Palma? I find myself hedging. This more dynamic side of Kevin is one I haven't seen before. He's a lawyer, I remind myself. He'd hardly be successful if he wasn't good at getting things done. But what's stranger is that after being so dismissive, he's suddenly interested. Or maybe it's the beer talking. 'We still don't know for sure that this is the same Luke we're looking for.'

Kevin sighs. 'Well, I can't find the others right now. So unless you have a better idea?' When I don't say anything, he goes on. 'Right. Let's look at flights.' He types on his keyboard for a minute. 'There's a flight from Gatwick tomorrow at midday. I'll book us on it.'

Just as I'm thinking his generosity seems out of character, he goes on. 'I'll send you my bank details so that you can transfer the cost.'

I get up. 'I'm going home. I'll call you in the morning.'

'You can't leave now.' Kevin looks outraged. 'This is just starting to get interesting.'

'Look, if we're flying to Majorca tomorrow, I need to pick up a few things – including my passport. I also need to get some sleep.' I pause. 'Can you manage on your own?'

'I can clean my teeth and piss, if that's what you're worried about,' he says curtly.

'Fine.' I start edging towards the door. 'I'll see you tomorrow.'

So now what?

As I walk down the track, a million thoughts crowd my head. That I've stuffed up, upset Luke at a difficult time in his life, and more to the point, Mackenzie. That I don't know this place; that I am totally alone here.

I come to the only conclusion I can. This was a monumental mistake and I should go home, my heart sinking as I imagine my mother's response, followed by her insistence that I call Moira and watch my entire life metamorphose into something I don't want. But as I ask myself what I do want, I don't know.

On either side of me, I recognise Aleppo pine trees and I breathe in their scent, turning my eyes to the sky for a moment. It's pale and clear, the air around me filled with birdsong and as I walk, it comes to me. Maybe, right now, I shouldn't go anywhere.

It depends on me finding a cheap enough hotel or B & B. But assuming I do, I could eek out some of my remaining funds and stay a while. Have an adventure – and at the same time, figure out what it is I'm going to do with my life.

Decision made, I turn onto the main road. And just like that, everything starts to change, as far from everything going against me, things take on a momentum of their own. Seeing a taxi come towards me, I wave it down and get in.

'Can you tell me where the nearest town is?'

'You mean Pollensa?'

'I think so. Yes,' I add, more decisively. 'Also, I need a place to stay. Not expensive.'

The driver glances at me in the rear-view mirror. 'I know somewhere. I will take you.'

At last, feeling like I've wrestled some semblance of control back, I gaze out of the window as we drive along quiet roads, as now and then, through the trees, the sea comes into view. Then, reaching the outskirts of a town, the driver turns down a narrow street of old buildings and stops at the end, nodding to a door on the corner.

'Is my friend's place. She will give you a room.' He gets out and opens the car door. 'Come. I will introduce you to her.'

* * *

Carmela, the driver's friend, is welcoming and after checking me in and offering me what seems like a really cheap rate, she shows me to my room.

'It is not fancy,' she says, standing in the doorway. 'We like to stay open. Winter is coming, but still a few people come here.'

The room is on the ground floor, clean and simply furnished, the bed made up with soft white linen. 'This is lovely. Thank you.' I walk over to the doors that open onto my own little private terrace, complete with bistro table and two chairs, taking it in, slightly dazed. It's little short of a miracle that it's me who's standing here. You see, things like this happen to the Saskias of this world.

After showering and changing into clean clothes, I'm feeling distinctly at odds with myself. Putting it down to not having eaten all day, I decide to go out.

'Adios, Bee.' Carmela waves as I walk towards the front door.

'Adios,' I call back, slightly proud of my one word of Spanish as I step outside into the street.

As I walk, I soon discover that Pollensa is a pretty place, steeped in history, with shady streets through buildings of pale terracotta and stone, a multitude of cafés and bars, all set against a backdrop of mountains.

After wandering for a while, as it starts getting dark, I find a bar, where I order a beer and some tapas. I pick at the food, my appetite suddenly deserting me as I think back over the events of today, and suddenly everything catches up with me.

So much for having an adventure. I'm irresponsible, I tell myself. Coming here on a whim, spending money on eating out when I don't have a job. I need to be sensible about this. Tomorrow, I'll go and apologise to Luke, then call my mother and tell her I'm coming back. I should probably also call Moira. The familiar is luring me back, reminds me how safe it feels; tightening its hold to make sure I won't get away again.

But what the actual? Picking up my phone to look at flights, I put it down again. *You're an adult, Bee,* I tell myself firmly. *You came here precisely to get away from the familiar. Yes, you might feel displaced. But get a grip. It isn't up to anyone else to dictate if this is right or not. You owe Luke nothing. And your mother won't care where you are. This might not be what you expected, but in many ways, it's a gift. Coming when you have time on your hands, it would be churlish of you not to embrace it.*

After ordering another beer, inspiration strikes. If I do stay on – and it still is very much an if, perhaps I'll look for a job online, work remotely. Meanwhile, apart from my online rants for the arboretum, I have my own social media. Maybe I should start a new profile about the trees on this island. Their symbolism and history, the myths surrounding them. Their magic and majesty. But my enthusiasm is short lived. Just thinking about it feels too much. But right now, after the day I've had, everything does.

* * *

The next morning, my head feels heavy, my thoughts an incoherent jumble. I step out onto my terrace and gaze across the garden as I give myself a pep talk. I'm on a Mediterranean island for however long. But while I'm here, there's no reason not to make the best of it.

After getting dressed, I go outside. It's a lovely morning. Sunny; optimistic. Gathering a baguette and a bottle of water from a mini supermarket, I hop on a bus to a nearby beach.

I've made a conscious decision not to think about anything other than the here and now, but as I watch the world go by, my mind starts to race, a level of panic setting in, because I can't afford this. I didn't come here to do nothing. To sit on a beach, to have an impromptu holiday. I came here to meet Luke Friday, and if that isn't going to happen, I need to go home and get a job.

Calm the fuck down and get a coffee, Bee, I tell myself. *Then you can start to make a plan.*

Ten minutes later, the bus stops beside a wide sandy cove, and after getting out, I stare at the brilliant blue of the sea for a moment, then around me, at people dressed in shorts and T-shirts, as I feel the sun start to soak into me.

Buying a takeaway coffee from a shack on the beach, I find a spot away from everyone else and sit on the sand. It feels a world away from October in England. From real life... As the thought enters my head, that's when the wheels of fate kick in again. Wedging my coffee cup into the sand, I'm getting my notebook out when a rather large and determined dog comes splashing out of the sea and makes a beeline for me.

Cavorting around, he catches my coffee cup and knocks it flying, as out of the corner of my eye, I glimpse a woman running towards it. 'Cato! Bad dog. Come here.'

Recognising the imperious tones of Augusta, I do a double take, then realise the dog is none other than the previously demure chewer of car seats. I push my sunglasses on top of my head and get to my feet. Thinking it's a glorious game, Cato jumps up at me.

'I'm so sorry.' Reaching me, Augusta sounds mortified. Then she frowns. 'Goodness. I didn't realise it was you, Bee. Wretched dog. You must be soaked.'

'A little damp, that's all. It's nothing. Me and coffee, it doesn't always go too well.' I'm thinking of the guy at the arboretum again, as Cato starts rootling in my bag. I pull it away from him.

'I don't know what's got into him. He isn't usually like this.' Augusta reaches for his collar, but he darts away, then charges into the sea. She sighs. 'I suppose I'll just have to let him get it out of his system.' She turns to me. 'How are you?' She frowns. 'Or rather, what I really should be asking is, how did it go with Luke yesterday?'

The wattage of this beautiful October day dims slightly. 'Not great,' I say carefully. 'I realised it was a really bad idea. He and Mack have enough to think about without a complete stranger turning up.'

'Oh dear.' Augusta looks concerned. 'Is that what he said?'

I shake my head. 'He said very little. But Mack was upset.

She ran inside and he went after her. So I decided to leave. It really wasn't the right time.'

'Am I missing something?' Augusta looks confused. 'I'm struggling to think of anything you could have said to upset Mack like that.'

'The thing is...' I break off. 'There was a reason. But it's complicated.'

Augusta glances at my upturned cup. 'Let me buy you another coffee. I'm not in a hurry this morning – which is just as well.' She glances at her errant dog cavorting in the water. 'There's a nice little place over there.' She points to a bar further along the beach.

Over coffee, Augusta listens as I tell her the real reason I've come here.

She's suitably shocked. 'And you've only just found out that Luke's your father?'

I nod. 'My mother didn't want me to know. She said he was in the past, and I didn't need him in my life.'

'Of course, I don't know your mother. But I'd say that's a little unfair.' Augusta sounds astonished. 'Not surprising you want to meet him. Your mother has nothing to worry about. Luke's a good man – and a wonderful father to Mack. It's why I find this so surprising.'

'I don't think she told him she was pregnant.' I shrug. 'She said they weren't together very long.'

'But surely...' Augusta frowns again. 'Luke had a right to know – unless she had a good reason not to tell him.'

'She didn't mention one.' But my mother lives her life on the surface. 'She has no trouble letting me know when she's annoyed with me. But she doesn't talk about emotions, or anything difficult. For as long as I can remember, she's always acted like everything is fine. Even when it isn't.'

'Too painful for her, I imagine,' Augusta says.

'Why would you say that?' I'm curious.

'Well, it's a classic distraction, isn't it? Acting like everything is fine means you avoid facing the reality that it might not be.'

As she speaks, there's a lump in my throat, because she's described my mother to a tee. Throughout my childhood, she never asked what was wrong, or comforted me when I was upset. Instead, I was told to keep my chin up, that disappointments were part of life. To just to get on with things – there was no point fretting over them. 'I think you're right.' A single tear rolls down my cheek. True to my upbringing, I wipe it away and pin on a smile. 'Sorry. But I suppose your words struck a chord.'

'Ah.' She makes a show of stirring her coffee. 'Odd creatures, aren't we? Humans?'

I look at her, astonished. 'I beg your pardon?'

'Well, part of being human is having emotions. Feelings. Not exactly natural to try to deny that. Anyway.' She pauses. 'What are we going to do about Luke?'

'I think probably nothing,' I say.

'Am I right in thinking that beyond a brief "hello, I'm your daughter", you haven't actually spoken?'

I sigh. 'Pretty much.'

'Oh dear,' she says. 'Does closing the door after the horse has bolted ring any bells?'

I stare at her, wondering what she means. But I suppose, now that Luke knows about me, there's no going back from that.

'My dear, don't you think he's going to be curious? If I know Luke, he'll be kicking himself. He isn't one to shirk responsibilities, you know.'

'He isn't responsible for me,' I say quickly. 'He doesn't even know me.'

'Quite.' She looks impatient. 'What I meant to say is now

that he knows you're here, almost certainly, he'll want to get to know you. Where are you staying?'

'At a little hotel in Pollensa. It's really nice.'

'I bet I know where. It must still be costing you, though. I'll have a word with Luke – if you'd like me to?' She takes out her phone. 'Give me your mobile number.' After programming it into her phone, she glances towards the sea where Cato is wreaking havoc in the shallows. 'Excuse me a moment.' She gets up. 'Cato,' she bellows, before at last her dog thunders over and sits obediently next to her. 'About time.' She clips his lead on. 'I'd better get him home before he does any harm. I'll call in on Luke on the way back. Just promise me – don't go rushing off? Not yet, at least.'

After our conversation, the focus of my day seems to change. Or perhaps it's the way I see it that starts to change. Augusta is right. Having turned up on Luke's doorstep and told him who I am, it doesn't seem right not to talk to him. If he wants to, that is.

Sitting on the beach, I watch some late season tourists, in particular a family with two young children. Running, laughing, they seem carefree in a way I never knew. But there was too much loss in our family, I remind myself, as it occurs to me that maybe that's why my mother could never let her hair down. Let go... Run splashing through the shallows with me. Reasons we both know, but even now, never speak about.

But things – life – losses – they happen to all of us. Take Luke and Mack, grieving the loss of a wife and mother. Suddenly there's a lump in my throat. It doesn't do to dwell. But it doesn't do to bury it away. I've heard it said that you should write about what you know. But instead of the state of happiness I subscribe to, what I do know, in abundance, is how being alone feels. Being lost. About sadness. Maybe that's what my new Instagram should be about.

I allow my mind to start to go there, until my conditioning kicks in, a knee-jerk reflex. *Write about trees, Bee. Who wants to read about sadness?* But as I look out across the sunlit sea, I silence the voice, because people write about almost every subject known to man. And when it comes to who would want to read about it, I know I would.

* * *

Later that afternoon, my phone buzzes, an unfamiliar number flashing up on the screen. Guessing it might be Luke, I'm cautious as I answer it. 'Hello?'

'Hi, Bee.' It's a man's voice. 'It's Luke. I, er, hope you don't mind me calling. Augusta gave me your number.'

'I don't mind. It's fine,' I say quickly. 'And I want to say how sorry I am – about yesterday... turning up like that... and upsetting Mack.'

'Mack's fine.' He pauses. 'I was hoping we could meet up – if you still want to, that is?'

Relief fills me. 'I'd really like that.'

* * *

That evening, I walk to the bar where Luke's suggested we meet, a little place in a square edged by historic-looking buildings, dominated by a gnarled old olive tree. When I arrive, he's already sitting at a table outside, a beer in front of him. Deep in thought, at first, he doesn't appear to notice me.

'Um, hi,' I say quietly.

He looks up, startled. 'Bee.' He gets up. 'Sorry, I was miles away. It's nice to see you. Er, will you sit down?'

'It's nice to see you too.' I pull out a chair opposite him and sit down, suddenly silent. I've thought for so long about this moment, now that it's here, I don't know what to say.

Luke gestures to a passing waiter. 'What would you like to drink?' he asks me.

'White wine.' I sit there while Luke speaks to the waiter. 'Where's Mack?'

'Augusta's with her. She wanted to come. Mack doesn't like to miss out on anything. But I thought it was best it was just the two of us – this time, at least.'

My heart lifts in hope, that this isn't a one-off. 'I hope she's OK?' I ask.

'She's fine. I suppose it was quite a surprise,' he says. 'For both of us. When you left, I was worried you might have gone home. I'm glad you haven't.'

'I thought about it.' My voice trembles. 'But right now, I have no urgent reason to go back there, so I thought I'd stay for a few days. I'm so sorry,' I say again. 'I really am. It didn't occur to me that you'd have a daughter.'

'Another one, you mean,' he says wryly. 'How could you have known?' He picks up his beer.

'I'm so sorry about your wife.' When he doesn't say anything, I go on. 'Augusta told me. I got a lift with her from the airport.'

'So she said.' He frowns. 'But I'm still not sure how she fits in to all this.'

'It was pure coincidence she happened to be there.' Now I think about it again, it really was some coincidence. 'But it was lucky for me. I left your address in England.' I falter. 'I only realised when I was trying to get a taxi. Augusta had just dropped her nephew off. He left his passport in her car and she came back to give it to him.'

'I see.' There's an awkward silence before he sighs. 'Look, to be honest with you, it isn't the easiest time.' He looks up, his blue eyes meeting mine for a moment. 'We're not at all ourselves, right now. Amanda... Well, she was the heart of everything.'

I watch him struggle with himself before he goes on.

'And I'm sure this isn't what you were expecting,' he says.

'I don't think I was expecting anything,' I say honestly. 'My mother refused to tell me about you. My mother's name is Cassandra,' I say, watching for a look of recognition to cross his face.

But he looks perplexed. 'Cassandra?'

I feel my stomach turn over as I stare at him. Have I got this horribly, terribly wrong? Has my mother got this wrong? 'Did you know her as Sandy? Or Cassie? She reinvents herself.' Cassandra is her latest incarnation.

He looks relieved. 'I know who you mean. She called herself Sandra in those days. You look a little like her.' He looks distant for a moment. 'You have to believe I knew nothing about you.'

I raise my eyebrows. 'You really didn't know she was pregnant?'

He shakes his head. 'She didn't tell me. But we weren't together that long. Four, five months as I remember. It was a lot of fun, but I don't think either of us was looking to settle down. She was pretty independent, as I remember her.' He pauses. 'So she hadn't mentioned me until recently?'

'No. I asked her. Many times.' I shrug. 'She just changed the subject. She said you belonged in the past.' Much to my frustration. 'Your name isn't on my birth certificate. I'd never heard of you until I found an old diary of hers. It isn't something I'd normally do,' I say quickly. 'But I was desperate to know who my father was. Your name was in there – and the timing seemed to coincide with nine months before my birthday. When I told her what I'd found, she didn't deny it.' I shrug. 'That was when I decided to come here.'

'She was always stubborn,' he says softly. 'How is she?'

'Still stubborn.' Our eyes meet in a moment of shared understanding. 'She's fine. Usually, I don't see her that often. But I've moved in with her for a while. I'm between jobs – and places to live. And boyfriends.' My voice wavers.

'It can't be an easy time for you,' Luke says. 'Still. Must be nice to spend some time with her.'

'I'm not sure about nice.' Realising how ungrateful I sound, I try to laugh it off. 'I know I'm lucky I can go there, but she's always on my case about one thing or another – she has strong opinions on how I ought to be living my life.'

Instead of amused, he looks curious. 'You don't share them?'

'Not exactly.'

He looks at me with interest. 'So what is it you do? For work, that is.'

'I used to work in an arboretum – as a receptionist. I was involved with marketing and social media... But I lost my job – they were cost-cutting.' I'm deliberately economic with the facts. 'Then a day later, my flatmate asked me to move out.'

'That's bad luck,' Luke says. 'So, what will you do now?'

'If I'm honest with you, I'm at a bit of a crossroads,' I admit. 'My mother's made it clear I can only stay with her for a short while. She has this cleaning job lined up for me with Moira – a friend of hers. I really don't want to take it. But that isn't why I came here.' I try to explain. 'I think growing up without you in my life has left me feeling I'm missing something – about who I am, if that makes sense?'

Luke looks thoughtful. 'I can imagine it would leave you with a lot of questions.'

'It's not so much questions...' I hesitate. 'I think it's more about having a sense of the parts of me that come from you. And maybe of my place in life.' Maybe it's because I'm talking to Luke, but it's the first time I've been able to put it satisfactorily into words.

Sitting there, he doesn't say anything. But right now, he has enough going on without having to think about my problems. 'I'm sorry,' I say quickly. 'You have other things on your mind. I'm fine. I really am. My hotel is booked for the next couple of days, but after that, I'll probably leave.' As I speak, real life rears its ugly head again; all my thoughts of working online, of staying on the island for longer, turning to dust. 'I need to face the music!' I'm talking about my ongoing life.

'Of course,' Luke says. 'You'll probably feel better once you have a plan in place.'

I nod. 'Probably. Maybe we could meet up again before I leave. Mack, too, if she still wants to.'

'You're quite different to your mother.' Luke's silent for a moment. Then he sighs. 'Look, I'm not very good at these things. But you don't have to leave so soon – unless you want to. If you think you can cope with us, you could come and stay. Who knows, it might even be good for Mack to have someone else in her life – once she gets used to the idea.'

My heart lifts in hope. 'Are you sure?' I pause. 'I don't want to cause any problems for Mack – or for you.'

'You won't. She just needs time.' Luke looks at me. 'She really misses her mother.'

'Do you mind me asking what happened?' I say quietly.

His eyes meet mine again. 'Amanda was hit by a car – the driver was drunk. She'd gone for a walk, like she did most days.' He sounds numb, as though even now, he can't take it in. 'They airlifted her to hospital. But she didn't make it.'

'God.' I'm horrified; imagine the shock they must have felt losing her; so suddenly, without warning.

'It just seems so senseless.' He stares at the table. 'We met on my fiftieth birthday. I'd given up on the idea of ever meeting anyone like her. I felt so lucky.' His voice wavering as he breaks off. 'Anyway, I should probably get back to Mack. No doubt she'll have a whole list of questions about you.' He finishes his beer, the conversation clearly over. 'Think about what I said – about staying.' He pauses. 'Why don't you come over to the house tomorrow? Around six, once I've got Mack back from her dance class? Stay a couple of nights – we can take it from there.'

'Sure.' I look at this man; search for likenesses with this stranger who's my flesh and blood; a peculiar mixture of emotions enveloping me.

* * *

Later, back at my hotel, as I lie in bed, moonlight shines through the window. I think of Luke again, of his obvious grief; of Mack, missing her mother, their lives changed forever and all because of a callous driver, a careless mistake.

Being here is so far from what I imagined and that's no bad thing. I didn't come here hoping to find a life like I have in England. I didn't know what to expect. But I'm already realising, it isn't for Luke to fix what's missing in my life. Only one person can do that – and that's me.

10

ALEX

Back home, thinking of the impending trip to Majorca with Kevin, I'm starting to question the wisdom of turning up on Luke's doorstep. I open my laptop and type in Luke Friday, finding it's as Kevin said; there's mention of only one. I look up Pollensa, discovering it's an old town in the north of the island, about six kilometres from the coast.

Closing my laptop, I sigh. Firstly, I can't help thinking it's still a long shot. There's also the prospect of travelling all that way with Kevin sitting next to me. If it was somewhere in the UK, I wouldn't have thought twice about it. But then I think of my mother, because this is about her. If this is what it takes to have a shot at getting the band back together, if in some small way it will help her, I have to do it.

* * *

I awake on Saturday as dawn is breaking; to an unfamiliar silence in the house as I pull back the curtains and watch the sun rise above the rooftops. Then, knowing my mother will be awake, I get my phone and call her.

There's a muffled sound before she answers. 'Alex. Is everything all right?'

'Everything's fine. How's it going, Mum?' I ask.

'I'm not sure where to start.' She sounds mystified. 'I suppose I'm all right. But Lorna has a man in her life. Can you believe that?'

'That's great, isn't it?' I say. 'Is he nice?'

'I suppose he is.' She sounds unsure. 'You'd think she might at least have told me.'

'Well, she has, hasn't she?' I reason. 'She was probably waiting until she saw you. Are you having a nice time?'

'Not too bad,' she says ungraciously.

I try to get her to focus. 'Mum, do you remember in the hospital, we saw Kevin? You know – the drummer from back in the days you were in the band.'

'Of course I remember Kevin,' she says.

'I saw him last night. He's going to lend me his recordings of some of the music you all used to play. I thought you'd like to listen to them.'

'Recordings?' She sounds mystified. 'I don't remember anyone ever recording us. I think you're muddled, Alex.'

It's clearly one of her more confused days and this conversation is going nowhere. But it can wait until I pick her up next week. 'We'll talk about it when you're back from Lorna's. Don't worry. It isn't important.'

'Recorded?' she says again, as if to herself.

'Mum, I'm sorry. I have to go. Send my love to Lorna. I'll see you soon.'

I end the call. Then I get out a bag and start packing a few things, wondering if Kevin's sorted anywhere for us to stay.

It's the end of the season; I can't imagine finding a hotel will be a problem. But for all his faults, Kevin is supremely organised. When I pick him up a couple of hours later, he taps his watch. 'You're late.'

'We didn't arrange a time,' I remind him. 'And our flight isn't until midday.'

'It's better to have time in hand. It isn't as though I can exactly hurry, is it?' he says acidly. 'Anyway, I've arranged a hire car for us to pick up when we arrive in Palma and I've booked us rooms in a small hotel in a town near to where Luke lives,' he tells me. 'Bloody expensive given it's out of season,' he grumbles. 'Get my bag, will you? It's at the top of the stairs.'

I'm starting to get an impression of what it must be like to work with Kevin. I can also completely understand why his wife left him. He seems to live in a world of facts and regulations, of clock-watching; of barking orders and switched off emotions.

At the top of the stairs, I notice a photo of Kevin with a woman, presumably his ex-wife. Pausing, I study it. Kevin looks younger, his face softer; a similar age to him, the woman is smiling. I wonder what happened, or if Kevin just became more of the Kevin he is now.

'What are you doing up there?' Kevin calls up the stairs. 'Time's getting on.'

'Coming.' I pick up his smart leather bag and sling it over my shoulder, then go back down. 'Right. Let's go.'

I turn down Kevin's offer of taking his car. I know him well enough to realise that it would expose me to a barrage of criticism about my driving, not to mention abuse of his car. As it is, he sits quietly, but only for the first ten minutes.

'Does Rachel know we're doing this?'

'No.' It would be too much for her to take in. Then she'd forget, only to remember again later a more confused version.

'I'll explain it to her, if – when – this comes to anything.' I pause. 'Did you speak to Leo – about Atlas?'

'Yes of course,' he says impatiently. 'He's going to speak to him.' He breaks off as his mobile rings. 'Excuse me. I need to take this.'

I try not to listen to the exchange between Kevin and someone who sounds like one of his colleagues. He's abrupt to the point of rudeness, before he ends the call.

'I work with fuckwits,' he announces unnecessarily. 'No common sense between any of them.'

Given he works for a law firm, I find it hard to believe. I say nothing, however; I have no wish to provoke another of his rants. Meanwhile, it's as if the gods are on our side, not least because for a while, Kevin falls silent. And outside, we're blessed with a beautiful day, the roads relatively empty as we drive to the airport.

'Where do you work?' I ask Kevin.

'Guildford,' he says. 'Talking of which, there's an email they're supposed to be sending me.' After putting on his glasses, he takes out his phone again, scrolling down it for a moment and typing a brief reply. 'Nothing they can't deal with,' he says, switching it off and putting it in his pocket.

'Has Miles replied?'

'Not yet.' He glances at the satnav. 'Head for the short stay car park.'

I glance at him doubtfully. 'It'll cost a small fortune. I'll drop you at the terminal and park in the long stay.'

'Don't be ridiculous,' he says curtly. 'If it's a problem, I'll pay.'

I want to tell him it isn't a problem. It's just to me, an unnecessary extravagance. But if he wants to pay, I'm hardly going to argue with him, though suddenly it strikes me wherever we park, there'll still be some distance to walk. 'We should have organised a wheelchair for you,' I say.

'For Christ's sake. I can manage perfectly well with crutches,' he snaps.

I open my mouth to tell him he'll have a devil of a job making it all the way to the departure gate, before sitting in a cramped seat for two and half hours. But rather than set myself up for more of his objections, I decide to let him find that out for himself.

'Can't stand flying,' he says. 'Just the thought of all that recycled air and people breathing down your neck. Did you know that an aeroplane is one of the worst places for catching a virus?' He glances at me. 'What do you do? For work? Or what did you do?'

'I'm a climate change researcher – I freelance.'

'Good God.' Kevin sounds disparaging. 'How long have you been doing that?'

'A few years.' I shrug. 'More specifically, I study the oceans – we monitor changing trends and analyse data. It's important. Not enough people realise how important.'

'It's bloody greenwashing if you ask me. Gets everywhere, these days,' he grumbles.

But for obvious reasons, climate change is a topic I feel strongly about; responses like Kevin's leaving me outraged. 'It's about time it did. We can't carry on the way we are, can we?'

'It's served us well enough so far.'

I shake my head, but too often, this is what I come up against. 'If you were to read anything other than the *Lawyers Weekly*, and whatever other right-wing rubbish you no doubt follow, you would be aware we're living in a time of crisis. Rising sea levels, forest fires, the destruction of the rainforests...'

'You actually believe all that hogwash?' He sounds incredulous.

'I do.' I pause. 'The reason being it isn't hogwash. It's science – and it's true. Saving this planet is possibly the only thing that matters right now. Or at least, it matters more than anything else.'

'I suppose you're fine with all these activists running wild, gluing themselves to motorways and wreaking havoc on the rest of us. Because from where I see it, society is breaking down,' he says cynically. 'People like you completely miss the point that human beings are basically savages. The law is what keeps society together,' he goes on. 'Without it, we'd descend into anarchy.'

I'm silent, taking in the reality that I am trapped in a car with my worst nightmare. A blinkered, narrow-minded human being, who doesn't care about anything beyond his small, bigoted bubble and his bank account. But as I know, there are millions of Kevins out there, who all feel exactly the same. 'Have you been to Greece?' I ask through gritted teeth, remembering the last time I went there.

'No.' He sounds exasperated. 'What's bloody Greece got to do with anything?'

'You should go. I stayed on an island. It was idyllic. Paradise.' I remember the pristine beaches and clear water. 'You could walk through an incredible forest and find yourself on the most stunning, wild beach. But one day, while we were out driving, we passed a landfill site. It was horrific. It was a sprawling mountain of rubbish that seemed to go on and on. You see, the rubbish we pile up doesn't decay and go away. It just grows, every year. And this is what's happening almost everywhere.'

'Which is all very well, but rubbish has to go somewhere,' Kevin says.

'You're missing the point,' I tell him. 'We've become a throw-away society. We generate far too much of it.'

'Thank God. There's the turning for the airport.' Clearly bored of our conversation, Kevin slides his chair back, wincing as he stretches his legs out.

People like Kevin infuriate me. He's ignorant, I tell myself. He doesn't understand, and he doesn't want to. But talking to him has helped remind me of something. I am passionate – about doing what I can to make a difference to this world.

* * *

As predicted, our progress through the terminal building is painfully slow, while with every passing minute, Kevin grows progressively more crotchety. We make it as far as security before a voice comes from behind us.

'Excuse me?' I turn to see one of the airport staff watching us. 'If you'd like to come with me, gentlemen, we can offer you assistance through the airport.'

'Fantastic,' I say at the same time that Kevin says, 'Absolutely not.'

The ground staff guy isn't put off. 'You're in luck. Usually you have to notify us well in advance. Where are you gentlemen going today?'

'Palma,' Kevin says. 'Be a good chap and get out of the way. As you can see, we're not exactly making rapid progress.'

'Gate 402.' The man glances at the departures screen, then shakes his head. 'Do you realise that's almost a mile away?'

* * *

'I absolutely detest making a spectacle of myself,' Kevin mutters under his breath in the electric special assistance buggy; a sentence that isn't entirely true, given that he regularly stands up in court in front of numerous, unknown people.

'I would feel grateful if I were you,' I tell him. 'You'd never have managed a mile on those.' I nod towards his crutches.

'We'll never know, will we?' He turns and looks the other way.

Mercifully, he stays silent as we weave past people on our way to the gate. To my amusement, when we reach it, Kevin's helped into a wheelchair, after which the ground staff insist on boarding him before anyone else. His manner is curmudgeonly at best, bordering on rude at worst, meaning I'm slightly embarrassed at being associated with him, both apologising and expressing my gratitude profusely to everyone, while Kevin appears oblivious to it all.

'After all that malarkey, I need a bloody drink,' he says.

'You'll have to wait until after take-off.' I'm starting to wonder if he has a drink problem. 'You really shouldn't be so ungrateful. Everyone is going out of their way to help you,' I remind him.

Sitting there stiffly, he manages a humph before turning silent.

Fortunately, we're not delayed. Once we're airborne, Kevin gets fidgety again, presumably because he's used to being in charge of his own destiny, not placing it in the hands of some unknown pilot.

'Bloody risky, isn't it? Flying?' he mutters. But after a double Scotch on the rocks, he starts to relax a little.

After a second, his head lolls and he starts to snore. Turning away, I take in the view from the window as we fly over France, then further south over the snow-capped mountain peaks of the Pyrenees.

It seems bizarre that just a couple of days ago, with the prospect of my mother staying at Lorna's for a week, I was imagining a quiet break at home, not a last-minute flight to Majorca. But as I should know by now, it's astonishing how quickly things can change.

Two hours after taking off, we overfly Barcelona, then start our descent into Palma, as I find myself hoping that Luke is less intransigent than Kevin is. Getting closer, I'm treated to a view of the rocky west coast of Majorca. Then about ten minutes before landing, I nudge Kevin. 'We're nearly here.'

One of the cabin crew comes up to us. 'If you would remain in your seats until everyone else has disembarked, someone will come and assist you.'

To his credit, Kevin doesn't argue. Just nods and says an abrupt, 'Thank you.'

The plane is less than half full, and after landing and taxiing in, Kevin grumbles half-heartedly as the other passengers disembark. But it isn't long before we're off the plane and being driven through security in another buggy, then out into the arrivals hall.

Finding the car hire desk, we finalise the paperwork, then go outside to pick up the car. After loading in our bags, I programme the satnav and we're away.

'Pretty painless, really,' Kevin says as we drive away from the airport.

'I think you were lucky,' I remind him. 'All that help you had?'

He doesn't respond, just changes the subject. 'I imagine you know where we're going.'

'I'm following this.' I nod towards the satnav into which I've programmed Pollensa. 'Do you have an address for Luke?'

'Not yet. Can't be too hard, though, can it? It's a little town in a little island, for heaven's sake. Someone's bound to have heard of him.'

The roads take us north, winding through stunning scenery of green hills, orchards, olive groves, of distant sea views, as it soon becomes apparent Majorca is much bigger than I'd realised. Even so, it's less than an hour later when we reach Pollensa.

Kevin fiddles with the satnav. 'The hotel is two minutes away.'

Following its directions, I turn up a narrow street, on either side of which are characterful townhouses with balconies of tumbling flowers.

'It's there,' Kevin says abruptly, pointing to an entrance as we pass it. 'For God's sake, Alex. You missed the turning.'

'I don't think so.' On this occasion, he's wrong. Slowing down, I turn through a narrow gateway into a small parking area in front of a large old house. 'I do believe this is where we're staying.'

Pulling over, I park under the shade of a tree. I get out and stand there for a moment. We're in the middle of the town, but it's wonderfully quiet, the traffic noise no more than a faint hum. Raising my arms, I stretch as Kevin levers himself out and reaches into the back for his crutches.

'Bring the bags, would you?' Without pausing, he starts hobbling towards the door.

I get out our bags and reach the door before he does. I hold it open, watching as he struggles up the stone steps and over the doorstep. 'Bloody hell,' he mutters.

'Take your time,' I advise.

'Can't do anything else, can I?' he snaps.

As he propels himself towards the reception desk, the

woman there raises an eyebrow. 'My name is Carmela. Can we help you, sir?'

'No. Thank you,' he adds. Reaching the bar, he rests his elbows on it. 'We have two rooms booked. The name's Carlisle.'

'Signor Carlisle,' Carmela says slowly, running her finger down a list of names on the screen in front of her. 'You're in rooms five and six. There's an adjoining door.' She glances at me, then back at him.

'That really won't be necessary,' he says.

She hands over the keys. 'Second floor, turn right at the top of the stairs.' She smiles at him.

'Where's the lift?' Kevin says.

Her eyes turn to his crutches. 'I am sorry. We do not have one. If you would like, I can ask someone to take your bag.'

'Now, look.' Kevin starts to bluster. Then he catches my eye. 'Look,' he says in a more conciliatory tone. 'I don't suppose you have a room downstairs, do you?'

'I can check,' she says doubtfully. Studying her laptop, she frowns. 'You are in luck. There is one. The customer checked out early – just a little while ago. It is a little on the small side, but it is on the ground floor – in the annex. Through there.' She gestures towards some double doors leading onto a garden.

'I'll take it,' Kevin says. He turns to me. 'Do you mind bringing my bag?'

* * *

Of course, the room is far too small for Kevin, as he tells me in no uncertain terms. In addition, the bathroom is dated, the view limited to the garden. But with his broken ankle, it's more palatable than attempting the stairs.

My room, on the other hand, is large; after too many hours

with Kevin, a sanctuary, with a newly modernised bathroom and a window that looks across town, with distant views towards the sea. I feel a pang of regret that my mother isn't here with me to see this. But whereas in the past, she loved to travel, it's a measure of the progression of her illness that with the best will in the world, I know how difficult it would be to get her here.

Having arranged to meet in the bar for something to eat, I'm relieved when Kevin tells me his ankle is hurting and he's eating in his room. It's also the perfect opportunity for a little solo exploring. I go downstairs and pause in reception.

'Do you happen to know someone called Luke Friday?' I ask the woman behind the desk. It's a long shot, but we have to start somewhere.

She smiles. 'I do, as it happens, though he hasn't been in for a while. Not since his wife passed.' A shadow crosses her face. 'So sad, it was. Signora Friday was a lovely lady.' She pauses. 'Are you a friend of his?'

'I'm not. But my mother was.'

'She is not with you?' The woman looks interested.

I shake my head. 'No. She couldn't make it.' I pause. 'You don't happen to know where Luke lives, do you?'

She must decide I'm trustworthy because she writes down the name of a nearby village. 'I do not know his house. But someone there will be able to help you.'

I go out and wander along the narrow streets. It's a long time since I last left the UK. Being here is already making me think, too long. The holiday in Greece I told Kevin about was three years ago.

Even though it's October, there's a gentle buzz of life, of small boutiques; cafés and restaurants with tables spilling onto the streets. Spoilt for choice, I settle for a tapas bar that Kevin would most likely have dismissed as too rustic; taking a moment to be grateful that I'm alone. But as I devour my food, my old friend, Guilt, is back, not least because I know my mother would love this. She's always loved welcoming places where people gather. My guilt is two-fold; I haven't told her where I am, or why I've come here.

Whether she would have talked me out of coming, or wanted to come, too, it's impossible to know. Dementia is an ever-changing picture; no two days are ever the same. But as I think about her, I feel another pang of protectiveness towards her. Yes, there are challenges, but for now, life is still good. It's why I'm here, doing whatever I can to help her make the most of the good days.

DEAR UNIVERSE

I'm writing to you because I don't think my last letter explained things properly. You see, I know I said I'd like a sister. But what I didn't say was I was thinking about a younger one. Like my dad getting married again, one day, not yet, then having a baby with someone. I wasn't expecting a grown-up sister I didn't know about.

It's my fault. I should have made it clearer. And I should also say thank you, because you did bring me a sister, even if she isn't the right age.

THANK YOU, THANK YOU, THANK YOU.

But if anything, my dad is sadder because he's only just found out about her. And he probably feels bad about that, too.

I wish life didn't have to be so complicated.

My mum said you don't always bring us what we think we want. You give us what we need. If that's true, maybe, I need Bee.

I hope that makes it clearer. Thank you again for being there.

Mackenzie Friday

11

BEE

That evening, I'm slightly trepidatious as Carmela's friend picks me up in his taxi. As I climb in, I frown as I notice a man walk down the street, not sure why there's something familiar about him.

'You do not stay long?' the driver asks as we head away from the town.

'I'm not sure how long I'm staying,' I tell him. 'I'm catching up with family.'

'Nice.' He smiles in the rear-view mirror. 'Family is important, isn't it?'

'It is,' I say. But an odd feeling comes over me as I'm realising I've never really known how that feels.

Instead of taking the track Augusta used, the driver turns up a smooth stretch of lane through an overgrown olive grove that comes to an end the other side of Luke's villa.

'We are here,' he announces.

'Thank you.' I hand over some euros, then open the door.

'You are welcome.' He hesitates. 'I hope you enjoy this time with your family.'

I get out, then lift my rucksack out just as Mack comes around the side of the house. As the taxi drives away, she looks at me shyly.

'Hello,' I say. 'It's nice to see you.' I pause. 'I hope it's OK I've come here.'

When she doesn't say anything, I go on. 'Is your dad here?'

She nods, then turns and starts walking back around the house. I follow her along the gravel path onto a wide sheltered terrace with breathtaking views across hills, of peach-coloured skies as the sun fades.

'Bee.'

I turn to see Luke, Mack beside him, holding on to his arm. 'Hi. I hope this is still OK?'

'Of course.' He eyes my rucksack. 'Let me take that.'

He carries it inside, Mack following behind. 'How long is Bee staying, Daddy?' she says quietly.

'I don't know.' Luke puts down my rucksack. 'I suggested a couple of days. Is that what you're thinking?' he asks me.

'It would be great – if you're sure.'

'Of course we are.' He glances at Mack. 'What do you think about letting Bee have the studio?'

Her eyes widen. 'No way.'

'I don't want to cause any upset,' I say, anxiously; aware that I already have and that right now, the last thing they both need is more. 'If you don't have a spare room, I'm really happy to sleep on a sofa.'

'What about one of the other rooms?' Mackenzie looks at Luke.

'They're a mess, Mack.' Luke's silent for a moment. 'At least the studio has a bed in it.'

Mackenzie shakes her head. 'No, Dad.'

He looks at his daughter. 'Do you have any better ideas?'

She shrugs. 'Bee said she wouldn't mind the sofa.'

But Luke also seems unsure. 'I think she should have the studio tonight. We can figure something else out tomorrow.'

'I suppose,' she says begrudgingly.

Slightly apprehensive, I follow them out of the kitchen along a passageway with an unevenly tiled floor, then at the end of it, up some stairs. At the top, Luke pushes open a door that's ajar and switches the light on.

Going inside, I find myself in a sparsely furnished room with white walls, on which various paintings are displayed. Then as I take in the shelves of artists' materials, I realise it's an artist's studio; it dawns on me, this was probably Amanda's room.

It explains Mack's reluctance. 'For a moment, I thought you were going to show me into a recording studio,' I try to joke.

'That's in the cellar.' Mackenzie doesn't smile. 'This was my mum's room.'

A strange feeling takes me over as I walk towards the easel, studying the painting she'd been working on of brown rocky cliffs and the bluest sea.

'I'll get you some bedding.' Luke's voice comes from behind me.

'Thanks.' For the first time, I notice the mattress in the corner, before my eyes are drawn to more paintings and sketches, some of which look incomplete.

'Do you like them?' Mackenzie says. Without waiting for a response, she points to a small, framed painting of an ethereal-looking mermaid. 'That's me.' She's quiet for a moment. 'Mum used to tell me I was part mermaid.' Her voice wobbles. 'She said we are all of the sea.'

'It's beautiful.' I stare at it, mesmerised, suddenly aware it's just the two of us here. 'I'm so sorry about your mum,' I say quietly.

She bites her lip; her eyes glisten with tears as they gaze into mine. 'My dad is always so sad,' she whispers.

The lump in my throat is unfamiliar. She's so young. Too young to lose her mother; to always be worrying about her father.

She glances anxiously at Luke as he comes in carrying an armful of sheets and pillows.

He places what he's carrying on the mattress, then turns to me. 'It isn't fancy or anything.' He pauses. 'Will you be all right up here?'

'I'll be fine.' I look at him gratefully. 'Thank you.'

'You're welcome.' He turns to Mack. 'Right. Mack, it's bedtime,' Luke says firmly. 'You can talk to Bee in the morning.'

They leave me alone and I go over to the window, pushing it open and breathing in the cool air. Through the dusk, here and there little lights twinkle, while there is no sound. Just the purest silence.

After making up my bed, I go downstairs and back to the kitchen. Seeing me, Luke goes to the fridge and gets out two bottles of beer. He opens them and passes one to me. 'Shall we take them outside?'

He goes outside and sits at the table near the edge of the terrace. Following, I pull out a chair opposite.

'Thank you,' I say quietly. 'For having me here.' It's on the tip of my tongue to ask how long I can stay. But each step at a time, I tell myself.

'You're welcome.' He pauses. 'Mack's protective – about anything to do with her mother.'

I take it he's talking about the studio. 'You don't have to explain. I understand.' I gaze at the view. 'It's so peaceful here.'

He looks surprised. 'I suppose I'm used to it. Amanda and I moved here six years ago.'

I'm curious. 'What made you come here?'

'Quality of life is the short answer. We didn't want to stay in England. And life's really different here. The pace is slower, there's the sun...' He pauses. 'We chose this house because we wanted somewhere quiet, but not too far away from it all. The village is a short walk – and there are good schools. And with the town being nearby, Amanda thought it would be a good place for all of us.' He pauses. 'Tell me about you. Where did you grow up?'

I'm not sure where to start. 'I was born in Brighton. But my mother never stays put for long. We've lived in Shoreham, Reigate, another part of Brighton. Now, she lives in Isleworth. She's a legal secretary. She mostly works from home.'

He shakes his head. 'I would have had her down as a creative type. Funny how we change over the years.'

But I don't want to talk about my mother. 'So you're a musician?'

He nods. 'I was in a band – that was when I met your mother. These days, I write pieces of incidental music and some of them get picked up.' He shrugs. 'It's enough – but only just. Amanda and I had plans for this place. She wanted to do up the rest of the house and run artists' retreats. There's also the olive grove. It used to be productive. But it's become run-down – as yet, we haven't got around to doing anything with it.'

'It would be good, though, wouldn't it?' I say politely. I know nothing about the production of olive oil, other than it's highly sought after, though I appreciate the beauty of the trees.

'It would be. I need to start looking into it. Why don't I get us some food?' Luke gets up. 'Would you like another beer?'

I sit on the terrace while Luke goes to the kitchen. The hills are silhouetted against the dark sky, the first stars appearing overhead. It's blissfully quiet, the occasional hoot of an owl breaking the silence, a random bat or two flitting past as Luke comes back out.

He puts a basket of bread and a plate of cheese and cold meats on the table. 'I hope this is OK.' He passes me another beer.

'It's perfect,' I say. The bread is fresh and I cut myself a slice of cheese.

We talk about little of consequence that first evening. I guess both of us are uncertain, feeling our way, while I'm awkward with the strangeness of being here.

Making my excuses, I go to bed early, creeping up the stairs to Amanda's studio, where it's as though her ghost is watching me. *What would she have said?* I can't help thinking. *Would she have welcomed me? Or would she have resented me unsettling the idyllic bliss they had?*

* * *

When I awake the following morning, for a few seconds I lie there, then as I open my eyes, it comes back to me, that I'm here – in Majorca. In Luke's house.

I get out of bed and go over to the window. The sky is pale, the sun still low over the hills, a layer of mist lying in the valley. Opening the window, I stand there for a moment. There's a depth of silence I've never known before, broken only by bird-song; the faintest of breezes through the trees and as I listen, I cast my mind back to the events of yesterday.

It seems impossible that two days ago, I was still in my mother's house in London. I think of her smoking in the kitchen, before going out to her office; obsessively cleaning her immaculate house, never stopping to glance at the clarity of the sky, to take a breath and let her mind still.

After pulling on jeans and a shirt, I open the door and go downstairs. There is no movement in the house as I make my way to the kitchen. It's cosy in there, heat radiating from a wood-burning stove. I switch on the kettle and hunt around for coffee.

I listen as a car pulls up, then as footsteps make their way around the side of the house before Luke walks in.

'Morning,' I call out. 'I was making coffee. Would you like some?'

'Hi.' He takes off his jacket. 'Thanks. It's in the cupboard above the sink.'

Opening the cupboard, I find it straight away. 'Got it,' I say brightly. 'Is Mackenzie up?'

'I've just dropped her at school.' He sits down. 'She wasn't too pleased. She was most insistent she wanted to take the day off.' He pauses. 'She's definitely curious about you – which I take to be a good sign.'

I pass him a mug then sit down at the table. 'What do you think I should say to her?'

'I'll tell her the truth about me and your mother.' Luke sounds matter-of-fact. 'It was a long time ago and Mack's smart. She won't dwell on it. I think she's already coming around to the idea of having a sister.' For a moment he doesn't speak. 'Bee, I've been thinking about the best way to do this. You can see where Mack and I are right now. If being here is too much for you, I'll understand.' He pauses. 'One option – and I can't help thinking it might be better for you – would be for you to stay somewhere else – while we get to know each other – just more slowly.' All the time he's speaking, he watches my face. 'What do you think?'

I gaze at him in shock; feel the colour leave my face. After what he said last night, I was counting on staying. 'Is that what you want?'

'Not at all. I suppose I'm not very good with these things.

Amanda would have known what to say... Anyway, I've been trying to think what might be best for you.' He pauses. 'And I suppose I'm giving you a let out.' He goes on. 'You didn't know what you were walking into. And as you can see, nothing's normal right now. Our lives have been turned upside down.'

'Oh.' My legs are suddenly weak.

'It isn't that I want you to leave.' He's quiet for a moment. 'I'm not putting this very well. If you think you can cope with us, and if it's what you want, I'd really like it if you stayed.'

It's the most roundabout explanation, but as he finishes speaking, relief washes over me. My eyes well up with tears as I look at him. 'Thank you,' I mumble. 'I would like to. You've no idea how grateful I am.'

'You're welcome. You're my daughter. I just wish it wasn't such a difficult time.' He pauses. 'Bee, if I'd known about you, I like to think I would have been in your life. But as you know, I wasn't given the chance.'

'Thank you.' The way he speaks makes me believe him. Not for the first time, I curse my mother's selfishness. But it's classic Cassandra not to think about the impact of her actions on other people.

Luke looks at me curiously. 'Let's see how the next couple of days go. I'm sure you'll want some time to explore a bit. But if you end up staying longer, it might be worth giving some thought to what you want to do while you're here.'

I blink at him; gratified that he's thinking about me staying. 'I will.' Until now, I've only thought as far as meeting Luke, but not knowing what would happen, I haven't planned beyond that. 'I should probably try to get a job.' But I'm aware the rules have changed since Brexit. 'But if I do, I'll need a visa.'

'We can look into that.' He pauses. 'Having family who are

resident might make a difference. I have a friend who's a lawyer. Let me check with her.'

'I'd really appreciate that,' I say, my imagination already running away with me. 'I could work online. But I'd consider anything, really – and just so you know, I'm not expecting to stay here for nothing.' An idea comes to me. 'While I'm not working, could I make myself useful? Maybe tidy up a bit or whatever else needs doing?' I stop suddenly, hoping I haven't overstepped the mark. 'Only if that doesn't sound rude.'

'It doesn't.' He pauses. 'You can probably see that, since Amanda died, I've let things slip.' He looks at me. 'If you really don't mind, I'd appreciate it.' Finishing his coffee, he gets up. 'I should get on. I have a meeting with our accountant later on. I'll try to remember to give my friend a call, too. I'm picking up Mack from her after-school swimming class, so I won't be back until this evening.' He looks around for his phone. 'Will you be all right here on your own?'

'Of course.' Looking around the kitchen, there's plenty to keep me occupied. 'Thank you,' I say.

He looks surprised. Then he smiles. 'For letting you tidy the place up?'

I roll my eyes. 'For letting me stay.'

It's the first hint of humour I've observed; Luke is otherwise very much a closed book. Meanwhile, what I thought would feel like the tentative start of the next chapter of my life, is more like turning back through sporadic, out-of-sequence pages. But it's a start, I tell myself.

After Luke goes out, I gaze around the kitchen, seeing it for a moment through his eyes, the untidiness a constant reminder that his wife isn't here. Normally I'd object to dealing with someone else's mess – Saskia being a case in point, with her strewn clothes, the unwashed plates and mugs she used to leave lying around. But if I can make a difference here, I'm more than happy to.

Noticing a speaker on the side, I get out my phone and connect to it. Very soon, my favourite music is playing. More than that, with no neighbours to worry about, I can play it loudly. In what seems like no time, the washing up is done and the surfaces are clear of clutter. After giving them a good clean, I start on the floor.

There's something joyous about loud music. But it's in my blood, I remind myself; that Luke is a musician is pretty much the only thing I know about him, as suddenly it occurs to me that maybe there's musical talent in me, too, as yet untapped.

I'm an ungainly dancer. I'm too self-conscious; my limbs are too long. I also have no sense of rhythm, or so I've been told. But today, it doesn't stop me. As I dance around the kitchen, I let myself go, until my eyes suddenly settle on the sympathy cards.

Turning the music down, my euphoria evaporates as I go over and pick one up, reading the poignant message inside. Then as I look at them all in turn, I find each one contains the loveliest, most moving message.

Amanda must have been so loved around here. Thinking of Mack without her mother, a tear rolls down my face. Then as I think of my own homeless, jobless plight, another tear follows, followed by another, until sitting down, everything hits me at once and I'm full-blown sobbing. As yet, Luke hasn't done more than hint at how long I can stay. A week, at best, two, wouldn't seem unreasonable. But if he's talking about work... Or talking to his lawyer friend... What if it all comes to nothing?

A knock on the window startles me. Still wallowing in self-pity, I think about ignoring it. But then there's another knock, this time, on the door.

Wiping my eyes, I go to open it, and find myself looking at Augusta. 'I'm afraid you've missed Luke.'

'Not to worry,' she says briskly. 'I'll catch him later.' She looks more closely at me. 'Are you all right?'

'I'm fine.' But my voice wavers. As more tears roll down my cheeks, I fish another tissue out of my pocket. 'Really I am.' My voice wobbles. 'I think I'm just tired. It always makes me emotional.'

'Hmm.' She doesn't look convinced. 'How about I make us a nice cup of tea? And you can tell me about whatever it is that you're obviously not fine about.'

Reluctantly I let her in, though from the look of things, I couldn't have stopped her. Augusta is clearly very much at home in this house. She closes the door and takes her jacket off, looking around as she stands there. An expression of shock crosses her face. 'Good God.'

'Is something wrong?' I say anxiously.

'Quite the opposite. It hasn't looked so clean and tidy in quite a long while.' She turns to me. 'You've done this, I take it?'

I nod.

'In that case, you really do deserve a cup of tea,' she says kindly. After filling the kettle, she switches it on, and while she waits for it to boil, she rummages in one of the cupboards and produces a packet of biscuits.

'Why don't you sit down,' she says.

I pull out a chair and perch on it, before taking the mug of tea she pushes towards me, then one of the biscuits.

'Now, tell me what's so terrible that it has you in tears this wonderful day.'

I gaze towards the window that frames a view of far-reaching hills, of a sliver of sea beyond. It is a wonderful day; it's like paradise out there. It makes no sense that I feel so desolate.

'I say every morning is wonderful,' Augusta says, following my gaze. 'It's all a matter of perspective. Even when it doesn't feel like it, there's something beautiful about the start of a new day.' She pauses. 'Anyway, back to your problems. Would you care to share them with me?'

'They're nothing, really.' Suddenly I feel like a fraud. 'At least, not compared to what Luke and Mackenzie are going through.'

'Oranges and lemons,' Augusta says briskly. 'Go on.'

I sigh shakily. 'I told you, didn't I, that I lost my room in Brighton? And my job?'

'You did.' Augusta frowns. 'You have been going through it lately, haven't you?' She pauses. 'Do you have a boyfriend?'

'Not any more,' I mumble, my tears coming thick and fast, as I think of Phil at the arboretum for the first time since arriving here. 'There was this guy – at work. But he had to go back to Australia.'

'Well, I'd say that's probably as well,' she says calmly. 'Men tend to complicate things, I find. Much easier when you don't have to worry about anyone else.' She pauses. 'It's a lot happening in a short space of time, though.'

I nod. 'It is. And right now, it's like I'm in limbo.'

Augusta is silent for a moment. 'Have you and Luke talked at all?'

'Yes.' I sigh. 'Last night, he said it was fine if I wanted to stay. Then this morning, it was like he'd backtracked. He said he hadn't, but I just get this feeling it would be easier for them both if I wasn't here.'

'Silly man,' she says crossly. 'One thing I will say about Luke is that he tends to say what's going on inside his head. Used to drive Amanda mad. It takes a bit of translating sometimes, but if he really didn't want you to stay, he would have said.'

'Oh.' It makes me feel mildly better, but that's all.

'Give it time,' she suggests. 'You've only just met each other.'

'But even if he says I can stay, I'll need a visa,' I say miserably.

'If you stay longer than three months, yes, you will.' Augusta frowns. 'Do you think you're staying that long?'

'I'm not sure.' The depths of my misery wash over me.

'Well, first you need to make your mind up,' Augusta says briskly. 'And cheer up. When it comes to visas, yes, it's a ridiculous process – thanks to Brexit. But it should be doable somehow or other.' She pauses. 'So what are your plans for now?'

'Get to know Luke. And Mack.' I shrug. 'Other than that, I don't have anything definite. Not yet anyway. At some point, I'm still going to have to go back to England and find somewhere to live – and get another job there.' My heart sinks just thinking about Moira's cleaning job. 'It's just that right now, it all feels a little daunting.'

'Unless you stay,' Augusta says.

'Yes.' Just now, every option sounds daunting.

'If Luke's looking into a visa for you, he's obviously thinking in terms of you staying longer.' She pats my hand. 'I'd park your worst-case scenario – at least for now.'

'You think?' Hope rises in me.

'Try to take things as they come,' she advises. 'It's clearly been quite an unsettling time – and on top of everything else, you have just met your father.' Augusta sips her tea. 'How did he take the news?'

'Quite well, really.' He's been remarkably calm about me turning up here. He hasn't even questioned if I am who I say I am.

'Good for Luke,' she says. 'But so he should. I mean, he is

your father.' She takes another biscuit. 'How long have you known about him?'

'Only for a couple of weeks.'

'Goodness.' Augusta arches her eyebrows. 'It's none of my business, of course. But was it your mother who told you?'

'No.' My cheeks flush pink. 'I found an old diary she kept – for the year I was born. I wouldn't have opened it, but I don't know how else I'd have ever found out. Whenever I asked about my father, my mother refused to talk about him.' I watch her face for a look of disapproval.

But it doesn't appear. 'Goodness.' She sits back. 'How's Mack finding you being here?'

'I think she's OK. Luke says she's coming around to the idea. It's a shock, though, isn't it? I mean, neither of them had any idea that I existed.'

'I'm sure Mack will be fine.' Augusta pushes the packet of biscuits towards me. 'Look, I'm sure all this uncertainty can't be easy to deal with. But my advice, for what it's worth, is to take each day as it comes. Especially right now. This is time for you to get to know Luke – and Mack. After all, she's your half-sister. That's rather nice, isn't it?'

'It is. She's really sweet. It's just that I don't really know any children,' I confess.

'Really?' Augusta stares at me for a moment. 'Well, I can assure you that Mack is not like most children,' she says. 'I mean, she is and she isn't. She can sulk like the best of them. But she's rather wise, I've always found. Though right now, she's far too young to be so worried about her father.' She pauses. 'Maybe you might be able to help her with that.'

I think back to last night, when we were alone in the studio. 'She said something to me – about how sad he is.'

'Did she?' Augusta pauses. 'Poor darling. She misses

Amanda dreadfully. If you'd come here two months ago, you would have seen this place at its best. Amanda would have been cooking something incredible or gardening, or painting in her studio... Luke would have been bumbling around being Luke. And Mack would have been wrapped up in whatever her latest obsession is. My point being, it was such a happy house.'

I try to imagine it, filled with love and life and family. A proper home – until it had the heart ripped out of it.

Augusta frowns. 'You know, far from the timing being bad, maybe you've come here at exactly the right time.'

I blink at her. 'You think?'

'Maybe. Anyway,' Augusta goes on, 'back to you. If Luke's happy for you to stay a while, why not make the most of it? The future can wait – it isn't going anywhere. So try not to worry about it.' She frowns again. 'I assume you have some money to tide you over?'

I nod. 'Enough for now.'

'Good. A girl should rely on herself, I've always said. And at least you're not paying for a hotel now.' She gets up and takes her mug over to the sink. 'I have to be on my way. Tell Luke to call me. You must come for dinner sometime.' She puts on her jacket. 'You're welcome to pop by. Any time – I'm usually at home.'

'Thanks.' I walk to the door with her. Then instead of closing it behind her, I leave it open, standing there taking in the glorious view, the hazy sunshine.

Feeling my mood lift, I venture out and cut a handful of late-summer flowers from the garden. After arranging them in a jug, I place them on one of the windowsills.

Back to my cleaning, after the bathroom, I explore more of the house. There's a large sitting room with a pair of sump-tuous sofas and one of Amanda's paintings hung above the very

Spanish-looking fireplace; a windowsill decked with vases of what I guess to be decaying sympathy flowers. My eyes are drawn to a family photo from happier times, of Luke with his arm around Amanda, her eyes radiating warmth, while between them, Mack looks as though she hasn't a care in the world.

As I carry on exploring, the house is bigger than it looks from the outside and I can see why Amanda imagined holding retreats here. A passageway leads to the front door and a large terracotta-tiled hallway, where there's a faded armchair and a tall leggy plant growing up beside a stone fireplace.

The door beyond that is labelled 'Mack' in bright pink letters. Pushing it open, it's like walking into a fairy tale. The walls are a pale shade of pink, one of them adorned with 'MACK' in large, ornate letters, each formed out of a delicately painted daisy chain – almost certainly Amanda's handiwork. The frame above the bed is festooned with sheer sparkling drapes, the bookcase filled with dozens of children's books, while near the window is a white-painted table covered in girly paraphernalia.

The door opposite is closed. Imagining it to be Luke's and Amanda's room, I pass it by. As I carry on, there are many other rooms, all of which look as though they're a work in progress, with furniture piled up, each of them with tiled floors and wooden beams, shuttered windows; uneven, white-painted walls.

I go up to the studio, pull on running clothes and tie my hair back. It's a perfect day for a run, and as I set off, I feel my spirits rise. Halfway down the drive, I turn onto a path between the pine trees. It's different to the running I'm used to, the ground slightly uneven, sloping gently uphill, the air wonderfully clean instead of filled with traffic fumes. I run until I'm out of breath, breaking into a walk as the path steepens. Then reaching the top of the slope, I stop.

The other side, the sea is not that far away, sparkling where the sun catches it. Gazing at it, I feel my heart start to slow, as a feeling of quiet euphoria creeps over me.

This could be my life, I suddenly realise. Yes, there are hurdles. But they can be overcome. When I think about where I am, then compare it to living at my mother's, or worse, with a stranger, it's a no-brainer. If I want it enough, there has to be a way to make it happen.

* * *

It's getting dark by the time Luke and Mack come home. Hearing the car stop outside, I'm apprehensive all of a sudden, wondering what he's said to Mack and how she's taken it. Then the door bursts open and Mack stands there.

'Hi,' I say. Her hair is damp from swimming, her eyes holding mine for a moment, before darting around the kitchen. Then dropping her bag, she bursts into tears and disappears along the hallway.

Luke looks tired when he comes in. He closes the door. 'Where did Mack go?'

'I think she went to her bedroom.' I pause. 'Did you talk to her?'

'Yes.' He sighs. 'She tore me off a strip for not knowing about you. There's not a lot I can do about that.' Looking around, he frowns. 'You've been busy.'

'I hope it looks OK,' I say hesitantly.

'It's much better. Thanks, Bee.' He stands there a moment. 'I should go and see where Mack is.'

'Shall I?' I offer.

'Are you sure? Mack can be quite... I was going to say obstinate, but that's a little unfair. Let's just say that once she makes her mind up about something, she can be quite determined.' He takes off his jacket. 'If you really don't mind, I'll get dinner started.'

I make my way along to Mack's room. Reaching it, I knock on the door.

'Go away,' she says.

'Mack? It's me. Bee. Can I come in? Just for a minute or two?'

'No,' she says tearfully.

'Mack. Please...' I say quietly.

There's silence. I hear her get up. Then she pushes the door open.

As she stands there, she looks so small and vulnerable, my heart goes out to her. 'I'm so sorry,' I say quietly. 'The last thing I wanted was to upset your lives. I realise you didn't know about me.' I hesitate. 'But the thing is, I didn't know about you, either.'

'Didn't you?' Her lip wobbles as she takes in what I've said. 'It's OK,' she says bravely.

I look at her anxiously. 'Are you sure?'

She goes back into her room and sits cross-legged on her bed, as I notice a tear roll down her cheek.

I follow her in and crouch on the floor beside her. 'Are you OK?' I say gently.

For a moment, she doesn't speak. Then her eyes fill with tears as she looks at me. 'When I came back from school just now, everything looked how it used to when Mum was alive. And then I remembered. She isn't.' Her voice breaks.

I reach towards her and put my arms around her. Leaning against me, she sobs as suddenly I realise, just as the untidiness was a reminder to Luke that Amanda has gone, for Mack, it's the opposite, the tidy kitchen reminding her of when her mother was still here. 'Oh, Mack,' I say softly, a feeling of protectiveness overwhelming me for my half-sister.

* * *

That evening, while Luke cooks, Mack sits on the sofa drawing in one of her notebooks until suddenly the back door opens and a familiar dog comes trotting in.

'Cato!' Mack's face lights up as she leaps to her feet. She runs over to him and hugs him.

For the second time today, Augusta walks in, this time carrying a bottle of wine. 'Thought I'd better check on you all.' After winking at me, she looks at Luke before her eyes rest on Mack. 'So what do you think?' she asks her.

'About what?' Mack looks up from hugging Cato.

'Having a half-sister, of course.'

Mack shrugs, then glances at Luke. 'It's OK.'

'I'd say it's more than OK.' Augusta places the bottle on the table and takes her jacket off. 'Family are really important, aren't they?'

'I know.' Mack rolls her eyes. 'That's why I'm not happy.'

Augusta looks confused. 'I don't follow.'

'He didn't tell me.' She glowers in the direction of Luke's back.

'Yes, well. I imagine he was as surprised as you were.'

'I suppose.' Mack glances at me, then back at Augusta. 'I do like Bee being here.'

'Thank goodness for that.' Augusta sounds relieved. She turns to Luke. 'Have you told Bee she has grandparents?'

Startled, I watch Luke freeze, before he turns around. 'That's right. I'm sorry, Bee. I should have mentioned them before.'

'Wow, Dad,' Mack breathes. 'You'll have to tell them. They'll be so excited. You'll really like them, Bee. Granny makes the best cakes.'

Until now, I haven't imagined any grandparents I haven't known about. 'That's really nice,' I manage, catching Augusta's eye as she goes over to the cooker.

'What are you making, Luke?'

'Paella.'

Mack's face lights up again. 'We haven't had paella in ages.'

Augusta winks at me again. 'I think he's doing it for your benefit.'

It's obvious Augusta cares greatly for them. But in tiny communities, I imagine neighbours take on greater importance. In any case, their closeness is heart-warming to witness, as that evening, the four of us dine at the big wooden table, with Cato installed underneath it. In the warmth of the kitchen, the atmosphere has thawed, the food is tasty and every so often I become aware of Mack's eyes resting on me, Augusta's constant vigilance as she dominates the conversation, while Luke says little.

I was naive to imagine this would be straightforward, I tell myself when I go to bed that night. You can't just parachute into the middle of someone's life and expect things to go on, just the same. But as I lie there, I can't help thinking about the sadness in this house; in Luke's silence, Mack's anxious watchfulness. An invisible void in their lives that needs time to heal.

I imagine being able to help in some way. Spending days with Luke and Mack – quiet days, just the three of us, as we get to know each other – in time, of course. These things always take time. The thought makes my heart warm. But as I should know by now. Nothing is ever that simple.

12

ALEX

'You are sure about this?' I ask Kevin as we turn up a drive.

'It's a bit bloody late in the day for that, don't you think?' He gazes out of the window. 'It really is the middle of nowhere, isn't it?'

Since leaving Pollensa, the road has taken us through the most glorious countryside, of rocky hills covered in pine trees, of green valleys and olive groves. The drive comes to an end in front of a white-painted villa. Pulling up, I park next to another car. 'This must be it.'

'Right.' Kevin swings the door open, cursing as he gets out then fumbles in the back of the car for his crutches. Standing there, he stares at the gravel path. 'How the devil am I supposed to manage that?' he says.

'Slowly,' I tell him.

'Don't state the bloody obvious,' he says rudely.

Biting back my reply, I walk ahead of him, briefly seeing a face at the window before reaching a terrace, where I see the door. As Kevin catches me up, I knock.

A few seconds later, it opens to reveal a man I imagine must be Luke Friday.

I open my mouth to speak but Kevin shoves past me. 'Luke. It's Kevin. Kevin Carlisle.'

Luke looks confused. 'I don't know a Kevin Carlisle.'

'For Christ's sake, of course you do. We were in the band. Back in the day.' Kevin sounds impatient.

'You have to be kidding.' Luke looks at him incredulously.

Kevin goes on. 'Leg's killing me. Can we come in?'

As he pushes past Luke, I hold out my hand. 'I'm Alex. I'm Rachel's – Roxy's – son. I'm sorry to turn up like this—' I glance past him to where Kevin is already pulling out a chair and sitting down at a big wooden table. 'If it isn't a good time, perhaps we could meet up when it is?'

'It's fine.' Luke looks dazed. 'You better come in.'

As I walk in, I notice a girl with long hair, her eyes wide as she watches us. She goes over to stand next to Luke.

'This is my daughter, Mack,' Luke says.

I watch Mack's eyes, like saucers as she stares at Kevin's unwieldy plastic boot.

'Would you like tea?' Luke says.

'Don't have anything stronger, do you?' Kevin says, then turns to look at Mack. 'Hello. Name's Kevin. This...' He nods towards me. 'This is Alex.'

'Hi.' I smile at her. 'I hope we're not interrupting anything.'

'Not in the least,' Luke says. 'What happened to your leg?' he says to Kevin.

'Tripped and broke my ankle. Damn thing,' Kevin mutters, as he stretches the leg with the boot on out in front of him.

Mack's eyes catch mine fleetingly as she tries not to laugh.

Luke brings over a teapot and some mugs. Then disappears

and comes back with a bottle of Scotch and a glass, which he puts on the table in front of Kevin. 'Will this do?'

'Just what I need.' Kevin helps himself to a generous glass. 'You're not having one?'

'Not for me,' Luke says firmly. 'I've no idea what's brought you here, but I want a clear head when you tell me why.'

'Yes, Daddy,' Mack hisses. 'What are they doing here?'

'It's Alex's doing,' Kevin says loudly. 'I met him in the hospital. His mother was in there at the time… Everyone's fine, by the way – except for this.' He nods towards his boot. 'Anyway, as I was saying…'

'I know Kevin from a long time ago,' Luke explains to Mack. 'We were in a band together. And I knew Alex's mother, too. She was our singer.'

Mack stares at him. 'Your band?' she says incredulously. 'The one on your CDs?'

'That's the one.' Still taking it in, an expression of disbelief crosses Luke's face as he looks at Kevin. 'I can't believe you've come all the way here. It must be twenty-odd years since we've seen each other.'

'It's only because of this ankle. And it's more like thirty. Anyway, I've suddenly found myself with rather a lot of time on my hands,' Kevin goes on. 'I suppose I should tell you why we're here. You see…' He pauses. 'Alex has this ridiculous idea about getting the band back together.'

Mack claps her hands in glee. But Luke folds his arms. 'The band was a long time ago. I'm not at all sure it's a good idea.'

'Thank you,' says Kevin. 'That's exactly what I said.'

I look at them both, wishing Kevin had left this to me. 'What Kevin hasn't explained is why.' They all stare at me. 'To be honest, it's about my mother. Rachel. Roxy,' I remind Luke. 'You see, I'm trying to find ways of helping her. Her memory is getting worse. She gets confused about the simplest things she never would have thought twice about.' I hesitate. 'These days, I look after her.'

'Rachel has dementia,' Kevin says loudly.

'I'm sorry.' Luke looks taken aback. 'She's too young, isn't she, to have that? She's our age.'

'Yes. But early-onset dementia happens more often than you'd think.' I hesitate. 'She's on medication and hopefully it's slowing it down. But it's still really tough on her.'

Mack sits down next to her father, and as I go on, they listen as I describe my mother's illness; how music can reach people even when the condition is advanced; that it taps into another part of the brain.

'I'm hoping it will help her remember more about her past,' I say.

'Has she forgotten it all?' Mack sounds worried.

'Only some parts of it.' I try to reassure her. 'But she does forget a lot of things. If I can get her interested in music again, especially the music that was part of her life, as more time goes by, I hope it will keep reminding her.' I look at Luke, then Kevin. 'It doesn't have to be a big deal. I just thought if we could get everyone together – and she could sing again, it would make a massive difference to her.' I frown at Luke. 'But with you living here, I'm not sure how practical that is.'

Luke shakes his head. 'You're not making this easy.'

'That's what I said,' Kevin adds with feeling.

'Does Rachel know what you're planning?' Luke asks.

'I haven't told her,' I say. 'For all kinds of reasons. She forgets things and gets confused. I thought I'd keep it quiet until I know whether it's going to happen.'

Luke rests his head in his hands. 'What about Miles? And Atlas?'

'I've found Miles,' Kevin says brusquely. 'He presents a radio show. I've emailed his producer – or rather, Alex has. Come to think of it, they still haven't replied.' He glances at me. 'I suppose we could phone in when he's on the air. That only leaves Atlas.'

Leaning towards Luke, Mack whispers to him, 'Who's Atlas?'

'He was our bass player,' Luke says. 'And Miles was our guitarist,' he explains to her.

'But we're working on finding him. We saw Leo the other day,' Kevin says. 'In the hospital. Remember Leo the roadie? He and Atlas stayed in touch after the band split up. Apparently Atlas moved to Glasgow, but seems to have completely disappeared.'

Luke's silent as he takes it all in. 'Not looking hopeful, is it – unless we can find him, I mean.'

'I have an idea or two about that.' Kevin pauses. 'But I need to get back to the hotel and put my feet up.' He winces as he moves slightly. 'There's rather a nice bar where we're staying. Shall we meet for a drink tonight?' He suggests. 'We can talk about it further.'

Luke shakes his head. 'I can't. I have Mack to think of.'

'Bee can stay with me,' Mack says. 'We'll be fine, Daddy.'

Luke looks hesitant. 'We'll have to ask her when she's back from her run.' He doesn't say who Bee is. 'Can I let you know?'

'My card.' Kevin fishes one of his pocket. 'Bloody hot out there.' He glances towards the window. 'Is it always like this?'

But Kevin's dressed for October in England. He didn't have the imagination to consider it wouldn't be the same here.

* * *

As we drive back to Pollensa, Kevin is irritable. 'Bloody long way to come if this is a wild goose chase,' he grumbles.

'We don't know if it is,' I point out. 'And it was your idea to come here.'

'Everyone's spread across Europe,' he says. 'Doesn't exactly make it easy, does it?'

'It isn't impossible.' In the rear-view mirror, I glimpse a girl with long fair hair turn out of a path, then continue running in the opposite direction.

'It will be once I'm back at work,' Kevin says. 'I can't just drop everything on a whim, you know.'

'No one's asking you to.' I don't remind him that in coming here, that's exactly what he's done. 'Tell me,' I ask, because I want to know the answer, 'if you're so against the idea of the band playing together again, why did you suggest coming here?'

Kevin's silent for a moment. 'Actually, it was what you said about your mother.'

I push him. 'You are sure? Because there's no point in trying to do this if you're going to pull out at the last minute.'

'I absolutely would not do that,' he says angrily.

It's what I wanted to hear. 'Good,' I say quietly.

As we come into Pollensa, Kevin glances around. 'I need a drink.' He points through the window. 'Over there will do. Drop me outside. Then you can park and come and find me.'

I do as he asks, watching him hobble towards a bar, before driving back to the hotel. After leaving the car there, I make my way slowly back to the bar, taking in the lovely old streets, savouring some time without Kevin bending my ear.

If it wasn't for the sadness of losing his wife, Luke's life would look idyllic. The island feels uncluttered, the pace of life slower; people like Kevin noticeable by their absence. In another lifetime, I could live here, I muse, just as my phone buzzes in my pocket. Taking it out, I answer the call.

'Where the devil are you?' Kevin sounds irritated.

'On my way. I won't be long.' I switch off my phone and put it in my pocket again.

But I deliberately don't rush. It isn't often I have time to myself and I refuse to be beholden to anyone, least of all Kevin.

When I reach the bar, he's halfway through a carafe of red wine.

'Took you long enough.' He pours me a glass and pushes it towards me.

'I was enjoying the chance to walk,' I say, pointedly staring at his wine glass. 'Don't you think it might be wise to slow down a bit?'

'A few glasses of wine is nothing,' he says. 'Not that it's any of your business. I'm hardly going to sit here waiting for you, without a drink.'

'I was twenty minutes,' I remind him. 'Hardly a long time.'

It seems that while I was on my way here, Luke had called. 'He's coming at seven,' Kevin tells me.

I glance at my watch. 'That's two hours away.'

'Exactly. I've asked for menus. It's not like we have anything better to do.'

Kevin orders steak and chips. But I hesitate. 'You know, I think I'll go for a longer walk. I'm not particularly hungry – and I should probably give my mother a call.'

'Fine.' He tops up his glass, then stares at me. 'Off you go then.'

Leaving him, I make my way through the streets of the old town. Finding a bench in a square, I get out my phone, noticing several missed calls from my mother.

'I've been calling you all afternoon,' she says indignantly when she picks up. 'Why didn't you answer?'

'I've been busy,' I say. 'I don't know if you remember, but I went to meet up with Luke.'

'I know all that,' she says impatiently. 'But when are you coming to pick me up?'

My heart sinks. 'Soon, Mum,' I say. 'It must be nice being at Lorna's, though. You don't see each other that often.'

'It's nice enough. But I want to come home,' she says.

'You will be – in a few days.' Then before she protests, 'I'm sorry, Mum. I have to go. I'll call you soon.' After ending the call, I switch my phone off. Almost immediately, guilt takes me over. But after too much time with Kevin, I'm craving peace.

After a beer on my own in a quiet tapas bar, I head back to where Kevin is. When I get there, he isn't alone. Luke is with him.

'Hi.' I sit down with them. 'I must have lost track of time.'

'Easily done,' Luke says.

'Hardly.' Kevin doesn't look impressed. 'Anyway, to business. Assuming we can track down Atlas and he's up for this charade of a reunion, how do you propose we're going to do this?'

13

BEE

'That old guy was weird. He said it was hot. And it isn't,' Mack says that evening, while Luke gets changed before going to Pollensa. 'He was wearing winter clothes. And he was rude.'

'Are you talking about the man with the boot on his foot?' I ask. She hasn't stopped talking about him.

'Yes. His name is Kevin.' She sits there watching as I go over to the sink and start washing up. 'You should have been here.' She pauses. 'Do you always run for hours?'

'Sometimes. It depends.'

'You'll have to meet them next time. The young one seemed nice. He's called Alex.' She sounds thoughtful. 'He says his mum can't remember things.'

'Some people can't,' I say. 'Usually when they get older.'

'Augusta's quite old,' Mack says. 'And she remembers absolutely everything.'

'And don't you forget that,' Luke says as he comes back in. 'Though I wouldn't tell her you think she's old.'

Mack rolls her eyes. 'Of course not, Daddy.' She pauses, looking at him. 'Are you going now?'

'Trying to get rid of me?' he jokes. Then he adds more soberly, 'You're sure you'll be OK?' He pulls on his jacket.

'Please don't ask me that again,' Mack says. 'It's quite annoying.' She looks up at him. 'Dad? Do you think you're going to get your band back together?'

'Probably not.' Luke ruffles her hair. 'No one knows where Atlas is – it wouldn't be the same without all of us. And we live in different countries now. It's a nice idea in some ways, but completely impractical.'

'But, Dad. They could all come here,' Mack persists. 'We have literally tons of room. We have those other bedrooms – we just need to clear them out.' She turns to me. 'Me and Bee can do it. And you have your recording studio. Mum always said...'

'Mack... Slow down. We're a long way from doing anything like that. And it's just you and me, now. I'm not sure I want a house full of strangers.'

'They're not strangers, Dad,' she says obstinately. 'They're your band.' She glances at me again. 'And it isn't just you and me any more. We have Bee.'

A warm feeling comes over me. Mack including me means everything.

Luke looks cornered. 'People change, Mack. Take Kevin, for example.'

'The rude one?'

'You know perfectly well who I mean. He was our drummer. Believe it or not, he used to be fun in those days.' Luke shakes his head. 'And now, well. He's a middle-aged, rather annoying lawyer, who likes the sound of his own voice.'

Mack's eyes widen. 'Dad. I can't believe you said that.'

'I didn't mean to be unkind,' Luke says hastily. 'I suppose the point I'm making is he's changed. We all have. I'm certainly not the same.'

'It's sad about Alex's mum,' I say. 'Not being able to remember things.' I'm all too aware of what it means, having watched my grandmother after she was diagnosed with dementia.

Luke nods. 'It is. It's the only reason I'm entertaining the idea, to be honest. Roxy was a firecracker – with this incredible voice. She was born to be on stage. I guess becoming a mother, her priorities changed.' He sighs. 'They really were good days.' His eyes become distant for a moment. Then as he stands there, a gust of wind blows the door open and there's a clattering sound as it catches the sympathy cards, knocking them over.

After hurrying to close the door, Luke crouches down to pick them up.

But Mack doesn't move. Instead, her eyes are wide as looks at me. 'It's a sign,' she whispers.

After rearranging the cards, Luke leaves for the pub to meet Kevin and Alex – somewhat reluctantly, I can't help noticing. After listening to his car drive away, there's a strange look on Mack's face. 'I've been thinking,' she says quietly. 'About everything that's happening.' She pauses again. 'It's the Universe,' she says, looking at me.

I frown. 'What is?'

'All of this.' She waves her arms around expansively. 'Them coming here. Maybe you coming here, too. Especially now.' She pauses. 'Do you talk to the Universe, Bee?'

Her words remind me of what Augusta said, about the timing of things. As for talking to the Universe... 'Not really.' Under her scrutiny I feel awkward. 'Do you?'

She nods. 'You see, before you came here, I asked the Universe to give my dad a piano. I know he already has one. But it's electronic, and it doesn't work very well.' She frowns. 'I thought if he had a new one, he wouldn't be able to resist playing it. But I don't think that's the point.' She folds her arms. 'My mum said the Universe doesn't always give you what you ask for. It has a way of giving you what you need.' She gazes at me expectantly.

'Are you saying your dad doesn't need another piano?'

'He does... But maybe what he needed more right now was a reason to get him playing again. Like Kevin, and Alex's mum. And Atlas,' she says conspiratorially.

I'm curious. 'What else did you ask it for?'

'Well.' She considers her answer. 'At the moment, I've asked it to help my dad. I don't want him to always be sad.' She pauses again. 'Sometimes I write it letters. It's easier to put in everything I want to say.'

'Have you had any answers?'

She giggles. 'Kind of. Only not in the way I was expecting. A bit like with the piano.' She hesitates. 'OK. I'll tell you something. But it's a secret. You have to swear you won't tell anyone. Even Dad,' she says earnestly.

'I swear,' I tell her. 'I promise, Mack. I won't say a word.'

'OK.' She takes a deep breath. 'A few days before you got here, I asked the Universe to find my dad a girlfriend. And then...' She gazes into my eyes. 'This is the really weird bit. Because I asked, if they really liked each other, maybe I could have a sister. And then...' She waves her arms in a flourish towards me.

'I turned up,' I say, slightly amazed.

'Exactly,' Mack says. 'I was a bit shocked at first.' Her brow is furrowed. 'I suppose I was thinking of a younger sister – it's why I was upset. But now, it really is OK.'

'That's lucky,' I tease, then add more seriously, 'Don't you think it's a little soon to be thinking about finding your dad a girlfriend?'

'Probably.' She shrugs. 'Anyway, it's out there – in the hands of the Universe. I'm not asking for it to happen now... It will take as long as it's meant to.'

Her confidence astounds me. 'You sound very sure. But after losing your mum... your dad needs time. You both do.'

'That's what Augusta said.' She's silent for a moment. Then she goes to get one of her books. Bringing it back, she opens it. 'This is my favourite book. It's about the sea and the universe. I really like this.' She shows me a page with a quote on it: 'Be careful what you wish for. The Universe is listening.'

Taking the book, I slowly turn the pages.

'You don't have to tell me if you don't want to.' Mack sounds hesitant. 'But there must be something you really want.' She pauses. 'I've been thinking. You really should start talking to the Universe, Bee. In fact, you should have started way back,' she says knowingly. 'But it isn't too late.'

'I'm not sure what I'd say.'

She shrugs. 'Mum said the Universe is always listening to us. You can ask it things. And it gives you answers, but you have to really listen. It isn't always in the way you expect it to – a bit like Dad and the piano.' She pauses. 'I talk to it a lot,' she says in a small voice.

I take in the curl of her eyelashes, the hair that's a mass of tangles again that need gently combing out. 'I've never asked the Universe for anything.'

She raises her eyebrows, then does this exaggerated little sigh. 'Then it's about time you did, don't you think?'

'Maybe.' I'm silent for a moment. After leaving Saskia's flat, all I wanted was a job and a home. But since coming here... What do I want?

'Bee,' Mack says impatiently. 'Have you decided what you're going to ask yet?'

'Give me a minute,' I tell her. 'I'm not used to this.' I close my eyes; the thought there almost immediately.

Universe, show me how to build a life here.

Opening my eyes suddenly, I stare at Mack. 'Oh my God.'

'What is it?' She looks curious.

'I think I've just asked for something a bit scary,' I tell her.

Mack's eyes widen. 'Don't worry. It's out there now.' She pauses. 'You just have to be patient.' She adds wisely, 'It's in the hands of the Universe.' Then she grins. 'Exciting, isn't it?'

Unconvinced, I changed the subject. 'Is there anywhere to order in pizza from?'

'Oh, wow. Yes.' Her eyes are like saucers. 'There's this place on the way to Pollensa. It isn't a restaurant, but they make pizzas and deliver them.'

'Sounds perfect.' After my long run, I'm ravenous. 'Shall we call them?'

After a little research, we find a telephone number. In fluent Spanish, Mack orders a Neapolitan for her and a Margherita for me. While we wait for our order to arrive, she takes my hand. 'I want to show you something.'

She opens a door, switches on the lights and leads me down some stairs into a cellar. At the bottom, she stands there. 'This is Dad's recording studio.'

'Wow.' I look around, taking in the keyboard, the two acoustic guitars and single electric one, the amps on the floor, the panel of dials and switches in the furthest corner; the microphone resting on the side. 'This is where he works?'

She nods. 'He used to. But not so much, these days.' Going over to a shelf, she picks up a CD. 'We'll play this one. He won't mind,' she assures me.

I follow her back up the stairs and into the kitchen. She climbs onto the work surface, opens one of the cupboards and takes out a CD player. Sitting there, she plugs it in and slides the CD into it.

'If you haven't heard any of his music,' she says with the confidence of one who's grown up with it, 'some of it's rock. But I like this one.' She fast-forwards, then presses 'play'. Swinging her legs over the side of the work surface, she watches my face as the music starts.

I listen, transfixed. It's a ballad, and at the same time, sort of rocky. And a little dated, to my ear, but the vocals are raw, the singer's voice at times powerful, at others ethereal.

'She's an amazing singer,' Mack says knowledgeably as it finishes.

'She really is. Can you play some more?'

As the next track starts, there's a knock on the door.

'Pizza!' Mack cries, the music forgotten as she slides down and rushes to open it.

It's another interlude of normality – of pizza and chatter about which movies we like. Mack tells me about her friends, declaring she's going to teach me to be fluent in Spanish. By the time Luke gets home, Mack and I are on our second movie, the empty pizza boxes open on the table in front of us.

Luke looks slightly anxious. 'Is everything OK?'

'Everything's fine.' I glance at Mack. Curled up on the sofa next to me, I hadn't noticed she'd fallen asleep. 'She's been on great form. How was your evening?'

'Interesting.' He pauses. 'Alex is a really nice guy, but Kevin...' He shakes his head. 'Never mind Kevin. I should get this little one to bed.'

He comes over, leans down and scoops up Mack. Instinctively, her arms go around his neck as she nuzzles against him. 'Be right back,' he whispers.

Five minutes later, he comes back. 'Not a peep out of her,' he says. 'She must be exhausted.' His eyes wander over to the CD player.

'She played me some of your music,' I say. 'I hope you don't mind.'

'Little monkey,' he says quietly. 'Of course I don't. I didn't even know she knew where I kept it. Amanda must have shown her.'

'I loved it,' I say. 'Alex's mum had an incredible voice.'

'She really did.' He's silent for a moment. 'Alex told me some more about her tonight – when he could get a word in. Kevin couldn't stop talking,' he says wryly. 'We've arranged to meet for lunch tomorrow – you and Mack included, if you'd like to?'

Suddenly I feel apprehensive. This is Luke's life – and Mack's. I'm on the fringes, rather than a part of it. But I don't want to seem rude. 'That would be nice.'

* * *

I awake the following morning to a noise outside my room, like a shuffling sound; then the quietest of knocks.

'Hello?' I call out.

The door opens and Mack stands there. Still in her pyjamas, she's carrying a book and has a unicorn under her arm. 'Can I come in?'

Studying her, I notice her face is tearstained; any trace of last night's exuberance gone. 'Of course,' I say gently.

She comes over and perches on the bed.

'Mack? What's wrong?'

Sitting there, she doesn't speak as a tear rolls down her cheek.

I wait as she reaches into a pocket for a tissue. 'This is my fault, isn't it?' I say quietly. 'For turning up like this, and sleeping in your mum's studio. I'm so sorry, Mack. The last thing I wanted was to upset you.'

'It isn't that.' Her bottom lip trembles as she stares at the floor. 'I just really miss my mum.' More tears roll down her face.

My heart twists in anguish for her. 'Of course you do.'

She's silent for a moment. 'It isn't just that. It's my dad.' She takes a shaky breath. 'I went to the kitchen just now. He was sitting on the terrace, just staring. At nothing.' Her voice wavers. 'I don't know what to do about it.'

It's as Augusta said; Mack's taking on her father's well-being as her responsibility. I wish there was a way to take her pain away. 'This is so hard, Mack. For both of you.' I pause. 'But maybe you can't do anything. Your dad misses your mum, just like you do.'

'I just want things to go back to how they were,' she says tearfully. 'But they can't. Not ever.'

'No,' I say quietly. 'It's going to take a little while to get used to that.' I pause. 'Your mum wouldn't want you to be unhappy, would she?'

'You didn't know my mum.' Mackenzie sits there, hunched.

'I know I didn't. But it's obvious she loved you both – so much, Mack. When you love someone that much, you want them to be happy again.'

'I'll never be happy,' Mack sobs. 'Not ever. How can I be?'

I put my arms around her; wish yet again I could take this away from her. 'I'm here for you, Mack,' I whisper into her hair. 'Any time you want to talk about it.' There's a knot inside me as I hold her, feeling sobs rack her body, until eventually, they stop. I let go of her, take her tissue and gently wipe her face. 'You know, maybe I might be able to help a little bit. Like perhaps together, you and I might be able to cheer him up.'

There's despair in her eyes. 'I've tried. But it hasn't worked.'

'Well, maybe it's time to ask the Universe again. And don't forget, there are two of us now.' I awkwardly stroke a strand of her hair off her face, suddenly feeling this love for her that's almost instinctive. 'You'll probably find out for yourself, but anyone who knows me will tell you, I don't give up easily.'

Her eyes search my face. 'Can I ask you something?' She pauses. 'Only I don't understand how you didn't know him before – Dad, I mean.'

'Me neither.' I shrug. 'He and my mum clearly split up well before I was born. I don't think they were together very long. He didn't know she was pregnant. And my mum... Well, she wouldn't tell me anything about him, my whole life.'

My mother's exact, unnecessarily blunt words were 'You wouldn't want a man like that in your life. And nor did I.' Foolishly, I never questioned her, instead building a picture of a man who wasn't a nice person; a picture that it turns out was inaccurate.

'Does she know you're here?' Mack looks at me curiously.

'Yes.' I pause. 'She tried to talk me out of coming.'

Mack screws up her face. 'Why?'

'Probably because I would have found out that your dad – and my dad – is a really nice man. It would have made her feel bad for not telling me about him before.' But it's only a half-truth; the real reason being my mother would have been forced to admit she'd lied to me.

'She sounds different to my mum,' Mack says.

'What was your mum like?' I ask.

'Pretty.' Mack's eyes fill with sadness. 'She was really happy and kind.' Her voice wavers. 'I miss her.'

She leans towards me and I put my arms around her again, holding her tight, breathing in the scent of her hair. 'I know, Mack.'

But the fact is, I don't know. We can never truly know how it feels to be someone else. Only Mack knows how it is to have this well of grief inside her, for the woman she loved most in the world, who was the heart of this home, of her family.

* * *

Extraordinarily, Mack rallies and at her insistence, Luke does, too, and drives us all to the beach. The colours are vibrant, the sun casting shadows across the valleys under a cornflower blue sky, while everywhere I look is a lush green. 'It's beautiful,' I say.

'It's been a dry summer,' Luke says. 'But we had rain just before you got here.'

'We do get storms. And sometimes it rains forever,' Mack says emphatically. 'It's like it's the end of the world.'

'Not very often, Mack,' Luke says.

'Often enough.' Mack rolls her eyes exaggeratedly.

'You're spoilt. You should try living in England,' Luke says.

'I'd like to go to England. But not to live there. We get a lot of tourists, too,' Mack tells me. 'Too many.'

'Stop moaning. The island relies on tourism. Tell Bee about the sea.' Luke glances at her in the rear-view mirror.

'I love the sea,' she says wistfully.

It's the typical banter you'd expect between a father and a daughter, another of those rare moments of normality, as for a short while, it's possible to forget their loss, that both of them are grieving. Similarly when we reach the beach and after slipping off her shoes, Mack runs towards the water.

'She's a sea creature,' Luke says as he picks up her trainers. 'It doesn't scare her. It never has. But she's careful, too. Amanda used to say she has a sixth sense about the ocean. She said something had happened to Mack in another life, and that Mack had learned from it. Amanda believed there was more to this life than the here and now. To her mind, it made sense.'

From the way he speaks, it seems Luke is less sure. When we catch Mack up, she's still standing at the edge of the sea, gazing out across the water. 'I'm looking for mermaids.' She flashes a smile at me, then a more anxious one at Luke.

'Seen any?' he says softly.

'Not yet.' Turning to gaze out to sea again, Mack's silent for a moment. 'Look!' she cries. 'There's a dolphin!' She jumps up and down. 'Look, Dad!'

I strain my eyes, catch a streak of silver as it arcs out of the water. Then as we watch, it's followed by another.

'Two!' Mack shrieks excitedly. 'Bee! Did you see?'

Still transfixed, I nod. I've never seen dolphins in the wild before. But as I watch them, there's something almost joyous about their presence, before just as quickly, they're gone again.

'I wish we could swim,' Mack says longingly.

'We'll come back soon and you can,' Luke says decisively. 'Now, how about we take Bee somewhere for a late breakfast?'

As we walk back to the car, I feel Mack's little hand take mine. 'Do you like it here, Bee?'

'The sea? Or the dolphins?' I tease. 'Only kidding, Mack. I love all of it.' I pause. 'I really do. I think it's magical.'

Luke drives us to a café off the beaten track. Sitting outside at wooden tables under the shade of pine trees, we order coffee and tostadas, a hot chocolate for Mack.

'We should go into town,' Luke says. 'Show Bee around Pollensa. Tell you what – you girls could have a wander while I go off and do the boring shopping. Just quickly, though. We have about an hour before we need to go home and change before meeting Alex and Kevin.'

'Yay!' Her worries parked temporarily, Mack claps her hands in glee.

* * *

While Luke goes to the supermarket, Mack and I while away an hour wandering the narrow streets of Pollensa, taking in the pretty, pale stone houses as she steers me towards the shops.

'We won't go in that one.' She points to a shop with racks of jewellery on display. 'They rip off the tourists, Mum said.' As she says 'Mum', her voice wavers.

'So show me the good places,' I say. 'For example, let's just say we wanted to buy you a new notebook. Where would your mum suggest?'

She smiles, her cheeks flushing pink as she takes my hand and leads me up another narrow street, stopping outside a shop with a window crammed with artists' supplies. 'In here,' she says.

Going inside what looks like a treasure trove of creativity, we peruse the boxes of coloured pens and pencils, as well as paints and notebooks. 'How about this one?' I pick out a notebook with a dolphin on the cover. 'Kind of perfect for today, don't you think?'

She nods. 'I can buy it.' She reaches into one of her pockets and takes out a little purse.

'My treat,' I tell her and, while she isn't looking, I add a packet of felt-tip pens. Then after, we walk a little further and stop for an ice cream, and by the time we meet up with Luke again, she's still smiling.

'Look what Bee got me.' Her eyes are bright as she thrusts her notebook at Luke. 'And these.' She shows him the pens. 'We went to the shop Mum used to take me to.'

'That's really nice.' Luke turns to me. 'Thank you,' he says quietly.

* * *

Having seen a little of the town, I feel a new appreciation for being here; a warmth inside that comes from Mack's apparent acceptance of me. Back home, she insists I come to her bedroom where she changes into a dress. Any remaining awkwardness between us gone, she turns to scrutinise me.

'How old are you, Bee?'

'Twenty-nine. How old are you?'

'Nine. I'll be ten in July. It's funny.' Mack hesitates, then adds shyly, 'I've always liked the idea of having a sister.'

'Me too. I'm sorry I'm so old,' I joke.

'One day, I might still have a younger sister...' She hesitates. 'Then I'll have two!' She starts brushing her hair.

'Would you like me to do it?'

She passes me her hairbrush. 'OK.'

Mack sits on the floor in front of the large mirror leant up against the wall. Her hair is windswept from the beach and sitting behind her, I carefully tease out the tangles. When I've finished, she turns to look at me, then smiles. 'I really like you being here.'

I feel my heart warm. 'I like it too.' Another surge of love fills me. 'I suppose I should go and get ready.'

'Yay!' Mack beams. 'Can I help you?'

Suddenly I feel dizzy. 'Why don't you put your shoes on?' But instead of going upstairs to change, I go to the kitchen to get a glass of water. As I'm standing there, Luke comes in.

'We should be going,' he says.

This time, I don't just feel dizzy. It's more like I feel daunted, that things are moving so fast when I still don't know where I fit in with it all.

'Are you OK, Bee?' He looks worried.

'I'm not sure.' Going over to the sofa, I sit down. 'I don't feel that good.'

Luke looks concerned. 'Can I get you anything?'

'I don't think so.' Disappointment washes over me. But at the same time, I have a need to be alone. 'I think it's probably best you go without me.'

14

ALEX

After the evening with Luke, I'm left with an impression of a quiet man. One who has fond memories of the days with the band, but who gives little away about himself or his family; is private – a fact that Kevin seems oblivious to.

In fact, they couldn't be more different, and even though Luke has potentially agreed to come to the UK, I can't help wondering how realistic my plan is.

By the time I get down to reception on Sunday lunchtime, Kevin is already there.

'Ah, Alex. I was just about to book a table. There's a Michelin-starred restaurant a twenty-minute walk away. Quite an interesting menu.'

Is he for real? Firstly, Mack's about eight or nine. Secondly, he's only thinking of himself again. 'Kevin, I think we should go for something more informal – like tapas, perhaps – or something that would appeal to everyone.'

'Tapas?' He says it like it's a dirty word. 'A bit basic, isn't it?'

'It's food of the region,' I say firmly. 'There'll be plenty of choice for Mack – and everyone else. I found a nice place the day we got here. It's about a five-minute walk.' I find it on my phone, then show him. 'It's here.'

'Doesn't really matter what I think, does it?' he says drily.

'That isn't what I'm saying,' I tell him. 'Anyway, I would have thought it's less about the food and more about being together,' I remind him.

'I'm afraid I have to correct you on that score. The food is critical,' he says firmly. 'Always.'

'You'll like this place. We can try yours another time.' I call the restaurant and book a table. Then after texting the address to Luke, I look at Kevin's crutches. 'Are you ready?'

We make our way slowly along the streets, our progress slowed by Kevin's painful hobbling. But unlike his Michelin-starred restaurant, fortunately it isn't far. Reaching the tapas bar, Kevin heads for the first available chair.

'I asked them to reserve a table by the window,' I say. 'You stay there. I'll go and check.'

The restaurant isn't busy and despite my booking at the last minute, they have indeed given us what looks like their best table. Staggering to his feet, Kevin winces as he puts his injured foot to the ground. 'Fuck. Sorry. I keep forgetting.'

We make it inside, Kevin settling uncomfortably onto a chair just as Luke and his daughter arrive. In a grey dress dotted with sparkles, with her hair neatly brushed, she's clearly made an effort.

'Nice to see you again,' Kevin says impatiently, glancing over his shoulder. 'Come and sit down. What do we have to do to get a drink around here?'

Luke catches my eye briefly as he slides into a chair, while Mack sits next to him, and opposite me. 'Can I have a Coke, Dad?' she asks.

'I should think so.' Luke opens a menu.

'Is this OK?' I ask them. 'I'm not sure what you like to eat,' I say to Mack.

'Pizza.' Her eyes gleam.

'You had pizza last night,' Luke tells her.

Mack rolls her eyes. 'Bee ordered it.'

'Bee?' I ask.

'She's my sister,' Mack says.

My ears prick up. It's the first I've heard of Mack having a sister.

'She's your half-sister,' Luke reminds her.

'It's almost the same.' Mack looks at Luke. 'Can I have tortilla? And chips?'

Between us, we order an array of tapas, a carafe of Spanish wine, a Coke for Mack. As I find out, she might be young but nothing gets past her.

'I've heard your mum sing,' she confides in me as we eat. 'On Dad's CDs. My mum played them for me.'

Suddenly I remember she's just lost her mum. 'You've probably heard more of the band's music than I have then. Maybe, sometime, you can play them to me.'

Her face lights up. 'OK.' A quizzical look crosses her face. 'He must be on them too.' She glances at Kevin. Too intent on attracting the attention of a waiter, he doesn't notice.

'He probably is,' I say quietly.

Her face lights up with a smile, before she puts a hand over her mouth, trying to stifle her laughter. 'I don't know why, but that's really funny,' she whispers.

'What is?' Luke asks.

'Mack was just telling me something,' I say. And she's right. It's hard to equate the Kevin sitting at the table with us with the supposedly talented drummer from the band. Over lunch, Kevin does little to redeem himself, talking non-stop, mostly about himself, breaking off now and then as he knocks his boot against one of the table legs, his face creasing up in pain. 'Ouch. Fuck. Sorry...' Turning away from us, he tries to hide the agony he's in.

'Are you OK?' Mack asks innocently.

'It's my foot,' he manages. 'Apologies. Excuse my language.'

'It's OK,' Mack says. 'Daddy says fuck sometimes.'

'Mack.' Luke gives her a warning look. Then winks at her.

As more tapas dishes are placed on the table, Mack looks at me. 'How long are you staying?'

'I'm not sure,' I say cautiously. 'Kevin booked our flights. I suppose we'll be leaving in the next day or two.'

'Oh.' Mack's face falls. 'What about getting the band back together?'

'Well...' I say, glad that she at least is interested. 'That's why we have to go back – to try and track down the others.' Plus there are only a few more days before my freedom ends and I have to start looking after my mother again.

'Miles and Atlas,' Mack says.

'Yes. Them.'

'So...' Stabbing a chunk of potato, Mack dips it into the *alioli* on the side of her plate. 'How will you find them?'

'Damned good question,' Kevin interrupts. 'I was thinking Alex and I should fly from here to Glasgow. Try and track down Atlas.'

I stare at him, wondering where his determination stems from. 'I only have a few more days before my mother comes home.'

'Presumably she could stay with your aunt a little longer.' Kevin sounds matter-of-fact. 'But all the more reason to crack on with this.'

When he hasn't even discussed it with me, it's easy to guess what kind of lawyer he is. 'Kevin found out where Miles works,'

I tell Mack. 'We've emailed him – we're just waiting to hear back.' But my heart sinks as I think about leaving Majorca, because I'm loving it here; when it comes to going home, I'm not ready.

Mack's face suddenly lights up. 'Dad, can we all go to England? Bee can come, too.'

'Don't get ahead of yourself,' Luke warns. 'You have school to think about – and we haven't found Atlas yet. This might turn out to be a wild goose chase.'

Mack looks deflated. But not for long. 'Ask him about his stories,' she says to me. 'About when they went on tour.'

'Oh?' I look at him quizzically; my mother's recollections are increasingly fragmented. 'How long were you together?'

'We were in our late teens. We played on and off for ten years. I suppose when your mum knew she was pregnant, we all knew things were going to change.' For a moment, there's a gleam in his eyes. But only briefly, before it's gone again. 'We worked really hard, but we had a lot of fun, too. Roxy – your mother...' He shakes his head at me. 'She used to love a prank. Caught you out a couple of times, didn't she?' He looks at Kevin. 'She told him we'd been picked out for a tax inspection. You should have seen his face. You see, we were all paid cash most of the time – but even then, you were a stickler for the law, weren't you?'

Kevin looks put out. 'That wasn't at all funny,' he says. 'Cash has to be declared, like anything else. That's the trouble with most people. They seem to think...'

He breaks off mid-flow when my phone buzzes. Picking it up, I see the number on the screen. 'Excuse me. I have to take this.'

* * *

Apparently my mother has had another fall, resulting in Lorna calling an ambulance, which, as a precaution, promptly whisked her off to hospital. 'I'm going to have to go home,' I say to everyone. 'She doesn't cope well when something unexpected happens.'

'What, already?' Kevin sounds put out. 'Damned nuisance, having come all this way.'

'My mother's had an accident,' I remind him, irritated by his comment, by his overall selfishness; a sinking feeling coming over me. But the reality of her illness is never far away. 'These things happen now and then.' Even though, if she'd been at home, if I'd been there, this might not have happened, I can't help thinking. But her mobility isn't what it used to be; she's become more frail. 'You don't have to come with me,' I say to Kevin.

'I thought we were going to Glasgow,' he reminds me. 'Together, I seem to remember.'

'I hope she'll be OK,' Mack says anxiously.

'Why not wait till the doctors have checked her over?' Luke suggests. 'If she's discharged, she can go back to your aunt's house and you might not need to rush back.'

I hesitate. He may well be right. But I can't shift the feeling of responsibility that hangs over me.

* * *

'You're worried about her, aren't you?' Luke says as we leave the tapas bar.

'Yes. She's dependent on me.' I'm silent for a moment. 'I can't help thinking if I'd been there, I might have been able to prevent it.' But it hadn't stopped the fall she had before I came away.

'You don't know that,' Luke says.

'No.' But it's like the sun has dimmed; it feels wrong that when she's in hospital, I'm here.

'At least you know she's being looked after,' he says.

'You're right.' But it doesn't stop the guilt I feel.

'We go this way,' Kevin says brusquely as we reach a junction, nodding in the direction of the hotel.

'If you have time, call in for a coffee before you leave.' Luke shakes his hand, then mine.

I turn to Mack. 'I hope I see you again.'

'Me too,' she says shyly.

As Luke and his daughter walk back to their car, Kevin and I make our way back to the hotel. Back in my room, I speak to Lorna again. It turns out my mother has a badly sprained ankle and a superficial cut on the side of her head. She's been discharged back to Lorna's, albeit with a care package in place.

'She isn't at all happy about it,' Lorna says. 'But she can hardly walk at the moment. It's probably best she stays a little longer – at least until she's back on her feet again. Would you like to have a word with her?'

'Of course.' I pause. 'Are you sure you're OK with that?'

'It's no problem,' Lorna says. 'The care staff will be helping. And you need a break, Alex. Don't worry about us. We'll be fine.'

'This is the problem with the NHS,' my mother complains bitterly when I speak to her. 'It's a waste of resources. I don't need carers. I'm fine. And Lorna's here.'

'Let them help you,' I persuade her. 'Just until your ankle's better. Lorna isn't getting any younger.'

'What about Alex?' she says suddenly. 'Where is he? He said he was coming.'

'You're talking to him, Mum,' I tell her, suddenly worried again. 'It sounds like you had a bump on the head. It's no wonder you're a bit confused.'

'Oh,' she says vaguely. 'Am I at Lorna's?'

'You are. Just for a few more days,' I remind her. 'Kevin and I have gone to see an old friend of yours. Remember Luke Friday?' I don't tell her we're in Majorca.

'You're with Kevin?' she says disbelievingly.

'Yes. We've come to see Luke,' I repeat.

'I know. You've already told me that,' she says impatiently. 'But why is Kevin there?' She goes on. 'Be careful, Alex. You do know he can be quite ruthless, don't you?'

I've no idea why she would say that about him. Nor do I ask. After the call ends, I weigh up my need to be there, against my relief that she's with Lorna, before deciding to do as Lorna said and make the most of having a break. Until she's over this crisis, for want of a better word, Lorna's right. It's best she stays where she is.

'Seems like I have a few more days,' I say to Kevin in the hotel bar that night, after explaining what's happening. 'Can you try to contact Miles again?'

'I'll email him now.' Getting out his phone, he types a message and sends it. 'None of my business, but don't you think it's time you found a live-in carer for your mother?' Kevin says abruptly. 'Let's be honest. Your life isn't your own, is it?'

I'm astonished at the lack of empathy in his voice; that he shows no sympathy whatsoever for her. I shake my head in disbelief. 'She has an illness, Kevin. If I can help her, it's what I want to do. If we're going to find Miles and Atlas, we need to get on with this.'

Little more is said after that. Kevin realises he's overstepped the mark, though I don't suppose he's worked out how, exactly. For all his monetary success, in Kevin's world, compassion and sensitivity towards his fellow humans appears somewhat lacking.

I finish my drink. 'Let me know if you hear anything from Miles.'

'Of course,' he says abruptly. 'Goodnight.'

I don't respond. Having tolerated Kevin for most of the last three days, my patience is running short. It isn't just his lack of sympathy for my mother. Not once has he expressed any sensitivity for Luke's loss, nor has he shown any interest in either of Luke's daughters.

In summary, Kevin is interested only in himself. I think of my mother's comment, about Kevin being ruthless. He's certainly focused about getting things done. But I have a feeling he's cynical and lonely; embittered by life. Either way, however, his behaviour does nothing to endear him to people.

I don't sleep well that night. It's the fall my mother's had; the feeling that I've dipped into her past, one that as I glean more knowledge of, she's increasingly losing track of.

At some point in the night, I dimly register my phone pinging with a text. It's from Kevin.

> I have an address for Atlas. Thought you'd want to know.

Knowing there's hope on the horizon, after that, I doze intermittently, falling deeply asleep just as it's getting light, so that it's 10 a.m. by the time I awake properly. Then as I come out of the shower, I see Leo is calling me.

'Alex. It's Leo. I got your number from Kevin. How's your mother doing?'

'Not so bad.' Then I remember, when I met Leo, he was in the hospital, too. 'How are you?'

'Could be better. But can't complain,' he says cheerily. 'That isn't why I called, though. Don't know if Kevin told you, but I have an address for Atlas. He lives in a hostel.' Just as I'm imagining Atlas being homeless, Leo goes on, 'He never could bear to see folks having nowhere to go. He bought the place years back to give homeless people a roof over their heads. Apparently, he's still there. Running it has pretty much become his life.'

I'm stunned. 'I had no idea. But thank you. I'm going to try to go and see him.' I pause. 'Why don't you come too? We could meet in Glasgow.'

There's silence from the other end of the call. 'That's a fine idea.' He bursts into a fit of coughing, that becomes muffled for a couple of minutes, before he speaks again. 'Sorry about that.' His voice is hoarse. 'It's best you go without me.' He pauses. 'I've a horrible feeling I picked up Covid when I was in hospital.'

'Of course.' I'm frowning, thinking how unwell he'd looked. 'I'm sorry,' I say. 'I'll be back in England soon. Let me know if there's anything I can do to help.'

'Bless you.' His voice is rough. 'About Kevin...' He hesitates. 'I know he can be a bit of a miserable bugger. But his heart's in the right place.'

'I'm kind of working that out,' I say. 'But he doesn't do himself any favours, does he?'

'You could say.' Leo chuckles, before it turns into a coughing fit. 'You're a good lad, looking after your mother. But don't forget to look out for yourself, too.'

I have the oddest sensation of a lump in my throat. When you're constantly caring for someone else, you tend not to think about yourself too much. 'I'll let you know how we get on,' I say.

'I'll look forward to it,' Leo says. 'Cheers for now.'

Checking out of the hotel, I'm sad to be leaving. But we have time to spare and drive over to Luke's.

'Leo asked for your number. No idea why,' Kevin says.

'He called before we left. He wanted to talk about Mum.' Though I think it was more to see how I was coping with Kevin.

Reaching Luke's place, I park and get out. Standing there, I soak up the peacefulness of the surroundings. The hills in every direction, the valleys of pine and olive groves. A world apart from everything I know, quite simply, it's a little corner of paradise.

'Come on,' Kevin says impatiently, as he hobbles towards the house. 'We don't have long.'

We make our way around the side of the house to the terrace where Luke is sitting at his laptop.

'Morning,' he says. 'Have a seat. How are you both?'

'Been better.' Kevin eases himself onto a chair, while I look around wondering if the elusive Bee is here this morning.

Closing his laptop, Luke gets up. 'Coffee all round?'

'Great,' I say, as Kevin says, 'Fine.'

Luke comes back with a cafetiere and cups. 'How was your mum?' he asks me.

'I spoke to Lorna – my aunt – again last night,' I say. 'She's all right. She's back at Lorna's. She was confused. She's always worse when something out of the ordinary happens.' I shrug. 'It's just how it is now.' I take the cup Luke passes me. 'Where's Mack?'

'At school.' Luke sits down. 'So, just so we're all on the same page... We're going to wait until you've spoken to Miles and Atlas, and then try and get some dates in place.'

'Sounds sensible,' Kevin says. 'No point planning anything just yet.'

'When are you going to tell Rachel?' Luke asks.

It's the million-dollar question. 'If I tell her too soon, she'll worry, then forget. And if I don't tell her, she'll accuse me of planning it behind her back. Plus, there's no point saying anything until we know for sure it's going to happen.' I shake my head, wondering if Luke realises how complicated my life is.

'But if we can get everyone together, I genuinely believe she's going to be over the moon about it.'

* * *

Twenty minutes later, we're on our way to the airport. For once Kevin doesn't argue about using a wheelchair. One hour after that, we're on the plane. The strangest thoughts are whirling inside my head, one of them dominating.

The fact is, I've loved being here. Meeting Luke, getting a taste of another way of life, has reminded me how small my own little world is. Of course, I want to see my mother. To pick her up and take her home. But one thought dominates all the others.

I don't want to leave here.

DEAR UNIVERSE

I'm writing to ask for your help again.

I know this a really, really long shot. But I've had a really brilliant idea. It's about my dad. I don't think I told you he used to be in a band. Anyway, some of them are talking about getting back together. It's because Roxy, who was their singer, can't remember things and they think music will help.

So. This is my idea. It's more of a wish really, but I watched this TV programme about festivals and how cool they are. And I hope you don't think this is too much, but it seems really important and I can't just forget about it. So, I'm just going to ask. If there was any way my dad's band could play, even on the smallest stage at the smallest festival, just for a few minutes, it would be everyone's dream come true.

I know that magic exists and that amazing things happen. We live in Majorca and magic is everywhere on this island. I just wish my dad could see it.

By the way, my dad doesn't know I'm writing to you and I know it's a big ask. But all I want is for him to be happy again. And for Roxy to hear the music.

If I can do anything in return, I'm up for that.

Thank you.

Mackenzie Friday (aged 9)

15

BEE

I put my malaise down to the stress of the last few weeks catching up with me. It seems to pass otherwise unaccounted for and the following morning, while Mack's at school, I go for a walk, heading further up the track past Luke's house. Not entirely aimlessly, you understand. Partly, I need to think. But also, it's where Augusta lives.

There's more warmth in the sun today, the air around me resounding with the sound of cicadas. Now and then, lizards dart across my path and as I walk, I try to unravel the thoughts in my head.

First and foremost, Mack is there. A warm feeling comes over me as I think of the bond growing between us. Then, of course, Luke. It's understandable he's preoccupied just now. And he's nice, don't get me wrong. But it's like his grief is impermeable, closing him off from everyone around him. It's early days, I tell myself. Two, three months is nothing when you lose someone who meant the world to you.

My thoughts turn to my mother. In a hundred lifetimes,

she'd never contemplate doing what Luke or Augusta have done, moving their lives and starting again in an unfamiliar country. But nor would most people, I tell myself.

Out of nowhere, Phil is on my mind. Let him go, Bee, I tell myself firmly. He doesn't belong there. Then I'm thinking of the guy at the arboretum and how kind his eyes were; wondering if I stay here, if I'll ever meet anyone like that again.

Turning my face to the sun for a moment, I breathe in the scent of pine, suddenly realising I'm not missing the shops or parties I used to go to. It seems incredible how in such a short time, the potential for wide, all-encompassing change has entered my life.

I follow the track around a bend, then up ahead a small, white-painted house comes into view, in front of it a field in which several goats are grazing. Seeing me, they amble up to the fence, fixing their eyes on me.

A dog bounds up and I recognise Cato. Wagging his tail, he trots beside me as I walk towards Augusta's house, where I see her in the garden, digging what looks like a vegetable patch.

'Hello?' I call out.

Stopping when she sees me, she waves, then puts down her fork and comes towards me. 'This is perfect timing,' she says. 'I have so much to do, but it really is far too warm for gardening.' She wipes her hands on her jeans. 'Come in. I'll make us a drink.'

Her house is smaller than Luke's. Following her into her kitchen, it's cosy and homely, with a dining table at one end, a fireplace at the other, close to which two sofas are arranged.

'I spend most of my time in this room,' she says. 'When I'm not out there.' She nods towards another door that leads to the back of the house.

Going over there, I open it and step out onto a terrace. It's smaller than Luke's but with a view that's equally stunning, my eyes widening as I gaze across the hills; at the distant sea glimmering where the sun catches it.

Augusta comes out and stands next to me. 'Most mornings, I come out here to watch the sun rise. Just over there.' She points towards the hills. 'I find it grounding. Doesn't matter what's going on in our little lives. The sun will go on rising long after we're not here.'

I gaze towards the sea, thinking about what she's said. It's different here to England in the most obvious of ways. But what I've noticed most is the way people think. I can't think of anyone else who'd talk about watching a sunrise, or who would rescue a wounded dog at a roadside, or give a lift to a total stranger. 'It's really lovely,' I say quietly.

I'm aware of Augusta watching me out of the corner of her eye. 'I'll get the tea,' she says.

She goes back into the kitchen, then reappears carrying two mugs and takes them over to the table. 'Come and sit down,' she says.

I pull out a chair opposite her and take the mug she pushes towards me.

'So how are you settling in?' she says.

'In a way, it's like I've been here ages.' I tell her about the bond Mack and I already have, then about the son of one of Luke's old band members who's trying to get them all back together again.

'Goodness. It's all been happening,' she says. 'But I suppose what I should really ask is how are you getting on with Luke?'

I'm silent for a moment. 'OK.'

'Just OK?' She raises one eyebrow.

'There's nothing bad,' I tell her. 'He's been nothing but

friendly. He doesn't seem to mind me being here. But we still haven't really talked – at least, not about anything important.'

'Ah.' Augusta sips her tea. 'As you're finding out, Luke keeps things close to his chest. Poor Luke.' She pauses. 'I really think losing Amanda has broken him.'

Broken. It kind of sums up how he seems. A feeling of sadness fills me. 'It's no wonder Mack is so worried about him.'

'Of course she is. Mack's a little empath. She can feel his pain better than he can.' She pauses. 'I wouldn't mind betting that all Luke thinks about, more or less every second of every day, is Amanda. It's going to take time.' She pauses again. 'Have you decided if you're going to stay around?'

I sigh. 'I have no idea. I'm trying to do as you said – to take each day at a time. But I need to find a job before too long. Which in the absence of anything else, means going back to England.' My heart feels heavy as I say it, but much as I wish it were different, this isn't my real life here.

Augusta studies me. 'Have you found out any more about visas?'

'Not yet.' I shake my head. Right now, everything feels too complicated again.

Augusta rolls her eyes. 'Brexit has so much to answer for. It's utterly unfair on your generation, taking away free movement. But complaining isn't going to help.' She frowns slightly. 'What we need is a solution.' She looks at me. 'Life's an adventure, Bee. Don't let anyone ever tell you otherwise.' She pauses. 'Those of us who moved from elsewhere, we're all driven by a sense of adventure in some way.' She looks at me quizzically. 'Where did you grow up?'

'I was born in Brighton, but since then, I've lived all over the place. My mother was always moving around. She lives in London now.'

'Interesting.' She studies me. 'I didn't have you down as the city type.'

'That's because I'm not,' I say. 'I liked Brighton – though I'm not really a Brighton type, either.'

'So where feels like home to you?' Her voice is unexpectedly kind.

It's the million-dollar question; perhaps the reason I've never felt settled. You see, I'm not sure where home is. I swallow the lump that's suddenly in my throat. 'I don't know.'

'I didn't mean to pry, my dear.' She's silent for a moment. 'I've moved around a lot over the years, too. I was always looking for something. It took me a while to work out that home isn't a place. It's a feeling.' She pauses, watching me. 'If that makes sense?'

I nod. 'I guess I'd hoped meeting Luke would help a bit.'

'Of course,' she says sympathetically. 'And I'm sure it will. But it takes time to really get to know someone – though you don't need me to tell you that.' She breaks off as her phone buzzes. She reaches into her pocket for it, then glances at the screen. 'I'm so sorry, Bee. I have to take this.'

Leaving me on the terrace, she goes inside. The call goes on a while and in the end I poke my head through the door. 'I'll go,' I say quietly.

Augusta blows me a kiss, mouths, 'Sorry.' Leaving her, I go back outside and start heading down the track towards Luke's house, replaying Augusta's question in my head, about where home is.

Having moved around throughout my childhood, since then, I've stumbled from one flat to the next, driven by circumstance; Saskia's was the longest I'd stayed anywhere, but it always felt like Saskia's. I blink away the tears filling my eyes. I've kept my life busy; leaving myself little time to just think – until now, that is.

Yes, I can stay at my mother's. But we're not close. We never have been. The truth is, I've yet to find anywhere that feels like home – and if I'm honest with myself, deep inside, sometimes I feel very alone.

Not wanting to go back to Luke's just yet, I turn off the track and follow a path through pine trees, until they thin out and I find myself gazing across a valley. Augusta's words come back to me. *Life's an adventure*. Then I think of my mother's life. Working all hours, then when she isn't, her enthusiasm for getting dressed up and going out to some overpriced restaurant. Then I'm thinking of Luke, raising Mack on this gorgeous island; of his music career. Of Augusta; of the lives they've built in the wilds of the Majorcan countryside.

Meanwhile, what do I want? If coming here has done anything for me, it's already shown me how many ways there are to live. There are no rules, no shoulds. These people are following their hearts. Pursuing a way of living that has meaning to them.

And that's what I want, too, I'm suddenly realising. A sense of purpose; meaningful relationships instead of fickle men and fair-weather friends. I want to feel I belong somewhere. All things that so far have been missing from my life.

When I get back to Luke's house, I walk around the back to the terrace. The door into the kitchen is open and as I go inside, Mack's sitting at the table drawing in one of her notebooks. 'Hi,' I say brightly.

But as she turns, she looks preoccupied.

'You're home early,' I pause. 'Is everything OK?' When she doesn't speak, a feeling of foreboding comes over me as I go over and sit next to her. 'What is it, Mack?'

Her lip wobbles. 'Something's wrong with Dad.'

* * *

I find Luke outside in a part of the garden I haven't seen before, halfway down a grassy slope behind the house, populated by more of the olive trees that are prolific around here. Sitting on a chair, he's staring ahead of him, his eyes blank, his hands clasped in front of him.

'Luke?' I say tentatively. 'Are you OK?' I pull up a chair next to him.

'Not really.' He doesn't look at me.

'What's wrong?' I ask, trying to hide how anxious I feel.

Shaking his head, he sighs. 'If I knew, I could fix it.' He pauses. 'Everything feels impossible at the moment.'

'Your life has changed,' I say quietly. 'But you're doing great.'

'It doesn't feel like that.' His voice shakes.

'Mack told me you were out here.' I hesitate. 'She's worried about you.'

'I know she is. But I didn't want her to see me like this.' There's desperation in his eyes, in the way he speaks.

It's the first visible manifestation of the grief overwhelming him. 'It's early days.' I try not to let my worry show. 'Really early days.'

He doesn't say anything. I reach out a hand and awkwardly stroke the arm nearest to me as I notice a tear roll down his cheek. Then he turns to look at me and I see the depth of his sadness in his eyes. 'I miss her. So much. I don't know how to do this without her.'

As I place an arm over his shoulders, they start to shake. Then moving closer, I put both my arms around him. Silent sobs rack his body and I feel powerless. All I can do is sit there, just waiting, until they subside.

* * *

Sometime later, I leave Luke sitting amongst the olive trees and go back to the house. When I go inside, Mack looks at me anxiously.

'He's upset,' I say gently, trying not to show how concerned I am. 'About your mum. He'll be OK, Mack. He really will. It just isn't a good day.' But I can't help thinking, what if he isn't OK? Where does that leave Mack?

When Mack doesn't speak, I try to lighten the mood. 'I went to see Augusta earlier. I saw Cato – and her goats.'

She pulls a face. 'I wish I'd gone with you.'

'We'll go together next time.' I catch sight of an envelope on the table next to her notebook. 'What's that?'

Her cheeks flush pink as she thrusts it under a piece of paper. 'Nothing.'

Luke stays outside until night falls. After putting together a simple supper, I help Mack go to bed. Then later, Luke and I sit outside on the terrace, Luke in silence, staring across the valley.

'I'm sorry,' he says at last. Then out of the blue he adds, 'Do you know how long you're staying?'

'I still haven't decided,' I say tentatively. 'I suppose I don't have any definite plans at this stage.' Then my heart sinks as I realise what he's getting at. 'If it would be better, I'll book a flight. I don't want to outstay my welcome.'

'No, you've got this all wrong.' He folds his arms. 'Will you stay, Bee?' There's desperation in his eyes. 'I'll get through this. I have to,' he says quietly. 'I realise you need to find a job. And you'll need a visa. Remind me to speak to my friend. I forgot.

The thing is…' He breaks off, his voice wavering. 'I think Mack and I both need you here.'

Overwhelmed, I can't speak. Instead, a weight lifts, my eyes filling with tears as for the second time today, I get up and go over to hug him. 'Thank you,' I whisper.

* * *

'You look exhausted,' Augusta says the next morning when she calls around.

'When I left yours yesterday…' I go on, telling her how Luke had gone off on his own; how worried Mack was about him.

'Oh goodness. No wonder you're so tired. You need to make sure you get some rest, my dear. Is he feeling any better today?'

'I think so,' I say. He seemed together enough to drive Mack to school. 'He wants me to stay.' I look at Augusta. 'He said it would be good for Mack – and for him.'

'Hoorah,' she says quietly. 'Common sense has prevailed. You must be delighted.'

'I am. But also…' I hesitate. 'I'm really worried about him.'

'Luke will be fine,' she says firmly. 'He loves Mack far too much to let her worry like this. But for you… there's a matter of the paperwork and getting a visa sorted out.' Augusta smiles. 'Once it's done, we'll have to celebrate.'

'I'll need to find a job,' I remind her.

'Of course.' She looks thoughtful. 'All in due course. I have a feeling things are going to work out, Bee.'

True to his word, Luke speaks to his lawyer friend. But it seems there is no easy way to do this.

'If you were younger, we could have applied for family repatriation. But it looks like you need an income. Once you can prove that, we can get started.'

'What kind of income?' I gaze at him hopefully. But when he tells me the monthly salary I have to prove, I feel my heart sink.

'Don't get despondent,' he says. 'We have the best part of three months to find a way through this.'

Three months go fast, as I know too well. As the realisation settles over me that this isn't going to be simple, it's like the sun goes out.

But as another day passes, I watch the changing light across the valley, aware of a sea change inside me; feel lighter than I have in as long as I can remember. Grateful, too, that in spite of what is going on in his life, Luke has asked me to stay.

I have to channel my adventurous spirit, I tell myself. If other people have built their lives here, there's no reason why I can't find a way.

When I tell her I'm staying, Mack flings her arms around me, holding me tightly.

'I knew you would,' she says, beaming at me.

'You knew?' I arch an eyebrow at her.

'Yes.' She shrugged. 'I've been asking the Universe.' She pulls one of her faces at me. But so have I. Maybe I should take a leaf out of Mack's book. Be more specific.

Universe, show me how to earn a living here.

'So now...' Mack breaks off, looking slightly cagey.

'What is it?' I wonder what it is she isn't saying.

'Nothing,' Mack says innocently.

But already I know her better than that. 'Is there something else you've been asking the Universe for?'

She seems to think for a moment. 'Bee, if I tell you, you must absolutely swear on your life not to tell anyone.'

Reaching under her notebook, she shows me the letter she's written.

* * *

But when it comes to helping Luke, the Universe seems oddly reticent. I watch him go through the motions of a day, but it's as though a light has gone out. I try to hide my worry from Mack. But the following morning, I awake to find her shaking me.

'Bee? It's Dad. He says he can't get up.'

16

ALEX

On the flight from Majorca to Glasgow, in the seat next to me, Kevin restlessly scrolls through a series of documents on his laptop, now and then making irritated noises. Trying to ignore him, I feign sleep, in my mind replaying the events of the last few days. The chance meeting in the hospital between my mother and Kevin that sparked all of this. I mean what were the chances of that happening? Then seeing Leo, too. Going to Majorca, meeting Luke. And now this leg of our journey to Glasgow to find Atlas – all in the name of getting the band back together.

Cocooned in the house in Brighton, preoccupied with caring for my mother, I'm all too aware how small my world has become. But after the last few days, under the Majorcan sun, it's felt as though it's opening up again.

Until we land in Glasgow to overcast skies and heavy rain.

'Bloody depressing, isn't it?' Kevin says. 'I won't be staying a minute longer than absolutely necessary. I'll look up when the last flight leaves later tonight.'

I say nothing. Once Kevin has the bit between his teeth,

there's no point. Outside the airport, we find a taxi. Getting in, I show the driver the address.

'You're sure about this?' He speaks with a broad Glaswegian accent.

'Quite sure,' I say firmly, just as Kevin intervenes.

'For Christ's sake, man, can you get a move on?'

As the taxi-driver's eyes meet mine in the rear-view mirror, I glance away. It isn't for me to apologise for Kevin's behaviour. It doesn't get any better, either, as throughout the journey, Kevin mutters disparaging comments.

'Miserable place, isn't it? Can't imagine why anyone would want to live here.'

I'm too tired to enter into another pointless debate with him. I happen to know that as well as architecturally fascinating, Glasgow is a cultural hub – if Kevin could look past the end of his nose and his misconceptions, maybe he'd be able to see that. Though right now, it's impossible to see anything much through the rain lashing against the windscreen.

Eventually the driver pulls up at the side of a dimly lit street, outside a shabby door that's slightly cracked open.

Staring at it, Kevin looks put out. 'This had better be the right address.'

'Of course it is. Come on,' I say hastily, paying the driver and getting out, before Kevin says anything else.

I take our bags, while Kevin hobbles on his crutches. I push the door open and go inside. It's a wonderful building with high ceilings and what looks like an original tiled floor. The walls are in need of a coat of paint, but I'm guessing that's way down the list of priorities.

'Where the hell's Atlas?' Kevin's voice comes from behind me.

'Why don't you wait here? I'll see if I can find him.' Leaving the bags with Kevin, I start down a corridor towards a hubbub of voices coming from the end. Reaching a partially open door, I push it open to find a room filled with mismatched tables and chairs, and people.

A woman sitting at the nearest table looks me up and down. 'Can I help you, love?'

'I'm looking for Atlas,' I say. 'Do you happen to know where he is?' But as I speak, I notice a man coming towards me. Small and wiry, he has long hair and bright eyes.

Reaching me, he holds out his hand. 'Atlas,' he says. 'And you must be Roxy's son.'

* * *

Within the hostel, Atlas has a tiny flat. 'Can't justify the space, just for myself. In any case, I'm hardly ever in here. Here. Sit yourselves down.' Gesturing towards the small table, he goes over to a cupboard in what passes for his kitchen where he gets out a bottle of whisky and three glasses, before coming back and sitting down.

After carefully pouring the whisky, he passes each of us a glass before raising his. 'Good to see you,' he says, taking the tiniest sip before putting his down. 'But what I really want to know is what brings you here.'

For once, Kevin lets me speak and I tell Atlas about my mother. He listens sympathetically. 'Terribly difficult. For both of you. Has she been prescribed medication?'

I nod. 'It's hard to know if it's working or not. But she takes it. Time will tell if it slows things down or not.'

'Miraculous things happen,' Atlas says quietly. 'So you want her to hear the band play, is that it?'

He's the first person who hasn't opposed me and suddenly

there's a lump in my throat. 'I don't even know if it's possible. But if it was...'

Atlas smiles. 'My boy, it's amazing what is possible.' He turns to Kevin. 'What do you think about all this?'

Kevin knocks back the rest of his whisky. 'I have to say I tried to tell him that we've had our day,' he says pompously. 'But then he told me about Rachel. Couldn't bother you for a drop more, could I?'

Atlas silently passes him the bottle. 'And that's the point. Isn't it?' He looks at me. 'It's about connecting your mother to her past. Creating a memory of something that was important to her – only this time, it will be one you're able to share with her.'

I stare at him. He's summed it up. Beautifully. 'That's exactly it.' But the reality of Atlas's role in the community here is fast sinking in. 'Your life already seems full.'

'I like it that way.' He winks at me. 'But I kind of like your idea, too.' He sits back. 'I've a few people who can help me out here. Count me in.'

I breathe out, a sigh of relief. 'Thank you.' My words are heartfelt. 'So the next question has to be where.'

* * *

With the last available flight overbooked, Kevin checks in to a nearby hotel, the hostel being too basic for him; I spend the night on Atlas's sofa. My head spiralling with thoughts, mulling exactly how we do this.

I think of Luke's offer for us to gather at his house in Majorca. But however much I want to, I worry the journey would be too much for my mother. As I lie there, however, I have a much better idea.

* * *

'I think the band should go back to its roots,' I say to Atlas and Kevin the next morning, over breakfast in a nearby café.

Atlas's eyes widen. 'You mean Brighton?'

I nod. 'Why not? It's where you all started out from. I'm sure we could find a pub where you could play – just for a one-off.' I glance at them both. 'What do you say?'

'Not on your life,' Kevin says immediately. 'I have a law firm. I have my professional image to think of. Some of my clients come from Brighton.' He stares at us both. 'What have I said?'

'You make it sound as though playing in the band is a bad thing,' I tell him. 'Have you thought it might improve your reputation, rather than damage it?'

'Nonsense,' he says abruptly. 'Playing with a bunch of amateurs in a dodgy pub? I hardly think so.'

'There's nothing wrong in showing your human side.' Atlas and I exchange glances. 'But if that's how you really feel, perhaps we should do this without you,' he says calmly, turning to me. 'What do you think?'

I see exactly what he's doing. 'I agree. Kevin shouldn't do this unless he wants to. I mean, really wants to.'

'Now just a minute,' Kevin blusters. 'I've gone to a lot of trouble to get things this far.'

'Then stop being such a fucking snob,' Atlas says. 'Sorry, mate. But that's what it amounts to. You take yourself far too seriously. Lighten up. You might even find you enjoy yourself.' He picks up a fork and tucks into his bacon and eggs.

We tentatively agree that Brighton makes sense – as long as Luke can join us. Part of me is sad that Majorca is off the cards, not least because I loved it there. But this isn't about me. It's about my mother.

Later that morning, I email Luke.

We've found Atlas and he's on for playing again. I know it's a
big ask, but is there any chance you could come to Brighton?
With Mack, of course. Let me know. All the best.

I spend the rest of the day sporadically checking my phone,
still waiting for a reply as Kevin and I drive to the airport.

'You'll probably never hear from him,' Kevin says. 'If you
lived in Majorca, would you honestly want to come to Brighton?'
Missing the point spectacularly as he always does.

But I refuse to let Kevin rile me. 'I'll let you know when he
replies,' I say.

The flight is short. After landing back at Gatwick, the same
buggy driver as when we left transports us through the terminal
back to the arrivals hall.

'God bless you,' he whispers to me, nodding his head in
Kevin's direction. 'If I were you, I would have left him by now. Or
worse.'

'What's that?' Getting his crutches organised, Kevin frowns
as one of them slips. 'Bugger,' he says crossly.

'Nothing to worry about,' I reassure him. 'Come on. I'll drive
you home.'

By the time we reach Kevin's house, he's uncharacteristically
silent. After parking near the front door, I get out then fetch his
bag out of the back. He fumbles with his keys, opens the door
and punches a number into the alarm, then just stands there.

'I'll bring your bag in,' I say, stepping past him. 'Would you
like me to carry it upstairs?'

'I can manage.' He's silent for a moment. 'Erm, if you wanted
to stay, there is a spare room. After all, it's been a long day.'

I try not to show my astonishment. It really hasn't been a

long day. But it's not just that. With his obsession for order and doing things his way, staying with Kevin would be unbearable. 'Thanks. But I should get home,' I say quickly. 'I'll let you know when I hear from Luke.'

'Yes. Of course.' He stands in the doorway as I walk out to my car. When I get in and glance in the rear-view mirror, he's still standing there, raising a hand as I drive away.

How odd, I can't help thinking. But I'm only a few miles down the road when it comes to me what that was about just now. Socially inadequate as he is, Kevin's lonely. I'm almost certain it's the reason he asked me to stay.

Back in Brighton, the house is cold and dark as I let myself in. But with the lights on, after the heating bursts into life, it isn't long before the chill starts to lift.

Six days have passed since I left here. Hardly the quiet break I'd imagined for myself, but it's been interesting. Not only that, but it's also brought new people into my life. I sink into the sofa and check my emails, finding as I'd hoped, there's a reply from Luke.

In theory, yes, I don't see why we can't come to England. I can see it makes sense for your mother. And I think Mack would like Brighton. We've one or two things going on right now, and Mack's school to work around. Do you want to let me know some possible dates?

Relieved, I put my phone down, wondering what's going on over there. Then as I sit there, I suddenly panic. No one's mentioned anything about where to practise.

I open my laptop and start a spreadsheet, of things we need to organise in order to make this happen. Number one being finding Miles. With no time to waste, I fire off another email to his producer.

Then we need dates, and a venue. But also somewhere for everyone to stay and practise. But the answer is so obvious I can't believe I haven't thought of it before. I pick up my phone, hoping he hasn't gone to bed, and call Kevin.

He answers straight away. 'Alex. How can I help?'

'More than you probably realise.' I tell him my idea about putting his big and empty house to use.

'Oh.' There's a silence at the other end. 'I had a feeling you were going to say that,' he says.

'You mean you've already thought about it?' I say, astonished.

'Obviously it had occurred to me. I mean, no one else has anywhere suitable.' He doesn't sound very happy. 'I have four spare rooms. I suppose they may as well be used.'

'That's amazing.' I'm completely blindsided. 'Thanks, Kevin. I can't believe you're doing this.'

'Nor can I,' he says drily.

'All we need now is somewhere to practise.' My brain is whirring.

'Yes, well, I've thought of that too.' He pauses. 'I'll probably regret saying this, but I have a cellar.'

I don't ask why he hasn't mentioned it before, simply put it down to a crisis of conscience, slightly shocked that firstly, Kevin has one, and secondly, that he isn't entirely selfishly motivated. As it turns out, Kevin's cellar is properly soundproofed. It seems he hasn't completely given up on music. He even has a drum kit down there, for the rare occasions he feels like bashing out one of the old tunes. 'Absolutely no need for anyone else to know,' he says.

'Of course not.' I don't point out that everyone will find out soon enough. 'I've emailed Miles's producer again,' I tell him. 'Once we've spoken to him, we're fit to go.'

'Yes. I suppose we are.' This time, instead of sarcasm, I'm almost sure I hear an element of surprise in his voice.

I barely sleep that night. In my mind, I conjure an image of my mother's face when she sees everyone back together again. I wonder if I'll get to hear her sing; what Mack will think of it all. My excitement is short lived, however. The following morning, I'm up and about bright and early when my phone buzzes and an unknown number flashes up.

'Hello?'

'Hello. Is that Alex?' It's a girl with a clear, calm voice.

'Yes.'

'You don't know me. I'm Bee.' She hesitates. 'Luke asked me to call you. I'm not sure how to say this.' She sounds a little anxious. 'But he isn't well.'

I grip my phone. 'What's wrong?'

'It's hard to describe.' She pauses. 'This may sound strange to you. I know you only heard from him yesterday. But he really isn't in a good place.' Her voice sounds taut. 'The other day I found him sitting on his own, just staring, at nothing. I tried to talk to him and he started crying. He isn't eating. Then this morning, when Mack tried to wake him, he wouldn't get up. I really don't see how he'd be able to travel. It's like even the simplest things are too much for him.' Her voice wavers.

'He must be feeling terrible.' I try to put myself in Luke's shoes, to imagine how it feels to lose your cornerstone.

'I'm trying to help. I'm just not sure how to.' There's anguish in her voice. 'It's like, right now, life is all a bit too much.'

'It's early days, isn't it?' I'm silent for a moment. 'We shouldn't have just turned up. He probably felt he didn't have a choice.'

'It isn't that,' she says quickly. 'I think it was really good for him, seeing you both. It's just the timing.' She hesitates. 'I think his heart is broken.'

I'm stunned into silence. On the one hand, a broken heart is a metaphor; describes the worst kind of human suffering. But on the other, it doesn't sound at all strange. Hearts feel pain; grief, loss, can be incapacitating. 'How bad is he?' I say. 'I mean, is he getting professional help?'

'At the moment, he's resting,' she says. 'He refuses to see a doctor, so I'm doing my best to look after him – and Mack, of course.'

'How is Mack?' I imagine how worried she must be. 'And what about you?' I add more gently.

'I'm OK.' Bee sounds tearful. 'And I think Mack understands that Luke is grieving.'

'Try not to worry.' Mentally I kick myself. How can she not worry? 'Maybe you need to give him a few days – just to rest. Then if he doesn't start feeling better, maybe you should call someone,' I suggest.

'I may.' She sounds uncertain. 'Anyway, I just thought you should know, because he may not be up to playing in the band – at least, for a while. And I know you're trying to arrange to get everyone together again.'

I swallow my disappointment. 'It doesn't matter. Please tell him I understand. There's no pressure. I just hope he feels better soon. And give him my regards.' I pause. 'Look after yourself, won't you?'

'Thank you.' She sounds relieved. 'I'm sure he'll call you himself when he's up to it.'

As the call ends, my heart goes out to Bee. Mack, too. And Luke. This can't be easy for any of them. But I'm floundering. Then I'm cursing the timing of this. Not of Luke falling apart, but of Kevin and I turning up at his house when we knew his wife had recently died. I should have ignored what Kevin said about there never being a good time. As decisions go, this was up there as one of the worst.

Sighing, I pick up my phone again and call Kevin.

'Alex. Glad you've called,' he says. 'I was going to call you. We need to do something about Miles, don't we?'

'Maybe not,' I say slowly. 'Bee called, from Majorca. We have a problem.'

Of course, he doesn't take it well. With my ears battered by Kevin's indignation, after the call, I switch my phone off. Regret fills me, that after coming so close, I can't rule out the possibility this isn't going to happen.

Pushing thoughts of the band out of my head, with a clear day ahead of me, I catch up on work, slightly horrified when I realise how behind I've got. By lunchtime, needing a break, I check in with Lorna.

'How's it going?' I ask.

'Fine.' She sounds calm, relaxed. 'Your mother and I are just having a cup of tea. Would you like to speak to her? Hold on. I'll pass you over.'

'It's Alex,' I hear her say before my mother speaks.

'Alex? Is that you?'

'Hi, Mum. How are you?'

'Rather good. Lorna and I have been having such a nice time. We're going out to lunch soon so I can't talk for long.' She seems perfectly calm. 'Where are you?'

'At home. Catching up on work,' I tell her. 'If you're going out, I'll leave you to it. I'll call you tomorrow. Have a nice time, Mum.'

I end the call, nonplussed. It's the most relaxed I've heard her in a long time. It's good, I tell myself. But it's also odd.

Having planned my life around her, it's as though all of a sudden, she doesn't need me any more.

Sitting there, it strikes me, that at this moment, my life really is my own. I'm like anyone else who isn't a full-time carer. I have freedom – and the thing is, I don't know what to do with it.

DEAR UNIVERSE

The old band turned up! I think they're going to get back together! Hooray! THANK YOU!

But now, my dad isn't well. I'm really worried about him. I think he really needs to play music with them, but I don't think he can right now. Please can you show him what a good thing it would be? My mum would be so proud of him. So would I.

Also, you know I asked about a sister? I'd still really like a younger one, if it's possible, when my dad is feeling better. When the time is right – but you know all about these things.

Thank you.

Love and gratitude and hearts and stars,

Mackenzie Friday (aged 9, in case you've forgotten)

17

BEE

The weekend passes quietly; for the most part, Luke remaining incapacitated, incapable of the simplest parenting tasks, as I try to look after both of them.

On Sunday, he makes it out of bed to join us for lunch. But he eats little, says even less; Mack's delight turning to tears when he goes back to bed again.

'I don't understand,' she sobs. 'Dad is never like this.'

'He's sad, Mack. He can't help it.' My heart aches, for both of them. 'How about we go for a walk? Maybe call in and see Augusta's goats?'

For Mack's sake, I try to maintain an element of normality, to hide my worry. But I should know better; Mack misses nothing and by Monday morning, her initial excitement about the band getting back together has turned to anxiety.

'He isn't going to play in the band, is he?' Mack looks worried.

'Oh, Mack. I don't know.' I take in the sadness in her eyes, the dark circles beneath them. 'I don't think he can face it just now. But he might change his mind when he feels better.'

'I really want him to.' Her bottom lip wobbles. 'Don't you see? It will make him happy again.' She reconsiders. 'At least, happier, I mean.'

'I know. I agree... But right now, he just can't. He's really sad about your mum – and I think it's making him tired. He needs to rest at the moment.'

'He will be OK, won't he?' Mack's eyes glitter with tears.

'He will. You mustn't worry.' It's so unfair that Mack is burdened with all of this. 'Now, don't you have school to go to?'

'Who's going to take me?' Mack asks.

'I am – but you'll have to show me where it is.' I haven't driven Luke's car before, but I dimly recall him saying that in Spain, car insurance covers anyone. Besides, if Mack's going to get to school today, I don't have much choice.

'I don't want to leave Dad.' The anxiety is back in her voice, in her eyes as she looks at me.

'Don't worry. I'll come straight back. I'll look after him.' I look around the kitchen. 'Now, what do you need to take with you?'

Her eyes widen. 'Lunch. I can do it.' She starts delving into the fridge, then cupboards as I find the loaf of bread.

'I'll make you a sandwich.'

Following strict instructions as to what Mack likes, I make her lunch and with her directions, we find her school. I park and walk to the gate with her.

'*Buenos dias*, Mackenzie! Natalie is looking for you.' One of the mothers greets her, then turns to me. 'I am Daniela, Natalie's mother. She and Mackenzie are very good friends.'

I watch a girl run up to Mack and fling her arms around her. 'I'm Bee. I'm staying with Mack and Luke.'

'Ah.' She looks taken aback. 'How is Luke?'

'He's been better.' Suddenly it occurs to me she's thinking

I'm his girlfriend. 'Actually, he's not great.' I pause. 'I'm a relative. I'm staying at the moment.'

'I'm so sorry.' Daniela studies me for a moment. 'Why doesn't Mack stay with us tonight? I will pick the girls up after school, and bring them here in the morning. We often do this – just not so much since Amanda died.'

'That would be great.' It's a good idea, but Mack has nothing with her. 'She has no clothes with her.'

'Don't worry. These two, they wear each other's things all the time.' Her eyes glisten. 'It is so sad for them both.'

'It really is.' I hesitate. As Mack comes running over, I know it isn't really my decision to make. 'I should check with Luke. I'll give him a quick call.'

I'm not at all sure Luke will pick up when I call him. But fortunately, he does. When I tell him I've met Daniela, he agrees that if Mack wants to go, it would be good for her to have some fun. Ending the call, I turn to Mack. 'Mack? Daniela has asked if you would like to go for a sleepover tonight.' I watch her face for any sign of reluctance.

But her eyes light up. 'Yay!' Then a worried look takes its place. 'What about Dad?'

'Don't worry,' I say. 'I'll be there. Your dad will be fine.' I turn to Daniela. 'Thank you,' I say.

Then out of the blue, Mack says, 'Bee's my sister!'

Daniela's eyes widen.

'Half-sister. Long story,' I say hastily, feeling sure Mack will fill her in. 'I'll give you my mobile number.' I recite it and she programmes it into her phone. 'I should get back. Have fun, Mack. I'll pick you up tomorrow.'

On the way back to Luke's, I stop to pick up some bread and a few other things. When I go into the house, it's silent, the washing up left on the side, Luke clearly not having made it out of bed as yet.

I go along the corridor and stop outside his room, then knock quietly. 'Luke?' When there's no reply, I try again, then not sure what to do, I push the door open.

The room is in semi-darkness, Luke huddled under the bedclothes. 'Is Mack all right?' he mutters.

'She's fine.' I hesitate. 'I'll make you some coffee.' Without waiting for him to tell me not to, I go to the kitchen. Then as well as coffee, take him a hunk of the bread I've just bought.

Going back into his room, I switch on the light beside the bed, then put the coffee and bread on the bedside table. Then going over to the window, I open it and push the shutters partially back to let some air in. I turn to look at him. 'Is there anything I can do?'

When Luke doesn't move, I go closer to the bed and crouch down next to it. 'I'm worried about you.' My voice wavers. 'I think I should call a doctor.'

'No,' he says quickly. 'I'll be OK. Don't worry. I'll get up soon.'

Leaving him, I close the door behind me, then go to Mack's room, which is in its typical state of disarray. I pick up the clothes strewn on the floor, fold them and put them away, then tidy her bed, taking a moment to think of her carrying on with her day at school, when, at home, life is falling apart around her.

Maybe it really is a good thing I'm here. But if I'm going to stay and be eligible for a visa, the need to prove an income hangs over me. I go upstairs to the studio. My laptop is on the table in the corner, which looks as though it served as Amanda's desk. But when I get to it, for some reason, my eyes settle on a little notebook.

Don't even think about it, I tell myself, thinking of my mother's diary. But then I see the words written on the star-studded front of it.

For Mack

Picking it up, a strange feeling comes over me as I open it. Amanda's handwriting is gracefully formed and easy to read, and it soon becomes obvious this little book is an ode to her love of this island, of its magic, its secret places off the beaten track. In short, the island she wanted her daughter to know.

Clutching the notebook, I take my laptop downstairs. As I pass, there is no sound from Luke's room and I go into the kitchen where I make myself a coffee, then settle myself outside, on the terrace.

Sipping my coffee, for the first time this morning, I'm still for a moment. I take in this gorgeous view, the peacefulness, which are no help to Luke. But right now, I don't know if anything is.

I decide to give him until lunchtime, and in the meantime, I open my laptop and google remote jobs, scrolling through the listings as I try to find something that's suited to me.

A couple of hours later, I have a shortlist of social media related jobs and after updating my CV, start firing off applications. Then with that done, I find myself drawn back to Amanda's notebook.

A pang of guilt hits me as I pick it up. But it isn't a diary, I tell myself. It's for Mack – a list of magical places Amanda has found. A rock shaped like a dragon, a hillside in which quartz is embedded. A rare tree, a waterfall only found after rain has fallen; then what Amanda describes as the mirror pond.

Fascinated, I'm engrossed, my attention broken as I hear footsteps on the gravel. Hiding the notebook, I look up just as Augusta comes into sight.

'Hi.'

'Good morning.' She glances at my laptop. 'Hard at work already?'

'I've been applying for jobs,' I tell her. 'Actually, I'm glad you're here.'

She sits down and I tell her about Luke. 'I don't know what to do to help him.'

Augusta looks worried. 'It isn't like him to go to bed for no reason. Is Mack at school?'

I nod. 'I took her. She's going to a friend's tonight, for a sleepover.'

'Thank goodness. She doesn't need to be any more worried than she already is.' Augusta's silent for a moment, then says thoughtfully, 'The question is what do we do.'

'I was going to call the doctor, but he doesn't want me to.' I pause. 'I don't know what else to suggest.'

'Perhaps he needs some more time. He's had to keep going since Amanda died – for Mack's sake. Now that you're here, maybe subconsciously he feels more able to give in to his grief.' She sighs. 'I'm no psychologist, but it does make a kind of sense.' She looks at me. 'Are you OK? I mean, it's one thing coming to meet your father. But another altogether to end up looking after him.'

'It's fine.' I've long cast off any expectations I may have had. 'Maybe you're right. We should give him more time.' I'm out of my depth, hoping this doesn't go on much longer.

Augusta frowns. 'If things get worse, or he starts acting oddly, don't think twice about calling the doctor, my dear.' She gets up. 'I should leave you to your work. Good luck. Let's hope the perfect opportunity comes your way.'

After she's gone, I start to panic. I didn't ask her what she meant by Luke behaving oddly. But my fears are allayed when he makes it out of bed, albeit briefly. Coming out to the terrace, his hair is uncombed and he hasn't shaved.

He comes over to the table and sits down. 'I'm truly sorry about this,' he says awkwardly. 'Did you speak to Alex?'

I nod. 'He sends his regards. I told him you'd call him when you felt better.'

'Thanks.' He pauses. 'I'm really grateful to you for looking after Mack.'

'I'm happy to.' I take in the circles under eyes that are bloodshot. 'Would you like some lunch?'

He sighs. 'I suppose I should have something.'

'Leave it to me.' I go to the kitchen and cook him some eggs and mushrooms on toast. When I take it outside, he's clearly not hungry, only picking at it before he pushes the plate away. He gets up and walks to the edge of the terrace. Standing there, he wraps his arms around himself.

Quietly, I go over to join him. 'I haven't been through anything like this,' I say. 'I can only imagine how you feel. But you and Mack... You will get through this.' My fists are clenched. I want to – have to – believe it.

But as I stand there, the strangest feelings are coursing inside me. I'm not being entirely honest with him, because I have been through something like this. I've just always suppressed my emotions, kept a lid on how I feel – as I do about pretty much everything.

'I just feel sad,' he says dully. 'Like the sun has gone out. It's the only way I can describe it.'

I put a hand on his shoulder. 'It wasn't the same, but I know what you mean,' I say quietly.

'Do you?' He stares towards the hills.

Suddenly I feel stupid. 'I haven't lost a partner. But she was someone close.' Hot tears prick my eyes. 'It was a long time ago.'

I pull myself together. 'I should probably get on with some work.' I pause. 'I wish there was something I could do to help.'

He shakes his head. 'Thanks. But there isn't anything.'

It isn't surprising his mood is low, I tell myself. There are peaks and troughs in all our lives. And most of us try, but no one can be happy all the time. Even so, seeing Luke like this seems to destabilise me.

But I don't let it get to me. Turning to my tried and tested cure, I change into running clothes. Instead of heading into the hills, I follow the road for a couple of miles towards the village. After Pollensa, it's tiny. A scattering of stone houses set amongst the hills, with a single shop outside which there are boxes of oranges and tomatoes, next to which there's a rustic-looking bar.

Slowing down, I walk through the centre of it, taking it in. The faded paint on the shutters, the pots of brightly coloured flowers, the freshly dug earth and well-tended vegetable gardens; a microcosm of genuine Majorcan life away from tourists, behind which the dusty hills stretch into the distance. It's quiet, yes. But I can see why Luke and Amanda moved here. If peace is what you're looking for, it's in abundance here.

* * *

That evening, the house seems empty without Mack. It's dark by the time Luke wanders into the kitchen. He goes to one of the cupboards and takes out a bottle of wine.

'Like some?' he asks.

'Thanks.' I sit there as he brings it over. 'How are you feeling?'

'Tired.' As he sits down, his eyes settle on Amanda's notebook, on the table next to my laptop. 'Where did you find that?'

'In the studio. I hope you don't mind.' I pause. 'I should have asked you first. It's really lovely. It's for Mack.'

Silent, he picks it up and starts leafing through it, now and then a smile playing on his lips. When he's finished, he passes it back to me. 'I don't mind. She was always jotting down her thoughts. I should go through her things. I just haven't been able to face it yet.'

'It can wait.' I sip my wine. 'I've been job hunting today.'

His eyes register interest. 'Any luck?'

'Not yet.' I don't tell him how anxious I am; how much I want this to work out, so I can stay on. 'I also discovered the village – with the shop and the bar – in the hills. It's cute.'

'I told you not much goes on around here. You're sure you're not going to find it too quiet?'

I shrug. 'I haven't so far. I used to like always being busy – but everything's different here.'

Luke stretches his arms out. 'It is. I was thinking, tomorrow, I might drive down to Palma, then pick Mack up from school on my way back.'

'Are you sure?' I say anxiously. 'If you want another quiet day, I can get her.' As I speak, my mobile buzzes. 'Hello?'

'Bee, it is Daniela. How is Luke?'

'Actually, he's right here. I'll pass you over to him.' I pass Luke my phone. 'It's Daniela.'

Taking my phone, he gets up and walks to the edge of the terrace. He speaks in Spanish for a couple of minutes, before coming back and handing me my phone. 'Seems Mack's taken things into her own hands. She's invited herself to stay for another night.' He looks at me. 'Probably not a bad thing.' He pauses. 'I'm not sure what she's said to Daniela, but she's obviously been talking about you.' He's silent for a minute. 'I'm going to take that as my cue to have another quiet day, then drive down to Palma tomorrow afternoon. I might even stay there overnight. Some friends of ours live there.' He stops suddenly. 'Of course, you're welcome to come too.'

I shake my head. 'Thanks, but I have to job hunt. I'll be fine here. It will be good for you to go. To have a change of scene, I mean.'

But I feel a pang of something, as I think about being alone.

* * *

I spend the following morning trawling through more jobs. Then in another of life's unexpected turns, after Luke leaves for Palma early that afternoon, out of the blue my mother calls me.

'Have you decided when you're coming home?' she asks.

'Not yet.' I hold back from telling her that hopefully I won't be. 'Luke's asked me to stay a while. He has another daughter. Mack. She's nine.'

'Didn't I tell you what kind of man he is?' My mother sounds bitter. 'I don't suppose she's the only one. There's probably a few more of them scattered around the world. I told you, didn't I? People don't change.'

I'm stunned into silence. I mean, just who does she think she is? 'You couldn't be more wrong,' I tell her. 'For your information, Luke has just lost his wife. He's devastated. So is Mack.' I pause. 'What you just said is completely unfounded. And it wasn't nice.'

'Don't speak to me like that,' she says sharply. 'I'm simply telling it like it is. It's for your own good, Bethany. Waltzing off to Majorca like this… It's time you got yourself back here, got a job and woke up to the real world.'

I gasp in shock. 'You have this so wrong.' I can feel my heart thumping. 'I'm sorry, but I won't have a conversation like this with you. It's probably best we talk another time.' After ending the call, I switch my phone off, not sure what just happened; why my mother says such awful things. Worse, why she thinks it's OK to say them.

My hands are shaking. I've never spoken to her like that before. But it's the first time I've recognised the extent of her bitterness, her default to judge, unkindly; utterly thankful that both are a measure of the difference between us.

Knowing my mother, she'll feel wronged; be expecting me to apologise. It's the way it's always been. But not this time, when I've done nothing to apologise for.

Trying not to think about her, I open my laptop and check my emails. There are two rejections to jobs I applied for yesterday. Slightly downhearted, I click on Google and carry on as an idea comes to me.

Since coming here, I've almost completely ignored my own social media. Too much has felt uncertain in my life. But suddenly it occurs to me that just maybe, in wanting to stay here, I'm not alone. Maybe what I should be doing is documenting my discovery of this island and journey to residency.

It's a sure-fire sign that I'm onto something as my mind starts to race with ideas. And a new journey equals a new profile. Using a photo of me on Luke's terrace, in no time, I set one up. Then searching for Majorca-related profiles to follow, I'm away.

By late afternoon, my head is spinning with it all as I pull together images and words about the beauty of this island, even with the frustrations surrounding staying longer than ninety days here. But my idea is gathering momentum. As well as sharing my knowledge about how to acquire residency, there's work to do on this house, something else I can help Luke with.

It's times like this that I can easily feel overwhelmed, that running calms my head. After pulling on leggings and trainers, on impulse, I grab Amanda's notebook and decide to try to follow one of her hand-drawn maps. I lock the house, put the key underneath a plant pot and set off jogging down the track.

After turning onto the road, the map leads me onto a narrow path I haven't found before, hidden among pine trees and twisting around rocks up a gentle slope. On reaching the top, I gaze down into the valleys, the trees seeming smudged in the hazy light; breathing in air on which the scent of rosemary lingers.

I carry on along the path as it winds around some rocks, recognising one set alone as Amanda's dragon rock. More of her landmarks follow as I pass a tree which, thanks to the arboretum, I recognise as a giant Ficus macrophylla, or Moreton Bay fig tree. Stopping, I rest one of my hands against its massive trunk, taking in the roots that hold it strong here.

I remember Cindy telling me about the underground connections trees have; about the invisible network of mycelial threads, which is like a vast circulatory system. I lean back against the tree, suddenly homesick for the arboretum. Then, reaching into the pocket of my leggings, as I feel for my phone to photograph it, I realise with dismay I've left it at Luke's.

Resolving to come back again and bring it with me, I carry on, slowing to a walk as the path grows rougher, listening for the sound of the waterfall on Amanda's map. I'm aware that daylight is fading, but having come this far, I want to find it, to see what Amanda loved so much about this place.

Losing my footing on a rock I didn't see, suddenly I realise how dark it's getting and decide the waterfall will have to wait for another day. Turning to go back, I glance up to make out the first stars, in the dim light trying and failing to read Amanda's map as I start to panic.

I try in vain to find the fig tree I passed on the way, but every path leads to an unfamiliar vista until slowly I'm forced to acknowledge I've lost my way. As it sinks in that I've no idea where I am or in which direction Luke's house is, I try to think. Then it occurs to me. There must be villas around here. Maybe Luke's is closer than I realise. I need to wait until after sunset when I'll be able to see lights in windows. Maybe Luke will come home and wonder where I am. But then I remember Luke is out for the night. He won't miss me.

As the last of the sunlight fades, I'm uneasy. It's the thought that I'm alone, that no one in the world knows where I am. Suddenly the prospect of spending a night out here is terrifying. I scan the darkness for pinpricks of light from car headlights, but there are none. I undo the sweatshirt tied around my middle and pull it on, grateful I had the foresight to bring it with me.

Sitting down, I lean back against a rock. In the darkness, my eyes have adjusted enough to make out the shapes of trees, of silhouetted hills, as I consider there's every chance I'm going to be spending the night out here.

I berate myself for not bringing my phone. For not telling anyone where I was going. But with Luke away for the night, there wasn't anyone to tell. A feeling of despair creeps up on me, then all of a sudden, overwhelms me. I forget the row with my mother, instead thinking of my bedroom in her house, of the boxes of all my familiar stuff, craving the comfort they bring. Then I think of Mack; how desperately unfair it is that a freak accident took her mother away from her. A mother who had so much to give.

A tear rolls down my face, followed by more. I've always thought of myself as an optimistic person, someone who looks for the positives. Who tends not to let things get me down. But as I sit here, I'm swamped by what I can only describe as an overwhelming, crippling sense of grief.

Sitting there, I feel my body shake as thoughts of Olivia fill my head, the little sister I lost. The sister I never talk about, to anyone. Alone in the darkness, I rest my head in my hands. I was five when she died. Too young for more than the most fleeting of memories, my dim recollection of her face based on a few photos I once found, which my mother wouldn't talk about.

I was left to work it out for myself. And over the years, that's what I've done – from her birth certificate, a small bundle of sympathy cards tied with a pink ribbon, a letter from her doctor. Olivia had died at the age of two from leukaemia.

It makes no sense I've carried so much grief for the sister I never knew. But here in the darkness, I realise it's about far more than that. It's for a shared childhood I never had, a future that will never be. For the loss my mother must have felt but never showed.

But my mother never lets her mask slip. In a million years I can't imagine her sitting on a Majorcan hillside, alone with her thoughts. She works, cleans, moves house, goes out; in short, she never stands still, a pattern I never questioned until I came here. But that's how she's coped, I'm suddenly realising. Augusta was right. The truth is too painful; my mother's bitterness and unkind words are symptomatic of her deep, unresolved unhappiness.

Why us? Wiping my face with the sleeve of my hoodie, it's like I've taken on Mack's way of talking to the Universe. Why Olivia? Why Amanda? Why any of us?

As I wait for an answer, a calmness comes over me. Raising my eyes, I gaze into the depths of the sky. That's when I realise it's true. Only in the darkness can you truly see the stars. As they twinkle at me, I count them, one by one, a sense of awe over-flowing inside me, as suddenly I'm filled with gratitude for the blessings in my life. The people. This island. That I'm alive.

Above the hills, the faintest glimmer appears. Then the moon starts to rise. Magnificent, pale, it casts its silvery light. I forget everything else as I trace its movement behind the trees. Then a shaft of moonlight filters through their branches and around me the ground starts to sparkle as the realisation comes over me. I've found Amanda's quartz.

Any fear I had has gone as I wonder if, wherever she is, Amanda is watching over me. At any rate, I sleep, awakening the following morning to the distant sound of water. Remembering where I am, I get to my feet and try to loosen my aching body. Seeing Amanda's notebook on the ground, I remember what brought me here. Then suddenly I'm thinking of the waterfall she found.

Brushing the dust off my leggings, I follow the sound. I don't recall hearing it last night, but the air has shifted direction and there's a coolness that mercifully wasn't there before. The sound grows louder, then hidden amongst the trees, the waterfall comes into view.

It isn't big, but it catches the early morning sunlight, while below it a stream flanked with delicate ferns feeds off it.

My hopes rise that it will lead me towards someone's farm and I start to follow it. But then it opens out and I stop. I've found what Amanda called the mirror pond.

The water is crystal clear, my reflection undistorted staring back at me. I'm not a brave swimmer, but emboldened by the night I've just had, I strip down to my underwear and wade into water that's cold enough to make my skin tingle. After splashing around, I lie back, floating, suddenly not caring that I'm lost. After my night under the stars with nothing bar the clothes I was wearing, a feeling of sheer contentment fills me.

My sense of urgency has gone; I'm in no hurry to find my

way back. But as I gaze up at through the branches high above me, I hear the faintest of voices call out.

'*Bee...*'

I swim to the edge, climb out and pull on my clothes. 'I'm here,' I call out, hastily pulling on my shoes.

'Bee? Is that you?'

I scramble towards the direction it seems to be coming from. 'Hello...' I call out. 'I'm over here.'

There's a rustling sound, then I start to freak out as an animal comes bounding towards me, before I realise with relief, it's Cato. Crouching down, I hug him, just as I hear footsteps crunching through the woods. Then looking up, I see Luke.

* * *

Back at the house, after a hot shower, I sit on the terrace wrapped in a blanket, sipping the coffee Luke has made me.

'I'm just glad you're OK,' he keeps saying.

'I am,' I reassure him. I really am. A little shaken, maybe. And a bit achy. But alone in the dark, without any distractions, I came face to face with myself. Then again, this morning, in Amanda's mirror pond. But more than anything, I feel invigorated.

Apparently, Luke drove back early this morning just as it was getting light. When he realised I wasn't here, he commandeered Cato and came to look for me.

'I should have taken my phone.' I still can't believe I didn't. But in a way, I'm glad. Otherwise I wouldn't have experienced this.

'You could have fallen.' Luke shakes his head. 'I should have warned you, Bee. If something had happened to you...'

I want to tell him that nothing's going to happen to me. But I don't. Amanda probably thought the same; there are no guarantees.

'I came back early because I couldn't sleep,' Luke says. 'I suddenly felt so bad about letting the rest of the band down. But with everything else going on, it just isn't the right time.'

'You shouldn't worry.' I pause. 'Alex will have explained. I'm sure they'll understand.' Still exhilarated from the night I've had, I think about persuading him to change his mind. But then I take in the shadows etched under his eyes. Right now, he has enough to worry about looking after Mack, getting through each day. Maybe he's right. Maybe it isn't the time to be doing this.

18

ALEX

I awake early. Oddly restless for reasons I can't identify, I get up and make some coffee. By 10 a.m., I have a few hours work behind me and after going out to my car, I find myself driving towards the arboretum.

It's a typical English autumn day. Grey skies, a dampness to the air, a landscape that's bathed in a dusky half-light, that triggers a pang of longing for Majorca's blue skies and warm air.

When I reach the arboretum, only a handful of cars are parked in the car park. As I walk through the entrance, there's no one there. Pausing, I ring the bell, waiting until someone comes over.

'Quiet this morning, isn't it?' I pay the woman the entrance fee. 'I've been here a few times, but I've never seen it like this.'

'It's quiet most days.' She looks slightly anxious.

'Oh?' Sensing a story, my ears prick up.

She glances over her shoulder, then back to me. 'Someone left. She was brilliant at marketing – and social media. It wasn't that long ago, but there's been a noticeable decline in visitors.'

'But you have someone running that side of things now?'

The woman drops her voice. 'Someone who isn't that good at it. And I really shouldn't have said that to you. Should I?' Panic flickers in her eyes. 'Me and my big mouth. Could you do me a favour and forget we've ever spoken?'

I try not to smile at her overreaction. 'Don't worry. I won't say a word.' I pause. 'Sounds like you need your ex-employee back.'

'If it was up to me, she wouldn't have left. There you are, sir.' She hands me a leaflet. 'The boss,' she whispers just as someone appears through a doorway. Smartly dressed, her hair neatly styled, there's an air of authority about her as she comes over.

'Is everything OK, Cindy?' she says to the woman behind the reception desk.

'Absolutely fine.' Cindy glances at me. 'This gentleman was just commenting on how quiet it is.'

'It's early in the day. And talking about it isn't going to change anything.' The woman glances at me. 'Enjoy your visit, sir.'

'Thank you. I will,' I say. 'I always do.' I start walking away. Then, because I have no reason not to, I turn back to them. 'Do you happen to have a girl working here – around my age, with long fair hair?'

Cindy rolls her eyes but it's the other woman, her boss, who speaks. 'We don't. Would you excuse me?'

As she walks away, Cindy beckons towards me. 'That girl you're looking for... She's the girl I was talking about – who used to do our marketing and social media.' She lowers her voice. 'Geneva fired her.'

'Geneva?' I frown at her.

'Geneva.' Cindy nods in the direction of her departing boss.

It's a rare window into the politics of the arboretum, one to which I have never before been privy, having come here simply for the peace it offers – and of course, the trees. Today, the grounds are ablaze with the rich reds and russet golds of autumn, which before long will carpet the ground as winter sweeps in.

I wander for a couple of hours, aware of a handful of other visitors, but mostly mulling the plight the arboretum seems to have found itself in. I rack my brains for someone who could help. But social media isn't my thing and I come up with nothing. With no hope of bumping into the fair-haired girl, when it starts to drizzle, I cut my losses and drive back to Brighton.

I haven't been back long when my mobile rings. Picking it up, I see Luke's name flashing up.

'Luke.' I cross my fingers that it's good news. 'How are you?'

'I've been better, to be honest.' He pauses. 'I thought we should talk – about the band.'

There's something about the way he speaks that sets off warning bells. Panic rises in me; my first thought is that after all this, he doesn't want to do it.

'Fire away,' I say.

'Alex...' He sighs. Then he goes on, telling me how it had seemed like a good idea, but he was still coming to terms with losing Amanda. 'I not saying never. But maybe a lot further down the line,' he says.

I'm disappointed. It's hard not to be. But from his voice, it's clear he's struggling. 'Really, don't worry.' My heart goes out to him. 'If it happens in the future, that would be fantastic. But no pressure. You have enough going on. I completely understand it isn't the right time.'

'I'm sorry,' he keeps saying. 'I'm letting all of you down. I feel terrible about it.'

'Please don't,' I say. 'Everyone knows what you're going through. They'll understand.'

And I do understand. But there's no denying I'm gutted.

After the call ends, I think of Luke in his house in Majorca. How beautiful the island is, how his life is in many respects enviable. But what matters most is the people in our lives; that the person he'd give anything to be sharing it with has been taken from him.

Sighing, I pick up my phone and steel myself to call Kevin. Predictably, he's unsympathetic.

'Bit bloody selfish of him,' he huffs. 'He should have told us at the start.'

'He probably didn't realise how he'd feel,' I say. 'I mean, we did rather spring it on him.'

'I'm actually quite pissed off,' Kevin says. 'All that time I've wasted. Not to mention money. I really could have done without that.'

I'm speechless. I want to tell him he can afford it. To not be so tight and mean-spirited. To try to feel an ounce of sympathy for someone who, frankly, is swamped in grief. 'It's hardly as though you'd chosen to take time off work. You were off sick,' I remind him. 'And at the very least, you reconnected with old friends. Surely that has to be worth something?'

'That's beside the point,' he mutters. 'And what about your mother?'

I'm taken aback. It's the first time Kevin's shown any concern about my mother. 'She doesn't know what we were trying to do.' And now, she'll probably never know. However much I understand Luke's decision, when I think of my mother, it saddens me.

'Nevertheless,' he says arrogantly. 'Like I said, bloody selfish of him. Suppose I should call Atlas.'

'You probably should.' I change the subject. 'I imagine you'll be back to work soon.'

'As soon as I get rid of this flaming boot. Right. Better get on.'

Deflected, he ends the call in his typical manner, somewhat abruptly.

It's like listening to air escaping from an under-inflated balloon, as just like that my dream of getting the band back together deflates and normal life resumes. But no matter, I tell myself. There will be other ways to keep my mother focused. To fight the obstacles dementia brings her way. This is a setback, but I'm not giving up. All I have to do now, is find them.

* * *

None of us see the invisible twists and turns that go on inside our minds as they create ideas that can seem brilliant in the dark hours, yet ludicrous in the cold light of day. But now and then, one or two are turned up that are like unpolished gems. And the following morning, I awake to find myself mulling something new. A little strange, perhaps, but just possibly, with a little thought and refinement, something that in time could become brilliant. Something that could benefit my mother, and other people living with the same illness.

I wait for it to dissipate. In my experience, ideas often do, logic and reason silently dissolving them. But as I drive to the arboretum, it doesn't happen. If anything, over the forty minutes it takes to get there, it becomes embellished, so that I arrive with it shining brightly in my mind.

Going in, the same woman as yesterday is manning reception.

She looks surprised to see me. 'Back again?'

'Afraid so.' I glance around. 'Does your boss happen to be around?'

She looks at me quizzically. 'I'll try her office for you.'

While I wait, I walk over to the window, trying to imagine

putting my grand idea into practice. Expecting my mind to conjure objections, to my ongoing surprise, it doesn't.

'Good morning.' The voice comes from behind me. 'Can I help you?' I turn to see the boss woman I recognise from yesterday. She holds out her hand. 'I'm Geneva.'

I shake her hand. 'Hi. I'm Alex. Do you have five minutes? I have an idea I'd really like to discuss with you.'

She leads me away from reception to a corner with three comfy chairs arranged around a small table, next to a window with a view across the arboretum. 'Please. Have a seat.'

'Thanks.' Sitting down, I tell what I've been thinking.

She listens intently. 'I like your idea. We're always looking for new ways to bring people into the arboretum. I see no reason why we can't dedicate a day for people with dementia. Actually...' She frowns. 'I really like your idea. It taps into so many reasons a place like this exists. There's the healing power of nature, for one thing. And I'd always imagined it as somewhere to draw people together. But that side of things rather went by the wayside when Covid started.' She pauses. 'So how do you envisage this happening?'

'Well, a lot of that is down to you. But I was thinking about getting it out there that once a month, or once a fortnight, there's a dedicated day. There's a local newsletter – we could promote it in that. And notify support groups and doctors' surgeries. Make it clear that it's wheelchair accessible, and that people can have coffee and cake, or lunch, or whatever.' I hesitate. 'The only potential issue I can foresee is funding it. Some people will be able to afford the entrance fee, no problem. But many people who are already funding extra care at home are financially stretched. I'd like to try to find a way around that.'

Geneva looks unconvinced. 'Funding is always a challenge.' She shakes her head. 'We can discount it for the group. But another potential challenge is the weather. We're going into what's usually the wettest part of the year. Spring would be a better time to get something like this underway.'

I'd hoped for sooner, but it makes sense. 'That would give me time to approach local businesses – see if any of them would be interested in sponsoring a day a month, or something like that. To start with, at least – then we could go from there.'

She takes a business card out of her pocket. 'Email me,' she says. 'Put all your ideas down. Like I said, I like this idea. But I need to think about it.' She pauses. 'You do realise, don't you, that there's nothing to stop anyone coming here, as things are?'

'True.' I try to think how to put it. 'But we could make it about more than just walking around looking at the trees. We could have activities.' I glance out of the window at the carpet of fallen leaves. 'Right now, for example, we could have people making leaf collages. Or playing games, or music... But it wouldn't matter what exactly. Most of all, I think it's like you said. About bringing people together. People who understand each other, who won't think it's odd if someone turns up in pink shoes and a man's hat, or says things that are completely inappropriate, or starts making strange noises.' I shrug. 'It's about providing an environment that's healing, de-stressing – and completely accepting.'

'It's a shame, really.' Geneva shakes her head. 'Until recently, we had a brilliant girl here running our marketing and social media. She'd know exactly how to approach this.' She sighs. 'I let her go – for all the wrong reasons. And ever since, I've been regretting it.'

She's obviously talking about the same girl that Cindy mentioned. It's another blow. But I refuse to be down for long. After all, there are many reasons to be optimistic. And there's nothing like love as a motivator for finding solutions to the impossible.

And it's time life really did start getting back to normal. When I get back, I call Lorna. 'How are things? Only I was thinking, if it's OK with you, I'll drive down tomorrow.'

I work for the rest of the day. But after that, it's time for my mother to come home.

19

BEE

After Luke speaks to Alex, he's the strangest mixture of tired and oddly restless.

'Why don't you get some sleep?' I suggest.

'I've done too much sleeping lately.' He pauses. 'Do you have a moment?'

'I have plenty.' Meaning moments. I look at him. 'Why?'

Luke and I walk down the garden to the olive grove where I found him the other day. 'Amanda had this idea about making it profitable again.'

It's the first time he's mentioned it and I gaze somewhat dubiously at the trees. They're straggly and neglected, which could probably be fixed, given time. But there simply aren't that many of them. 'Don't you need more trees for a decent olive crop?'

'Come with me.' We carry on walking to the bottom of the valley. Then Luke spreads out his arms. 'We have all of these.'

My eyes widen. On the gently sloping land, hundreds of trees reach in every direction. 'Oh,' I say, slightly awestruck. 'I mean, this changes everything.'

'You think? I wouldn't know where to start.'

'Nor would I,' I tell him. 'But there must be plenty of people on the island who do.'

'They all have their own olive groves,' Luke says. 'I'm not sure how they'd feel about sharing their expertise with a couple of complete novices.'

'You could ask around.' I like that he includes me. 'But actually, I happen to know someone who would have an idea.'

OK. So arborists are not generally masters of olive production. However, what they do have is contacts and access to sources of tree-specific information, and when we get back to the house, I call Cindy.

'I wish you were still here,' is the first thing she says. 'It's been so quiet since you left, Bee.'

'Why?' I'm confused. 'I thought Geneva had everything in hand, with her super-rich investors and all that.'

'Those super-rich investors pay our wages, but have done sod all to drum up visitors,' Cindy says. 'By the way, a guy came in. He was asking about you. At least, I think it was you.'

'Who?' I say, mystified.

'He didn't tell me his name. I should have asked.'

I've no idea who this random guy could be, but right now, I'm not interested. 'Anyway, that isn't why I called.' I get to the point. 'I need some information about olive trees. Specifically, rather gnarled old, neglected ones and how to make them productive.'

'Goodness. I don't know. I'd have to think.' Cindy pauses. 'Where are you, Bee?'

'Majorca,' I say proudly. 'I'll fill you in sometime. If you have any ideas regarding the olive grove, can you get in touch with me?'

Luke, meanwhile, has come up with someone. An old man who's spent his entire life on the island, named Sebastian.

'He comes highly recommended,' Luke tells me. 'And he has no allegiance to any of the other farms, which makes him pretty much perfect for us.'

'That's good,' I say. 'Because I didn't get anywhere.'

'Sebastian's coming to see us this afternoon,' Luke says. 'You will be here, won't you?' He pauses. 'I was hoping this was something we could do together.'

I have a warm feeling inside. 'I'd love that.' I have an idea. 'I used to do the social media in my old job. If you're serious about starting olive oil production, why don't I start documenting the whole journey – from gnarled old trees to liquid gold?'

Luke looks doubtful. 'Is there much point?'

'Hey. I just said. It was my job. And I happen to know I'm good at it.' I pause. 'Look, it's up to you. They're your trees. But if we're doing this together... And if you're serious about turning this into a business, it's never too soon to start getting the word around.'

* * *

No matter I spent the night on a hillside; that I had only a little sleep. There's a lightness to my step, a sense of purpose that's been missing, as Luke and I await Sebastian's arrival.

He arrives half an hour late, which isn't a problem. But he doesn't speak a word of English, which is – at least, for me.

'You're going to have to start learning Spanish,' Luke says quietly.

'It's all in hand,' I say, remembering that Mack said she'd teach me.

The three of us walk among the olive trees, Sebastian stopping from time to time to gesticulate wildly and rattle something off in Spanish, to which Luke replies, leaving me feeling even less adequate.

When we get back to the house, while Luke goes to fetch Mack from school, I get my laptop. On opening my emails, I find one from Cindy.

> This is the best I can do. I haven't had a chance to check our
> library yet. But I'll keep thinking.

I open one of the links she's sent, then putting my feet up, start reading the beginners guide to olive farming. I'm halfway through when Luke comes back and Mack runs around the side of the house.

'Dad says you found the mirror pond.' Her eyes are hopeful. 'My mum told me about it. But I've never seen it. Can we go there, Bee? Please?'

I wonder if she's seen Amanda's notebook. Or whether her mother simply told her stories of the places she loved.

'It was this time of day the last time I went to find it,' I tell her. 'Do you want to know what happened?'

Her eyes are like saucers. 'Tell me. Now.'

'OK. Come and sit down.' I move my feet to make room for her. 'Shall I get us both a drink first?'

I fetch us both an orange juice, then sit back down.

'Tell me,' Mack says impatiently.

'Well...' I pause. 'While you were at Natalie's, your dad went to see some friends in Palma. There were some places your mum had written about in a notebook. It was on a shelf in my room,' I explain. 'It wasn't hidden – it's why I thought it would be OK to have a look at it,' I say quickly. 'So, I thought I'd go and check them out.'

'Did you find the tree?' Mack asks. 'Mum showed me it. It's massive.'

'I did.' I pause, remembering. 'It's like no tree I've ever seen before. And I found the dragon rock.' I'm guessing Mack's already seen it by the way her eyes light up. 'Then I kept going. I suppose I didn't really notice it was getting dark. The thing was, if it hadn't been, I'd never have seen the quartz. It was beautiful, Mack. Like the ground was sparkling.' Suddenly it occurs to me. 'Your mum must have gone there in the dark, too.'

Mack's eyes shine with unshed tears. 'She used to go on night walks. She said that was the best way to see the stars.'

'She was right.' I'm silent for a moment, remembering looking up at them. 'But unlike your mum, I don't know the paths very well. I didn't have a torch. And I'd forgotten my phone. I ended up spending the night out there.'

Mack gasps. 'The whole night? On the hill?' Her eyes grow even wider.

I nod. 'I didn't have much choice. I knew your dad wasn't coming back till morning. No one was going to come and find me. No one knew where I was.'

'Wow.' Mack looks shocked. 'You must have been so scared.'

'At first I was,' I admit. 'I was thinking all these different things, about how and why I ended up there. I even asked the Universe.' I glance at her. 'After that...' I break off, remembering. 'It was like the sky started to glow. Then I watched the moon rise behind the hills. That was when I saw the quartz. I stopped feeling scared.' I shrug. 'It just felt magical. Then...' I skip the bit about my grief coming out. 'The next morning, I found the mirror pond.'

'Can we go together?' Mack begs. 'We can take a tent and camp. And a picnic. It would be so cool. Please, Bee...'

I look at her, take in the light dancing in her eyes; hoping I can find the waterfall again. It's the perfect thing to do, to honour the way Amanda loved this place. 'I'd love to.'

* * *

We plan to go that weekend. Meanwhile, I carry on educating myself about reinvigorating and maintaining olive trees, walking down there the next morning to photograph them before Sebastian starts clearing the weeds that have grown up.

Later that afternoon, I get a positive response to one of my job applications. Setting up a Zoom meeting for the following week, a tentative sense of hope settles over me.

But by Friday night, change is in the air, and as the daylight fades, the rain starts, drizzle that slowly moves across the hills, then rapidly becomes torrential. Mack and I huddle inside and watch a movie until the power goes off.

'Don't worry, Bee,' Mack says calmly. 'This is why we have hundreds of candles.' But an hour later, when the power hasn't come back on, it seems like a cue for an early night.

Lying in bed, I listen to the rain hammering on the roof, suddenly reminded of England, more determined than ever that I want to make my life here. But in the darkness, my doubts loom, my problems seeming unsurmountable as they often do during the night hours. If I can't prove sufficient income for my visa, I won't be able to stay here.

My mind starts to catastrophise. I imagine myself forced reluctantly back to England, as suddenly I realise, I haven't told my mother what I'm planning. But since the call I cut short, we haven't spoken.

It seems impossible that I've been here just ten days. From arriving knowing no one, to staying in the hotel, to meeting Luke, Mack, Augusta; spending a night on the hillside, to the olive grove... It's such a different life, but one I already know makes me feel alive. It fires me, a new determination taking me over. I don't want to, can't, leave all of this.

The next morning, it's as though Luke has been awake most of the night, too.

'Morning. There's coffee in the pot.' He looks tired, but at the same time, I can't help noticing, the light has come back to his eyes.

'Thanks.' I pour myself a cup, then take it over to the table.

'I've been reading about olive oil cooperatives around here. To start with, I think that's going to be the way to go.' He seems energised, as though his life force is gradually finding its way back to him. 'In time, I'm hoping we can process our own here. Did you know, we have an old mill in one of the barns? Cold-pressed olive oil is at a premium. If we market it right, we could do well out of this.'

My ears prick up. 'I can take care of that side of things,' I say quickly.

'I hoped you'd say that.' Luke puts down his pen. 'Last night, I was lying awake thinking about all kinds of things – about what Amanda would say if she were here. Then, about the band.' He pauses. 'I need to call Alex again. I know I told him it isn't the best time. But there never will be the perfect time.' He goes on. 'If I haven't put everyone off, I think we should go ahead and do this.'

My heart warms. I've yet to meet Alex. But you can tell a lot about someone from their voice. And he was clearly concerned about Luke. 'Why don't you call him now?' I've a strong feeling this would be good for Luke.

'If we go,' he says carefully. 'And it's still an if...' He hesitates. 'Would you think about coming with us?'

I hesitate. 'I'd love to. But...' Going back to England will mean dealing with my mother. Fielding her objections about Luke. Potentially mediating in a reunion between them, one I'd really prefer not to witness. But maybe it would be good for us to talk. And besides, I don't want to miss what's probably the only chance I'll get to hear Luke play. 'No buts.' I smile at him. 'I'd love to.'

Going out onto the terrace, I think about calling my mother. Then before I can overthink it, I just do it.

'Hi, Mum.'

'Bethany.' Her voice is disapproving; she clearly holds a grudge about the way I spoke to her last time. But I said nothing wrong, I remind myself.

'I thought I should just tell you what my plans are,' I say calmly. 'I'm going to apply for a visa. I can stay at Luke's. There's plenty of room and he's happy for me to be here.' *Unlike you*, I'm thinking. But I don't say it.

'What about work?' my mother says sharply.

'I can work remotely. I have a job interview next week. Plus Luke wants me to help him restore his olive grove.'

She's silent for a moment. 'You do realise this is pie in the sky,' she says coldly. 'I understood you wanting to meet Luke. But don't you think it's time to come home?'

I hesitate. 'The thing is, I'm not sure where home is,' I say carefully. 'You've made it very clear it isn't in your house. But it wasn't at Saskia's, either. All I know is, this is a good place to be. I'm happy, Mum. I'm not sitting around doing nothing. I know life is different here. But that doesn't mean it isn't a good life.'

'You have no idea what you're getting yourself into.' She can barely conceal how angry she is.

But I don't understand why. 'Why is it so important to you?' I ask. 'Just for once, why can't you take an interest, or wish me good luck?' I can't go on walking on eggshells around her. 'I know you're unhappy. But it's because Olivia's gone – and I'm here, isn't it?'

There's a silence. Then as she hangs up, I realise I've spoken the words out loud; dared to mention Olivia's name, when she never has. The blood drains from my face as I immediately try to call her back. But it goes straight to voicemail.

'Shit.' I put my phone down just as Luke comes out.

'Everything OK?'

'No.' Shaking my head, tears fill my eyes. 'Things really are not OK. That was my mother.'

He comes over and sits down next to me. 'Want to talk about it?'

I sigh. 'Not really.' Then it pours out of me in a rush. 'I told her about my plans to get a visa and stay on here. She was really cutting about it.'

'Maybe she misses you,' Luke says.

'It isn't that.' I'm silent for a moment. 'OK. My mother isn't motherly. She never has been. She never asks me about my life. She isn't interested in my friends, or my job. All she cares about is the impact I have on her life. You've made me more welcome than she ever has. She's made it abundantly clear I can only stay at hers in the short term.' Tears fill my eyes as I look at Luke. 'But I didn't mean to upset her.'

He frowns. 'It sounds as though you're the one who should be upset. What happened just now?'

'It's a really long story.' My voice wobbles.

'I'm not going anywhere.' Luke watches my face. 'It might help to talk about it.'

'OK,' I say shakily. 'You see, I had a sister.' I swallow the lump in my throat. 'Her name was Olivia. She had a form of leukaemia and she died when she was two. I was five – I don't really remember her.' I wipe away the tears pouring down my face.

'I'm so sorry.' Luke looks shocked. 'I had no idea.'

I shrug. 'No one talks about her. After she died, her photograph was put away. It was like she'd never existed. For a long time, all I had was this hazy memory. But over the years, I found photos and her birth certificate. Then I found some sympathy cards and a letter her doctor wrote to my mum. I asked my mother what happened to her – just the once. But never again.' I shudder at the memory. 'She got angry, then she changed the subject. After that, she carried on as though we'd never had the conversation.'

'So, similar to the way she refused to talk about me,' Luke says.

I nod. 'There are similarities, aren't there? Anyway, when we were talking just now, it suddenly came to me why she's so cold towards me. I think she's unhappy.' My voice wavers as I gaze at Luke. 'And I think she subconsciously resents me – for being alive when Olivia isn't.'

He looks outraged. 'Surely not. You're as much her daughter as Olivia was.'

'I know.' A tear rolls down my face. 'The thing is, just now, I actually said it out loud to her. She hung up on me.'

'If that's how you feel, you didn't say anything out of place.' Luke shakes his head. 'Give her time, Bee. Sounds like your mother can't cope with her emotions.'

'She can't.' It explains why she lives in the moment, on the surface; why she refuses to engage in conversation of any meaning. 'She's always encouraged me to be the same. I've wanted, so many times, to talk to her. I know she lost her daughter, but I lost my sister. It's like I've never been able to grieve.' To my embarrassment, tears flood down my face; unstoppable, as I'm sobbing again.

Luke puts an arm around me and as I lean against him, all the sadness I've locked away is slowly unleashed. All my life, I've never had anyone just hold me and let me cry, just as I've never felt the comfort of someone who understands, who cares and just wants to be there for me.

At last, drained, I sit up. 'I'm so sorry.' I take the tissue he holds out and wipe my face.

'You have no need to be,' he says gently.

'Your shirt is soaked.'

'My shirt will dry,' he says. 'Are you OK?'

I nod. I feel emotionally wrung out, but at the same time, I feel lighter. 'I'm sorry. I really am. But...' I look into eyes that are filled with kindness. 'Thank you.'

'We're family, Bee. It's how it should be, isn't it?' He pauses. 'If I'd been there for you in the past, we would have talked about Olivia long before now. You wouldn't have been carrying it alone.'

'You're making up for it.' I manage a watery smile.

He looks curious. 'Who was Olivia's father?'

'His name was David Connelly. It was on Olivia's birth certificate. I remember him vaguely. I used to think he was my dad, too. He left a couple of years after Olivia died. I always wondered why I never saw him again. Now, I realise it must have been impossible for him.' I'm trying to think how he must have felt, dealing with my mother's emotional shutdown.

'You must have felt like you'd lost your father too.'

I stare at him. It must have been how it felt. And no one ever explained it to me.

Luke shakes his head. 'Life's really tough sometimes, isn't it? For all of us.'

'Yes.' I try to smile again.

He gets up. 'How about I make us some breakfast?' He stands there looking perplexed. 'I was about to do something, wasn't I?'

'You were.' Getting up, I pull myself together. 'I'll do breakfast. You go and make that very important call to Alex.'

20

ALEX

On Saturday morning, I'm up early, making coffee before setting off to pick up my mother when my phone buzzes. Surprised to see Luke's name on the screen, I pick it up.

'Luke. How are you?'

But he cuts to the chase. 'I've been thinking about the conversation we had.'

'It's fine, Luke. I understand,' I say. 'I really get this isn't a good time for you.'

'No, no.' He sounds taken aback. 'Look. I've had a bad few days. I know I'm not myself at the moment. I probably won't be for a while. But I've been thinking, Alex. The plan to get the band together... I'm in.' He pauses. 'I mean it this time. As long as everyone else hasn't changed their minds?'

After all the explaining I've done to Kevin and Atlas, it's an outcome I haven't anticipated. 'I don't suppose they will have.' I hesitate, hoping he isn't going to have second thoughts again. 'You are sure, aren't you?'

'Completely.' He sounds hesitant. 'I'm sorry. I realise how much trouble you'd gone to, before I screwed things up.'

'You didn't,' I say. 'It was just one of those things. Though we still haven't spoken to Miles. But I can sort that.'

'Can you? It would be great if you could. Should we fix some dates? And we'll need a place to stay and to rehearse, too, I suppose?'

I scratch my head. This is so not what I was expecting. I try to think on my feet. 'Well, believe it or not, Kevin had offered his spare rooms.' Hoping he hasn't changed his mind, I go on, telling him about Kevin's soundproofed cellar.

'Kept quiet about that, didn't he?' Luke says wryly.

'I think he was secretly looking forward to you all being together again,' I say. 'He was pretty snarky when I told him we'd have to put it off.'

'I can imagine. Sorry about that.'

'I wouldn't worry. Kevin will get over it.' Then I remember, he doesn't know. 'I didn't tell you about our meeting with Atlas. He couldn't have been nicer.'

As we go on talking, I get the sense that far from over-whelming him, playing with the band again will be good for Luke. That having lost his wife, he needs something life-affirming. And I like that far from being just about my mother, this will help Luke, too.

I'm expecting Kevin to be difficult when I call him to tell him Luke's had a change of heart, but to my surprise, he isn't.

'Glad he's seen sense,' he says slightly less abruptly than usual. 'Offer still holds. For my place, I mean.'

And just like that, it's all systems go again. The missing link in all this remains, however, as we wait for Miles to get in touch.

After speaking to Kevin, I send Atlas a message, then set up a WhatsApp group. Almost immediately, Kevin's on there.

Suggested dates, any three days between 5–15 November.

Consult your diaries and let me know.

Not surprisingly, no one rushes to respond and that evening, he sends another message.

Reply?

Not being part of the band, I leave them to sort it out, instead turning my attention to a venue for a gig. Just a very small one, you understand. It isn't something I've run by the others, but I have the feeling that staying, practising and playing all at Kevin's is too much power in his hands – and not just for me, but for all of us.

I call Lorna to ask her if she can keep my mother for another day. It turns out she's more than happy, so, that evening, I wander through the lanes in the direction of The Ship. It's a big old pub, not the most sophisticated of places. But it has a stage, and when I ask, they're open to a band playing there for free.

Getting out my phone, I check the WhatsApp group. So far, only Luke has responded.

Can book flights 10 November.

I take a deep breath, then start typing.

I have a venue in the Lanes, 14 November.

Of course, Kevin objects. But I could have said any date and Kevin would have objected. I have a sneaking suspicion he's watching the WhatsApp group constantly and when he calls me almost immediately after I post about the venue, my suspicions are confirmed.

'I made it abundantly clear that this was for three days, Alex. Now, you've already changed it to four – and without so much as running it by me. It's a bit off.' He sniffs.

But I'm ready for him. 'The way I see it, Luke and Mack will arrive on the 10th,' I say reasonably. 'Three days follow to practise, at yours, which is in line with what you suggested. Then the venue is booked for the fourth night.' I pause. 'Surely, there can't be anything wrong with that?'

'It's just...' he starts angrily. 'Dammit. You know perfectly well I said three days. We're now looking at five nights. In my house. You wouldn't be too pleased if it was your house we were talking about.'

'Honestly?' I'm starting to get fed up with him again. 'I wish we had room, Kevin. Because I'd love to have everyone here.' Which kind of takes the wind out of his sails.

'It's all very well saying that,' he starts.

I resolve never to become like Kevin. To never let myself inhabit a solitary, reclusive, selfish bubble such as he does. After all, what is the point of that sodding great house, just to rattle around on his own in it; if he never intends to share it? 'I'm sorry, Kevin. I have another call waiting.' I don't, but I hang up on him.

Miraculously by that evening, everyone has committed to the dates – bar one person.

> What about Miles?

Kevin's straight back to me.

> If he can't be bothered to reply, that's hardly our responsibility. I say we do this without him.

Which of course, is missing the point because it's us who want Miles, not vice versa. So, not for the first time, I take things into my own hands. My email having failed, while Miles is on air, I call his radio show, to find I'm rushed to the front of the phone-in, his producer clearly keen to know more about the band, or to wind Miles up, I'm not altogether sure which as I wait to speak to him.

I hear Miles say in jaunty, radio-presenter style, 'And our next caller is Alex from Brighton. Evening, Alex, you're live on air. What would you like to talk about?'

'Hi.' Suddenly I'm nervous. 'I wondered how many of your viewers know the power music can have?'

'I'm sure we all do, Alex,' Miles says smoothly. 'It's no secret, music can be potent. It's the backdrop to our teen years and our passionate love affairs. How else are there so many wealthy musicians out there?'

I can already sense he isn't engaging with me. 'Well, what I had in mind was a slightly less common benefit. Did you know that for people with dementia, for example, it's a powerful trigger to remember the past?'

There's a brief silence. 'That's, er, fascinating, Alex,' Miles says, clearly unmoved. 'I'm sure many of our listeners are interested to hear this.'

'Many of us have family members affected by dementia,' I say. 'In my case, it's my mother. Her name is Rachel, Miles. I think you knew her once. She called herself Roxy. She used to sing in a band with you, back in the day—'

Before I can go on, Miles interrupts. 'We're heading to a break. Thanks for calling in, Alex. Good to talk to you.'

The line goes quiet, as in the background I hear someone mutter, 'The switchboard's lighting up.' Then the producer comes on. 'Stay on the line, will you?'

I wait a few seconds, then hear Miles's voice.

'That was unexpected. Next time, send an email, will you?' He sounds less than pleased.

'We tried that. Twice,' I tell him. 'Your old band members are planning a get-together. To begin with, it was for my mother. But actually, it's turning into much more than that.'

'Sorry, but I'm far too busy,' he says quickly. 'But good luck with it all. Gotta go. I'm back on air any moment.'

And that's that. Miles is out – or so it seems he is, until the following morning when I get a call from an unknown number, who turns out to be no less than Miles's producer.

'You lit a fire last night.' He sounds excited. 'We don't get many calls about something that really matters. Miles tends to get the, er, less educated calls, shall we say.'

'Oh? That was good then, was it?'

'It was bloody good,' he says enthusiastically. 'I had a chat with Miles after the show. His ratings are down. But I reckon with a few more calls like yours, he'll be back where he needs to be. So this is what I'm thinking.'

It turns out the radio station want to follow our story – not so much the story of the band per se, but as an example of how music can help dementia patients.

'I'll have to ask everyone else,' I say. 'But honestly, I think it would be brilliant. And I think they will, too.' Anything to help widen the understanding of dementia, to help people realise it isn't always extreme. That life with it can and does go on – it's just a little different.

'If you're up for this, I'm thinking we'll contact medical professionals to get them involved, too,' he goes on. 'This has huge potential to reach people. You have my number, Alex. Let's keep in touch.' He hesitates. 'Miles is going to call you. Let me know if you don't hear from him.'

I take that to mean Miles doesn't share his enthusiasm. But he does get in touch, less than an hour later. Not quite so jaunty as he was on air, he's slightly apologetic.

'I've been thinking about what you said.' He sounds sheepish. 'I'd love to do it – for Roxy. Count me in.'

He makes it sound like it's coming from the goodness of his heart. But after the way he spoke last night, we both know that's not the case. Moreover, I'm not letting him get away with it. 'Thanks, Miles. Glad to have you on board. If you give me your number, I'll add you to the WhatsApp group.' I deliberately underplay how relieved I am. 'Your producer called me a little while ago. Said the radio station want to cover the story – specifically the dementia angle. He thinks it will be good for your ratings. Brilliant all round, isn't it?'

There's an awkward pause. 'That isn't the only reason I'm doing this.'

* * *

When I tell Luke about the radio station being involved, he's in complete agreement as I fully imagined he would be. Just as predictably, Kevin is less than happy, yet again, dragging out the old 'I have my professional reputation to think of' card.

'This can only be good for your reputation,' I point out wearily. 'Look how positive this is. Dementia affects so many lives. This is going to help raise awareness. Your clients will realise what a thoroughly decent chap you are.' Realising too late, I've probably said the wrong thing and that Kevin's clients probably hire him precisely because he's so heartless.

In all this, however, it preys on my mind that I've yet to break the news to my mother. Wondering how she'll take it, I make a cup of tea and take it outside. Raising my eyes, I gaze at the sky.

Up there in the darkness, myriad stars twinkle at me, not for the first time reminding me how surprising, how mysterious the workings of the Universe can be.

So it is that a day later than planned, I go to pick my mother up from Lorna's. The visit has clearly been successful and it's heart-warming to see the genuine affection between them. When they say goodbye to each other, Lorna sheds a tear.

'Don't leave it too long,' she says to my mum, then hugs her.

With my mother safely in the car, I turn to Lorna. 'I have news,' I say quietly, meaning about the band. 'I'll call you later and fill you in.' Then seeing the apprehension in her eyes, I add, 'Nothing to worry about. I promise.'

My mother is quiet on the way home. I try to draw her out, but when she isn't forthcoming, alarm bells start going off. 'Are you OK, Mum?'

'I don't know.' She sounds confused. 'I suppose it would help if I knew where we were going, Alex. But you haven't told me.'

'We're going home, Mum. To Brighton.' Already I've slipped into the habit of assuming she'll work things out; that what's obvious to me doesn't need explaining.

'Oh, I see,' she says in a different voice. 'For a moment, I was worried we were going somewhere else.' She pauses. 'How's Alex? I've been so worried about him.'

'He's fine.' It gets me every time, that confusing the past and present causes her so much angst. To distract her, I start to tell her about what's been going on the last few days – because that's all it is, even though it seems much longer. 'You know I told you I was going to see Luke Friday?'

'Luke.' She frowns. Then her frown clears. 'Luke – from the band. You did, didn't you? How is he?'

'He's good. Actually...' I glance at her. 'He's coming to England in a couple of weeks. He wants to see us.'

'But he lives in England. You've just been to see him,' she says blankly.

'Luke lives in Majorca.' I wait for the penny to drop.

'You mean—?' She turns to look at me. 'You went to Majorca? On your own?' As if I'm still six years old.

'Not on my own. Kevin came with me.'

'That was brave of you,' she says. 'Going all the way there with him.'

There's plenty I can say about Kevin, but given my mother's lack of filter these days, I keep it to myself. 'Then after Majorca, we went to Glasgow. We went to see Atlas.'

'Good heavens.' She sounds shocked. 'I don't believe this. Where does Atlas live?'

'Glasgow,' I repeat. 'He runs a hostel there. He's a really nice guy.'

'He always was,' my mother says wistfully. 'Unlike that... that...'

'Kevin?' I suggest.

'Yes. Him.' She lapses into silence.

'The thing is...' I hesitate. 'Atlas is coming to see us, too.'

'Oh goodness.' She sounds worried. 'We don't have enough bedrooms, Alex. Where are we going to put everyone?'

'Mum. They're not staying with us. They're staying with Kevin.'

'Kevin?' she says. 'Are you sure?'

'It was his idea, believe it or not.'

'Astonishing,' is all she says.

As we reach the edge of Brighton, it's getting dark, the seafront lit by street lamps, the white crests of breaking waves visible below us.

'I see what you're doing,' she says after a long silence.

'You do?'

'You want me to sing, don't you?' She sounds worried.

'Only if you want to, Mum. There are lots of reasons every-one's coming here. Luke's wife died not so long ago. It's good for him to have a distraction. And believe it or not, Kevin's shown another side to him – only once or twice, but it's a start. I forgot to tell you, Miles is coming, too. He works for a radio station. They want to follow the story of the band getting back together.' I can no longer go on skirting around the truth. 'They want to feature how music can help people with dementia.'

'Oh.' It's an unexpectedly, understated response, after which my mother is silent again.

I turn into our road, park outside the house and get her bag from the back seat, then help her out of the car.

'I can manage,' she says crossly, then immediately takes the arm I offer to help her up the steps.

We go inside and I close the door, locking it and taking the key out, while she stands there for a moment, looking around.

'Everything's the same.' Looking slightly bewildered, she slips off her jacket. Then she smiles. 'Shall I make the tea?'

'I made a shepherd's pie. I just need to put it in the oven,' I tell her.

'You think I can't cook,' she says accusingly.

'It isn't that at all,' I say. 'I thought you'd be tired. It's been a long day.'

'I suppose it has.' She goes over to the sofa and sits down.

Going into the kitchen, I switch on the oven and fill the kettle to make us both a cup of tea. When I take it out to her, there's a worried look on her face.

'What is it, Mum?' I ask gently.

'It's all this talk about the band.' Her eyes fill with tears. 'What if I can't sing? And just look at me. They all remember glam old Roxy.' Her voice trembles. 'Not middle-aged Rachel who can't remember anything.'

'I'd say Kevin's changed a bit since then, wouldn't you?'

She giggles. But then the worried look is back. 'I have dementia, don't I, Alex?' Her eyes are misty as they gaze into mine.

It's one of those heartbreaking moments. Maybe the most heartbreaking to date. I take her hands in mine. 'You do, Mum. But you're taking medication. And you're doing really well.'

A look of angst crosses her face. 'What if I can't remember any of the songs?' Her eyes glisten. 'What if I can't sing?' she whispers.

'Well...' I say quietly. 'Firstly, none of us have heard Kevin play the drums yet. What will happen if he's dreadful? And I know for a fact Luke hasn't touched the piano in months. As for Miles, I don't know how many years have passed since he last picked up a guitar. He'll probably be the worst of everyone.'

A ghost of a smile crosses her face.

'You know what, Mum?' I say gently. 'It's going to be different. But it's going to remind you all about those days when the band used to play. It isn't about being perfect. But it will be fun. And if you can't sing, it doesn't matter. Though I somehow think that isn't going to be a problem.' I remind her that I've heard her sing, in the shower. 'As for being middle aged...' I pause, looking at her. 'You're beautiful, Mum. You always have been – and you always will be.'

'You're a good boy, Alex.' Then her eyes light up. 'If I'm going to do this, I'm doing it in style. Roxy was sassy, I'll have you know.'

I groan inwardly; have a vision of my fifty-nine-year-old mother in a miniskirt and fishnets. But then I sit back. If that's what she wants, so be it. This is her show.

She goes upstairs and I hear the sound of drawers being pulled open. But as I sit there, I realise that in our hurry to get things organised, we've all forgotten someone.

Someone who was integral in getting everyone back in touch.

Leo.

21

BEE

Mack is elated at Luke's change of heart; at the thought of flying to England. Moreover, it takes her mind off our cancelled camping trip.

'I asked the Universe,' she tells me conspiratorially. 'See? I told you it works, Bee.' Her eyes grow round with wonder. 'It was really quick this time. It's obviously very important for us to go.' She frowns slightly. 'I have been to England – once. But I was a baby. I don't remember.'

After a weekend of rain and low cloud, I awake on Monday to clear skies; as I gaze outside and think of the week ahead, I feel daunted. There's the prospect of going to England with Luke – which on the one hand is really good. Don't get me wrong. But it also means I should go and see my mother.

It isn't just that, though. With each day that passes, the less I want to leave this place. But since Brexit, with Brits no longer free to live in Spain, my visa application is looming over me, with all the hoops I have to jump through.

My phone pings with an email – an offer of the social media job I applied for. It's part time, but it's a start. Three more just like it and I'm on my way to the income I need. But if it doesn't happen... A wave of despair washes over me.

I know what Mack would say. I glance up at the sky. The rain has cleared the air; there's a clarity to it as I send out my message.

Show me how, Universe. What do I need to do? I could really do with your help with this.

When I go downstairs, Luke is back from taking Mack to school and sitting, typing at his laptop.

He looks up briefly. 'Hi. I was going to book flights.'

'You must let me know the cost,' I say hastily.

He shakes his head. 'This one's on me. Do you have your passport to hand?'

'I'll get it.' I go upstairs. Then coming back, give it to him.

'Kevin's said we can stay at his,' he says. 'He lives in Midhurst. Will you be OK to share a room with Mack?' He rolls his eyes. 'She's so excited, she can't talk about anything else.'

'I'd love to.' I pause. 'I'm thinking I should try and see my mother – if it fits in.'

'Good idea,' he says. 'I was going to ask if you'd mind keeping an eye on Mack now and then? I'm going to be pretty busy – at least some of the time.'

'Of course I don't. I can show her around. It'll be fun.'

'Great. I'm going to hire a car, but I'll put you on the insurance, too. That way, you can come and go as you want to.' He pauses. 'I'm hoping to take her to see my parents. No pressure, but I know they'd like it if you came, too.'

'They know about me?' I say cautiously.

'I've told them about you coming here.' He taps away at his keyboard. 'Right. Our flights are booked. I'm going into town – I have a delivery to pick up. I'll see you later.'

It's the most motivated I've seen him in the time I've been

here. It's kind of an odd feeling, though, to think about going to England with Luke; but to know I'm not staying, that I'm coming back here.

In the kitchen, I'm making coffee when there's a brief knock before Augusta walks in.

'You look bright,' she says. 'I hope that means that all is good in your world.'

'It is.' I tell her about the social media job. 'I need to earn more. But it's a start.'

'Well, I might just be able to help.' Augusta pulls out a chair and sits down. 'My understanding is that in order to apply for a digital nomad visa, you have to be paid by a UK-based company. Am I correct?'

'Yes.' I wonder where this is going.

'I thought so. The thing is, the daughter of a friend of mine has started a glamping business. Somewhere in Dorset. She's put together a website, but it really isn't very good. Here. If you have your laptop to hand, I'll show you.'

I fetch my laptop, then sit down next to her and open it. When she brings up the website, I see what she means. 'It isn't so bad,' I say. 'It has all the information prospective customers will want. But she needs to make sure people find it.'

'So here's my idea.' Augusta sits back. 'You do social media, don't you? Well, I think you should do hers, or at least get her started. I'm no expert, but I've looked at what she's doing and it isn't exactly eye-catching.'

I get a sinking feeling. Augusta is well meaning. However, working on one website, isn't going to generate enough income for the requirements of the visa. But by her own admission, she doesn't understand how these things work. 'I'd be happy for you to pass on my mobile number. Then if she'd like some help, she can call me.' Then I realise she probably doesn't know. 'We're

going to England for a few days. Luke's getting back together
with his band.'

* * *

The next few days go very quickly.

'We're not going, are we?' Mack's face is solemn.

'Going where?' She's lost me.

'Camping.' She rolls her eyes, as if I'm supposed to be a
mind-reader.

'Of course we are,' I say. 'Though it's probably best we wait
until we're back from England.'

Mack's idea of packing is to pile her favourite summer
clothes into her little suitcase – not very tidily.

'It isn't going to be warm,' I tell her. 'You need cosy things.'

'But I really do need this dress, Bee.' Her voice is solemn as
she holds up a sparkly party dress with short sleeves. 'If Dad's
band are playing, I need to wear something special.' She frowns.
'What will you wear?'

I shrug. 'I don't know. Just normal clothes. I didn't bring that
much with me.'

'I know.' She sounds exasperated, as though she's noticed.
'We can always go shopping.' Her face lights up. 'I really think
we should do that.'

Luke notifies the school that Mack's going to be away for a
few days. In the context of Mack's recent loss of her mother, they
make no objections. So it is that five days later, Augusta drives us
to the airport in what feels like a surreal reversal of the day I
arrived as I take my rucksack out of her car.

It's as though she reads my mind as she gives me a hug.
'Funny, isn't it, how things work out?'

Travelling with Mack is fun. She's wildly excited about going on a plane, as well as being in England. Nor does she mind that our flight's delayed by two hours. Instead, she eyes up the various eateries, then glances at Luke.

'It's really good, Dad, because we have time for lunch. And shopping,' she adds.

The airport is quiet and as we walk out to our plane, she stands there, just staring at it, her eyes like saucers. 'It's really big. How does it fly?'

'I can't explain that,' Luke says. 'But I can assure you it will. Come on.' He starts walking up the steps. Mack takes my hand and we follow.

I see the flight through Mack's eyes. The wonder that this weight of metal can accelerate and become airborne; the bird's-eye view of tiny houses and boats. The faintest crescent moon, ethereal wisps of cloud.

Highly organised, she takes out one of her notebooks and starts drawing, then making notes under her pictures. 'I'm going to write everything down about going to England and the band playing. Then I'm going to give it to Alex's mum, so she can remember,' she says.

'That's the loveliest idea.' I'm touched that she's even thought about Alex's mother in all this. 'I haven't met her yet.'

'Me neither.'

Nor have I met Alex. Or come to that, Kevin.

On the other side of me, Luke is quiet, closing his eyes and my thoughts turn to my mother. I wonder whether I should call her again, or maybe just turn up and see her.

England greets us with grey skies and windblown cold. After the long walk through the airport, Luke sorts the hire car paperwork.

'Please feel free to make the most of using the car. You're not going to want to be stuck at Kevin's all the time.'

'See? We can go shopping,' Mack says gleefully.

I've never been to Midhurst, where Kevin lives. It's an old Sussex market town on the edge of which is Cowdray Park. Following the satnav along country roads, it isn't long before Luke turns into a quiet street, then through iron gates and up a drive.

As houses go, Kevin's is big. And stark, with wide, dark windows and a very sculpted front garden. Luke pulls up near the front door. 'OK.' He turns to me. 'A word of warning. Kevin can be a little...'

'Rude,' Mack volunteers. 'Because he is, isn't he, Dad?'

'I was going to say irritable.' Luke pauses. 'But he has invited us here. Maybe he won't be. Come on.' He gets out, as Mack scrambles out after him. I follow more trepidatiously, suddenly feeling out of place.

For someone described as rude and irritable, Kevin is welcoming towards us, albeit in his own somewhat limited way. 'Welcome, all of you. I'm Kevin. You must be Bee.' He holds out his hand, then he frowns at me. 'Good Lord. You remind me of someone.' He frowns. 'Damn shame you're so late. You've just missed Rachel and Alex. They left ten minutes ago.'

'Our flight was delayed.' Luke glances around. 'Where would you like us to put our stuff?'

'Ah. Yes. Upstairs.' Kevin limps up the wide staircase, then at the top, opens the door into a huge twin-bedded room. 'I thought this for you girls. Bathroom's through there.' He nods towards an en suite. 'Luke. You're this way.'

Mack sinks onto one of the beds. 'This is massive.' Going to the en suite, she flings open the door. 'Bee, you are not going to believe this.' She stands there. 'Kevin must be very rich.'

'Sshh,' I say, as I hear footsteps outside our door. 'Shall we unpack?'

'I'm going to see Dad's room.' Mack buzzes along the landing leaving me alone. Forgetting about unpacking, I go over to the window. This truly is the most manicured country house I've ever set foot in. Standing there, I stare at the view of the vast expanse of neatly mown lawn and sculpted plants, beyond which woodland stretches.

It takes all of five minutes to unpack my rucksack before I start on Mack's case. Opening it, I find her beloved furry unicorn, stuffed in at the last minute, and I arrange it on her bed, then hang up her clothes.

Downstairs, Kevin shows us into a palatial sitting room, where he stands, looking slightly awkward. 'Make yourselves at home. Can I get a drink for anyone?'

He goes to get a beer for Luke and a glass of wine for me, while Mack follows him into the kitchen and checks out his fridge, before she comes back carrying an orange juice.

'So what's the plan?' Luke asks.

'Good question. Miles said he'd be here sometime this evening.'

'And Atlas?'

'Oh. He got here hours ago. He walked into Midhurst.' Kevin frowns. 'I'm surprised he isn't back by now.' He pauses. 'Yes. Well. I may as well show you where we're going to practise.'

After a tour of his cellar, which is five times the size of Luke's, Atlas returns. From his bright eyes and ruddy cheeks, he's clearly been to a pub. But there's kindness in his voice; it's easy to imagine him running a hostel.

'So you're Bee.' He holds my gaze. 'It's really nice to meet you.'

Not long after Atlas gets back, there's the sound of a car, then the sound of gravel flying up as it brakes.

'Bloody Miles,' Kevin mutters, getting to his feet and hobbling to the door.

* * *

It's a strange evening in one sense, watching these people who used to know each other so well find their footing again, clearly aware that this is Kevin's house, a fact that he keeps reminding us of. We order a Chinese and eat it at the table in a kitchen that's kitted out like something out of *MasterChef*.

'We really need to formulate a plan for the next few days,' Kevin says. 'Alex has found us a venue – for Sunday evening.' He sounds most disapproving. 'The Ship – it's in Brighton. Not at all what I was expecting. But there it is.'

'That gives us three days. Blimey, mate. Not long, is it?' Miles looks slightly terrified.

'Plenty of time,' Kevin says. 'Probably best not to get our expectations up. This idea of playing in a venue...' A frown creases his face.

'It'll be fun.' Atlas's eyes twinkle. 'Isn't that what this is supposed to be? A few old mates playing a few tunes – to help Roxy?'

'Hear, hear,' Luke says. 'That's what we need to remember. Right?' He glances pointedly at Kevin.

* * *

The following morning, there's no sign of Mack when I wake up. I get up, go over to the window and pull back the heavy curtains to find a low sun under which frost is sparkling. After showering and dressing, I go downstairs to find Mack in the kitchen. Still in her pyjamas, she's giving Kevin a hard time as he attempts to make her breakfast.

'Don't you have white toast?' Mack's saying. 'Even in your freezer? It's just that I don't really like brown. I know it's supposed to be healthy, it's just a bit...' She makes a sound like sticking her fingers down her throat.

'That's quite enough of that, young lady. Firstly, I do not have white bread. And actually, I think you'll find this is very nice. Now, what would you like on it? Jam or Marmite?'

I go into the kitchen. 'Morning.'

'Morning. There's tea and coffee on the side. Pour yourself a cup. Ah, the Marmite.' Handing Mack the jar, he hurries out of the room.

'What are we doing today?' Mack lavishly spreads the Marmite on her toast. 'Kevin said they're going to practise. I want to listen. But all day might be too long.' She raises her eyebrows, adding casually, 'I suppose it might be a good day for us to go shopping.'

'I think we should talk to your dad first.' I pour myself a coffee.

'That's funny,' Mack says through a mouthful of toast. 'You said, your dad.'

I look at her blankly. 'I know.'

'But he's your dad too!' Mack glances behind me just as Luke walks in. He's followed minutes later by Miles and Atlas. Then Kevin reappears. In a Guns N' Roses T-shirt and faded jeans, a baseball cap around the wrong way – it's an image that's incongruous with everything I know about Kevin and as he stands there, everyone turns and looks at him.

'Right. Time we made a start.' He pauses, then glances at everyone in turn. 'What are you all looking at?'

I turn away to hide my smile as, going over, Atlas pats him on one of his shoulders. 'Absolutely nothing, mate.'

* * *

I still haven't called my mother and while Mack goes upstairs to change and brush her hair, I take my phone outside and walk around the side of the house.

The phone rings for what seems like ages before she answers. 'Hello.'

'Hi, Mum. How are you? Only I'm in England – just for a few days. I thought maybe I could drive up and see you.'

'Oh.' She's silent; there's no apology for the way she reacted last time we spoke. 'It depends when. I'm busy, as you know.'

'How about lunchtime? We won't stay long.'

'Who's we?' she says suspiciously.

'Mack will be with me.' I hesitate. 'She's my half-sister.' I have a sick feeling, as though I'm waiting for her to hang up on me again.

'I suppose that will be all right,' she says ungraciously. 'Come at 12.30. I'll make us a sandwich.'

As she's talking, I watch a car come up the drive and park next to Luke's. I see the back view of a man as he helps a woman out, then takes her arm as they head towards the front door. 'Thanks,' I say. 'I want to pick up a few clothes while I'm there.'

'So, you're going back to Majorca,' my mother says disapprovingly.

'Nothing's changed, Mum.' I pause. 'I just thought it would be nice to see you.'

After ending the call, when I go back inside, Mack's alone in the kitchen.

'They're all in Kevin's cellar.' She shakes her head. 'What happens if they're not very good?'

'They're enjoying it. That's the main thing. Was that Roxy who arrived just now?'

Mack nods. 'With Alex. They're in the cellar, too.' She slides off her chair. 'Can we go out now?'

Fetching my bag, we go out to the car. As we set off, I tell Mack we're having lunch with my mother. 'Don't be surprised if she's a bit grumpy. She doesn't mean anything by it.'

'Like Kevin?' Mack says.

'Much the same,' I say, not at all sure why I'm defending my mother. 'But lunch is ages away. I think we should stop in Guildford and do some shopping.' Glancing across, I notice she's clutching her notebook. 'You're still writing everything down?'

'Yes. It's important.' She jots something down. 'I'm trying really hard not to leave anything out. Like today, Roxy was wearing this glittery T-shirt and black trousers.' Mack frowns. 'They looked like men's trousers. Shall I tell you what I've written about Kevin?' She giggles.

'Go on, then.'

'"Kevin is wearing a very old T-shirt and a teenaged boy's hat. His jeans are a bit weird. No one said anything and I tried not to laugh. He doesn't have white bread in the house. And… he won't share his bathroom."'

'I beg your pardon?'

'It's true, Bee. Kevin has two bathrooms. One used to be his wife's, only she doesn't live here any more. He told me it isn't hygienic to share.' She doesn't say how they got onto the topic of conversation, just seems oddly fascinated by the detail.

But we forget about Kevin and his foibles once we get to Guildford as I discover Mack is a demon shopper. It's like all her Christmases and birthdays have come at once, as she rushes from one thing to the next, chattering excitedly. 'Look at these notebooks. Bee, they're so cool.'

'You have fifty pounds,' I remind her. 'And your dad said it has to last while we're here. If you spend it all now, that will be it, you know.'

'OK. Just these two, then.' Picking out two notebooks, she frowns. 'Can we go and find a shop that sells dresses?'

Mack has dozens of dresses, from everyday to flamenco style. But we still find one she falls in love with. It has pink and gold sequins and a full, knee-length skirt that swings as she twirls in it.

After buying it, with some reluctance, we drive on towards my mother's house. When we get there, my car is parked where I left it, on the drive, a sharp reminder of my old life. But there's another as I get out and my phone buzzes with a missed call. Checking my voicemail, I play the message.

'Good morning, Bee. It's Geneva. I hope you're well. I have a business proposition I'd like to talk to you about. Do you think you could call me?'

Utterly astonished, I stare at my phone.

'Who was that?' Mack frowns at me.

'Someone I used to work for.' I'm wondering what it is she wants to talk to me about. But it will have to wait.

We go inside to find my mother in the kitchen. 'Hi, Mum.'

'Bethany.' She comes over and gives me the shortest, most awkward hug before pulling away as though I've stung her.

'This is Mack.'

Mack gazes at her, unblinking. 'Did you call her Bethany?'

'It's her name.' My mother glances at me.

'Mack's short for Mackenzie,' Mack says.

'I'm Cassandra,' my mother says. 'Would you like some orange juice?'

After the conversations I've had with both Luke and Augusta, I realise how guarded my mother is. She shows no interest in the band, or how long we're here – which shouldn't be surprising. But after just a short time away, I'm realising how strange it is.

'Who's that?' As Mack points to a photo that wasn't here when I left, the blood drains from my face. It's a photo of Olivia.

'A little girl.' My mother's jaw is set. 'Would you like some ice cream?' Underplaying a moment that's monumental. After all these years, at last there's a photo of Olivia in this house.

I try to catch her eye, but she pointedly looks away from me, clearly still unable to talk about her.

After lunch, I take Mack upstairs with me. 'My clothes are up here. But it shouldn't take long. I sorted through them when I moved out of Saskia's.'

'Who's Saskia?' Mack follows me into the bedroom I was using.

'A girl I used to share a flat with,' I say, wondering how it already feels a lifetime ago. As I open my suitcase and take out some carefully folded items, a sharp intake of breath comes from Mack.

'I didn't know you had such cool clothes.' Her eyes are like saucers.

'Because I came to Majorca with shorts and T-shirts?' I say. 'To be honest, I wasn't sure how long I was going to stay.'

'But you are staying, aren't you?' Sitting on my bed, Mack swings her feet. 'You have to.'

'I hope so.' I pull out some jeans and a couple of cardigans, but the majority of my clothes are more Brighton-style than rural Majorca. 'What do you think?'

'OK,' Mack says. 'I'll help you.' Coming over, she starts rummaging, then pulls out a dress I've never worn before. It's long and oversized, a lightweight black fabric shot with silver thread. 'This is really, really beautiful,' she says almost reverently.

It's probably the most expensive item I've ever bought. 'There are some shoes somewhere.' I open another box that's filled with footwear and pull out some delicate, strappy silver flat shoes, then because it's so cold, find my boots.

As I finish, Mack's frowning. 'Don't you think you should bring everything?'

I hesitate. It makes sense. But I'm still not certain I can meet the visa requirements. 'I'll bring these things and come back for the rest. I should probably go through everything again first.'

It satisfies her for now and we go downstairs to find my mother still in the kitchen. 'I'll be back to sort out everything – one way or another,' I say.

'There's no rush,' she says, not meeting my eyes. 'If you're taking those, you'll need a bag, won't you?' She nods towards the clothes I'm holding.

She goes to the cupboard under the stairs and pulls out a holdall I've only seen her use a couple of times. Burnt orange, it's made of heavy canvas with printed straps. 'Will this do?'

'It's perfect.' Unzipping it, I'm oddly touched as I pack my stuff inside. 'I'll bring it back next time.'

'You can keep it if you like.' She glances at her watch. 'Goodness. Is that the time? I have a call in a few minutes.' She looks at Mack. 'It was nice to meet you.'

'Thank you for lunch,' Mack says politely.

'Bye, Mum.' There's another brief awkward hug. 'Thanks for having us.'

Small steps, I tell myself, as we go out to the car. OK, so she couldn't bring herself to mention Olivia's name. But, having her photo on the wall just a few weeks ago, was unimaginable. As is the unexpected gift of the orange holdall. My mother isn't one for impromptu gifts.

'I didn't know your name was Bethany,' Mack says as we drive back to Midhurst. 'Why doesn't she call you Bee?'

'I don't know.'

'Is she going to come to Brighton on Sunday? To see the band?' Mack says hopefully.

'Honestly? I don't think she will.' But after today, who knows what my mother will do?

* * *

Back at Kevin's, when we go into the kitchen, for the first time I meet Rachel – or Roxy, as she used to be known. She has fair hair streaked with grey and eyes that don't seem to miss anything.

'Do I know you?' She frowns at me.

'I don't think so. I'm Bee.' I watch her try to work it out before her face clears. 'Luke's daughter.'

But then she frowns again. 'You don't look much like him.'

'We both have blue eyes.' Mack stands next to me. 'Look.' She flutters her lashes at Rachel. 'We're the same, aren't we?'

'I suppose you look similar in some ways.' Rachel looks impatient. 'Where is Alex?'

'He's gone to Waitrose,' Kevin says. 'Come on, Roxy. Sit yourself down and I'll make you a cup of tea.'

'I'd much rather have coffee.' She sounds disgruntled.

Leaving them together, I take my mother's orange holdall and go upstairs. I carefully unpack my dress, and other things I've picked up. Then hearing a car arrive, I go over to the window. In the dim light, I watch a man get out, who I assume must be Alex. He opens the back and gets out several shopping bags, then takes them into the house.

Then he comes out again and as he locks the car, he turns and I see his face. I'm still staring, shock washing over me when Mack comes bursting in. 'Bee? Can you do my hair?'

'Um, yes.' Still dazed, my brain is putting together the most bizarre of realities as I'm taken back to a day at the arboretum. I'd been coming out of the coffee shop, this guy walked into me, spilling my coffee. A guy who looked remarkably like Roxy's son. Alex.

It can't be him, I tell myself.

But equally, it could be. In the semi-darkness it's impossible to be sure.

22

ALEX

Back at Kevin's, I find my mother in the kitchen drinking tea.

'There you are,' she says impatiently. 'Shall we go home?'

'I've only just got here.' I lift the last of the bags onto the worktop. 'Besides, I've just bought food for everyone.'

She starts ferreting in the bags as Kevin says, 'Can I get you a drink?'

I watch him fetch a couple of beers from the fridge. 'So how did the practice go?' I ask.

'Bloody terrible,' he says, just as my mother says, 'Amazing!'

Not sure what to say, I pull out a chair. 'Where's everyone else?'

'Atlas and Luke are still working on something. Not sure about Miles.' Kevin looks nonplussed. 'He disappeared a little while ago.'

As I look at her, my mother suddenly turns pale. 'I don't feel very well. Alex? Could you take me home?'

Alarm bells start going off. 'You've probably overdone it.' I glance at Kevin. 'Sorry about this. I think I should take her home.'

'Of course.' He comes over and takes her arm. Despite everything, it's a comical sight watching him hobble as he helps her to the door.

Back in the car, my mother's colour starts to return. 'You're sure you're OK?' I ask, still worried.

'Stop fussing. Of course I am,' she says, sounding much more like herself.

But it's been a long day – and busy, when she's used to life being quiet, to it being just the two of us. 'You haven't really told me how it went,' I say. 'How was it? Being with the guys again?'

'Strange,' she says. 'Not in a bad way. I mean, we're all so much older. But we played some old songs, and some of them really weren't bad. Of course, Kevin doesn't agree. You know what he can be like.' She pauses. 'And I sang.' She's quiet for a moment. 'I could remember the songs, Alex. I was so worried I wouldn't. But they were all there, in my head.'

Hearing the relief in her voice, it's like my heart is bursting; it's everything I'd hoped for her. 'I'm so pleased, Mum.'

It's as though the music has reconnected her to something that's been missing. She's unusually calm when we get home, changing into her fleece pyjamas and gratefully eating the supper I cook – she even has a celebratory glass of wine. But what I notice most is the light in her eyes.

While she washes up, keeping half an eye on her, I find my phone and call Leo.

'I thought you'd want to know we managed to get in touch with everyone. They're staying with Kevin for a few days. I know they'd love to see you.'

'Thanks for thinking of me, but not sure I'll be able to make it. I'm a little busy just now.' Leo doesn't say how exactly.

'How about Sunday?' I persist. 'The plan is to play at The Ship in Brighton.' I hesitate. 'I can pick you up, if it's any help.'

'I remember The Ship.' He collapses into a coughing fit that sounds terrible. 'Sorry about that,' he says when it stops. 'Bloody Covid. Can't get rid of it. But afraid I can't do Sunday,' he says, regretfully.

* * *

The following morning, I drive my mother over to Kevin's. On the way, she starts warming up her voice.

'Are you sure you're feeling OK today?' I ask.

'Of course I am. Why wouldn't I be?' she says indignantly.

But when we get there, instead of going in, I have other plans. 'I want to go and see Leo,' I tell Kevin when he opens the front door to us. 'I spoke to him last night. I tried to persuade him to join us, but he sounds a bit out of sorts.'

'Right,' Kevin says. 'Got his address, have you?'

'Not yet. I was going to call him and tell him I'm on my way.'

'Come in a moment. I'll get it for you.' He disappears and I watch my mother waltz down the hallway, singing loudly to herself as Kevin comes back.

'Here you are. Would have gone over there myself, if it wasn't for my flaming foot.'

'Er, right.' I'm mildly astonished by the thought of Kevin doing something selfless. 'Is he OK? Only he didn't sound too good.'

'I think he's like the rest of us. Getting older.' He goes on. 'He used to take a lot of photos. I gave him one of my old T-shirts back in the day. I wanted to ask if he still had it.' Which knowing Kevin, makes much more sense, as he's just the sort of person who would want a thirty-year-old T-shirt back.

* * *

I set off towards Worthing where Leo lives, still thinking of the conversation last night.

Thanks for thinking of me, but not sure I'll be able to make it. I'm a little busy just now.

The call had been punctuated by coughing fits, which Leo had dismissed.

Bloody Covid. Can't get rid of it.

But he'd looked far from well when I met him in the hospital that time.

Leo lives in a terraced house in a quiet street. Parking outside, I find his house and knock. For a few minutes, there's no reply. But then the door opens.

Standing there, Leo blinks at me. 'Thought you were the district nurse,' he says.

His skin is grey. But it isn't just that. It's as though I can tell by looking at him that Leo is sick. Really sick. 'I'm sorry. I should have called first. Have I come at a bad time?' I ask.

Leo sighs. 'There's no such thing as a good time,' he says. 'Not these days, at least. Come on in. Good to see you again.' Closing the door behind me, he has a coughing fit.

'Is there anything I can do?' I ask.

'Not unless you're a bloody miracle worker.' He turns and starts walking along a passageway. 'But you can come and have a cup of tea with me.'

Leo's house is surprising, the passageway leading into a large airy kitchen with a window onto a narrow garden.

'So they're all together again,' he says, meaning the band; filling the kettle and switching it on.

'They are.' Glancing around, I notice the cups in the sink, the dirty plates stacked on the side. 'Why don't you sit down? I can do this.'

Leo shuffles over to one of the chairs at a wooden table. 'Tea bags are in the cupboard right in front of you.'

While I wait for the kettle to boil, I fill the sink and do the washing up, then make us both a cup of tea. 'Sugar?' I ask.

'May as well,' he says. 'It's not like it's going to make any difference.'

I carry the mugs over to the table and sit down opposite him. 'What's going on?' I ask.

He shrugs. Then he sighs. 'I suppose you may as well know. It's cancer.'

'I'm so sorry.' I pause. 'That's why you were in the hospital, isn't it?'

He nods. 'I'd been for a scan. Then they sent me for more blood tests... Anyway, I won't bore you with the details. Upshot of it all is I'm on palliative care.' He picks up his mug and sips his tea. 'Everyone's so kind. The nurses, my neighbours... I'm pretty good, considering. Just hoping things stay like they are. But when they don't... Anyway, my GP has referred me for hospice care.'

I'm silent as I sit there. 'Do you have any family?'

'No. There's just me. I suppose, in many ways, that makes it easier. Doesn't feel like it, though.' His eyes mist over. 'But enough about me. How's your mother doing?'

'Not bad, really. She's forgetful – that's how it is now. But being with her old bandmates has put a spring in her step.' I can't stop thinking about Leo. 'You know, when I first had this idea, it was about helping her reconnect with music – and the past. But it's been good for Luke, too. He lost his wife a couple of months ago. It's even brought out another side of Kevin, believe it or not.' Suddenly I'm wondering, if in some small way, this could be good for Leo, too.

'Funny bugger, isn't he?' Leo shakes his head. 'He rattles

around in that sodding great house, has more money than he knows what to do with. Hasn't made him happy, though. In fact, I'd go as far as saying he's the most miserable bloke I've ever met.' He pauses. 'How's Atlas these days?'

'He's great,' I say.

'He's one of the good ones,' Leo says. 'You got hold of Miles, then. He was a pretty cool guitarist, back in the day. Then he got all these ideas about making it on the radio. Not sure it quite went according to plan.' He shakes his head. 'I've been in touch several times over the years. But he's always been too busy. Bit of a miracle you managed to speak to him.'

'That's a story in its own right.' I tell him how I called in to the radio show, how the producer called me back. 'Which reminds me. I don't know when they're coming to interview the band.' But I can worry about that later. I look at Leo. 'I'm really hoping I can change your mind – about Sunday. I can pick you up and drive you to Brighton. And take you home after.'

He reaches across the table and pats my hand. 'You're a good boy,' he says. 'Shall we see what Sunday brings? If it's one of the good days, then maybe I will.' He pauses. 'Keep this between us, OK?' He winks. 'There's no need for the others to know what's going on with me.'

* * *

It's early afternoon by the time I get back to Kevin's to find a black van emblazoned with the name of Miles's radio station. When I ring the bell, nothing happens. Then there's the sound of footsteps and Kevin opens the door.

'You're just in time. They want to interview your mother. To be perfectly honest with you, I'm worried what she's going to say.'

'You needn't be. They know she has dementia,' I remind him.

'And that's all very well.' He marches as fast as he can with his booted ankle. 'But this interview is going to affect all of us.'

'Actually, it really isn't,' I tell him. 'This is solely about raising awareness about dementia. The band is secondary to that.'

'I'm not sure you've got that right.' He opens the door to the cellar. 'Come on. Hurry up. They're down here.'

In the cellar, my mother is sitting on a piano stool swinging her legs. 'Alex! Did you know? I'm going to be interviewed for the radio! Isn't it exciting?'

'It's great, Mum.' I turn to the guy who's setting up a microphone. 'Hi. I'm Rachel's – Roxy's – son.'

'I'm Jack. We're ready to get started,' he says. 'We probably don't need everyone down here. Perhaps you,' he says to me. 'And obviously Miles, because he's running the interview.'

'I should stay,' Kevin says loudly. 'After all, it is my house.'

'If you don't mind, sir,' Jack says to Kevin. 'We'd like to keep this simple.'

Kevin glares at him, then makes his way to the stairs and follows the others. Hearing the door at the top close, Jack turns to Miles. 'OK. Over to you.' He fiddles around with another microphone and sets it up in front of my mother. 'Shall we get started?'

Miles settles in his chair. I'm on edge, hoping he's going to be more sympathetic than he was when I first spoke to him.

'Today we're talking to Rachel. We've known each other a long time, haven't we, Rachel? In fact, we met in our teens and went on to form a band called The Rhythm Sheds – with some success, wouldn't you agree, Rachel?'

My mother nods. Then looks at her microphone. 'Yes. We did, didn't we?'

'Just recently, Rachel's son got in touch with me. You see,

Rachel has memory problems – like so many of us. I don't think she'll mind me saying she's fifty-nine. But unlike most of us, she has a diagnosis of early onset dementia.'

I watch my mother pull a face as Miles goes on.

'Her son, Alex, lives with her and helps her with things that have become more difficult. Isn't that right, Rachel?'

With her unreliable filter, I'm slightly anxious as to what my mother will say, how she'll react to her diagnosis being talked about.

'He's very good. I suppose I do forget rather a lot of things,' she says. 'And sometimes I say the wrong things. The words just aren't there. And I know I get muddled about what time of day it is. Poor Alex. I wake him up in the middle of the night – I don't mean to.' Her eyes mist over.

I reaching across and take one of her hands.

'Anyway, I'm so sorry, Alex. But time doesn't seem important the way it used to.'

Miles jollies her along. 'Tell us how it is singing with our old band again.'

'Wonderful. It's like it was only yesterday.' She pauses for a moment. 'I was worried I wouldn't, but I can remember the songs.' Her eyes start to light up. 'I don't know how, but I remember every last one of them.'

'Tell us what music means to you.' Miles pauses.

'Well, it can make you happy. Or sad… Maybe sometimes that isn't a bad thing. And it reminds you – of people and places, don't you find that?'

'I think we can all relate to that. Music's wonderfully evocative. So is spending time with our band again bringing memories back?' Miles asks.

'Oh yes.' My mother smiles. 'Of course, everyone is different and we all live so far away. Atlas lives in Glasgow and Luke's in Majorca. Then there's you, of course,' she says to Miles. 'You still play a mean lead guitar.' Her eyes twinkle at him. 'And Kevin. I think he's changed the most.' It's as well no one can see her roll her eyes. 'Though it really is nice of him to let us all use this house,' she says. 'It's a bit of a takeover, isn't it?' She winks at Miles.

'Absolutely it is. Cheers, Kevin. We couldn't have done this without you.' He smiles at my mother. 'Back in the day, you were quite a rock chick, weren't you, Roxy?'

'Well, I've been remembering some of the dresses I used to wear. Mostly short.' She winks at Jack. 'With high-heeled shoes. Can I say something?'

'Er, by all means.' Miles sits back. 'What is it?'

'I suppose...' She pauses, frowning. 'If we're talking about dementia... I didn't really want any help – at first. I was probably quite grumpy about it. But I suppose I have realised I'm lucky – to have Alex. And to be meeting up with you and the rest of our band again.'

'I think you'll find it's been good for all of us,' Miles says gently. 'Thank you, Rachel, so much, for talking to us.'

Jack leans forward and switches my mother's microphone off.

'That's it?' She sounds put out. 'I have so much more I wanted to say.'

'It was perfect,' Miles says. 'Just what we wanted. Isn't that right?' He looks at Jack.

'Absolutely.' Jack starts putting his equipment away.

'Shall we go upstairs?' I say to my mother.

'I suppose so.' She gets up and walks towards the stairs.

'Thanks, Miles.' I pause. 'You handled that really nicely.'

'Glad you think so. If the recording's OK, I'll probably play it on the show tonight.' He glances at his watch. 'Talking of which, I need to get going.'

I follow my mother upstairs then along to the kitchen, where Kevin is standing looking what I can only describe as fidgety.

'I hope that was successful,' he says drily.

'Very much so. Wasn't it, Mum?'

She looks at me vacantly. 'What are you talking about?'

'The interview you just did – with Miles.' But then I break off as Mack comes in, followed by a girl. My jaw drops as I recognise her. It's the girl from the arboretum, the one I spilled coffee over. Gazing at her, I wonder what on earth she's doing here.

23

BEE

As I walk into the kitchen, I see the guy from earlier, the one who brought the shopping in, my cheeks suddenly hot as I realise, it really is him. The guy from the arboretum.

'Alex, this is Bee,' Kevin says.

Alex looks at me quizzically. 'We spoke on the phone, didn't we?'

I nod, my mind putting everything together. It was Alex I called about Luke; who is Rachel's son. It's unbelievable that we met before – albeit briefly. But though I've been here two days, it's the first time our paths have crossed. In the flesh, he's calm, the kindness I heard in his voice radiating from his eyes. 'Nice to meet you,' I manage, slightly dazed.

'Cup of tea, Bee?' Kevin says.

I'm aware of Mack beside me, pulling on my arm. 'No thanks,' I say, still dazed. 'Actually, Mack was wondering if you had a Coke.'

'Dreadful stuff. But as it happens, I do.' Kevin goes to the fridge, takes out a can and passes it to her.

'How was the interview?' I try to pull myself together.

'Good.' Alex looks relieved. 'Miles is talking about playing it on air later tonight.'

On cue, Miles stops in the doorway. 'Got to go. Show starts at ten. Don't forget to tune in! See you all tomorrow?'

'I think we should go, too,' Rachel says. 'All this practising... I don't remember it being so tiring.'

'That's because you used to be younger,' Alex says. 'Come on. I'll take you home.' He smiles at me. 'Nice to see you again.'

'You too.' I watch, partly not wanting him to go; slightly envious of the easiness between them. Of Rachel's obvious affection towards her son as she takes his arm. 'See you tomorrow.' As Rachel catches my eye, it's as if she's guessed as she winks at me.

Mack, of course, misses nothing. 'Bee! You know him? Why didn't you tell me?'

'I bumped into him once – where I used to work. I didn't know his name.' I shake my head. 'Today was the first time I've seen him since.'

'That's crazy.' Mack rolls her eyes exaggeratedly.

When Kevin comes back after seeing them out, he's frowning. 'I should have insisted on hearing the interview first,' he says. 'I have no idea what Rachel's been saying.'

'Alex said it was good. But Miles is a professional,' I remind him. 'He's only going to want the best on his show.' As I've already realised, Miles is just a little bit up himself. 'Where's Luke?'

'He and Atlas went to the pub.' He pauses. 'Shall we join them?'

Under Kevin's instructions, I drive us to a pub on the outskirts of Midhurst, up a quiet country lane. Getting out, I breathe in the scent of woodsmoke, taking in windows lit with fairy lights.

Inside is just as welcoming – a log fire burning in the hearth, the air filled with the smell of home-cooked food. I notice Luke and Atlas at a table in one corner, deep in conversation.

'I'm starving,' Mack says as we go over to join them.

We order delicious food and we're still in the pub at 10 p.m. when Miles's radio show starts. Getting out his phone, Kevin finds it online. But even with the volume turned up, we can barely hear it over the background sound of voices.

He turns and addresses the pub. 'Be quiet all of you, will you?' He holds up his phone. 'Trying to listen to an interview – about our band.'

'You're in a band, Grandad?' It comes from a tipsy-looking boy, before laughter ripples around the group he's with.

'As a matter of fact, we are. Young people are so rude,' Kevin say crossly. 'Present company excepted, of course.' He glances at me, then gets up just as one of the staff comes over.

'You can listen in the snug if you like.'

They lead us into a quiet room away from the crowded bar. Sitting down, Kevin puts his phone on the table. Miles is already on air and there's a phone-in underway, before he goes to a break.

'Coming up – we talk about the reunion of my old band – and to our wonderful singer about her experience of music and dementia.'

Mack's face lights up. 'This is really exciting.'

'God, it'd better be good,' Kevin says under his breath.

'It will be great.' Atlas smiles. 'It's Rachel. How could it fail to be?'

After the break, Miles starts talking. 'As you know, over the next few days, we're talking about dementia and earlier today, I spoke to Rachel who has been diagnosed with early onset dementia. Rachel used to be known as Roxy, back in the day, when she played in a band that became well-known locally. A band I just happened to play guitar for. And just recently, the band got back together. We are called The Rhythm Sheds and earlier today, I asked Rachel what difference music makes to her condition.'

It becomes apparent early on in the interview, just how much Alex does for his mother.

'Miles is good, isn't he?' Luke sounds surprised.

Kevin shushes him. 'I'm trying to listen.'

At the end, Miles goes on. 'In case you're interested, Roxy and The Rhythm Sheds – featuring yours truly! – are playing at The Ship in Brighton this Sunday evening. A one-off. Don't miss it. Coming up, we're taking your calls on how dementia is affecting your life, or that of someone you love...'

'Bloody hell.' Kevin sounds pissed off. 'Half the world will be there.'

'What's wrong with that?' I look at him, then at Luke. 'This is amazing – can't you see? Getting people talking about dementia. So many people don't understand it.'

'It isn't something most of us like to think about,' Kevin says.

'But they should.' Memories of my grandmother's illness are flooding back to me. 'There's medication available now. What matters is that it's picked up before it becomes advanced.' I'm thinking of Rachel again. How brave she was, talking about it. How brilliant Alex is, for helping her.

* * *

Saturday arrives. As I lie in bed, I realise how wrapped up in the band I've become these last few days; how little thought I've given to my own life. One that's fast looming once this interlude is over.

Suddenly I sit up. I've forgotten about Geneva's call. How could I have? But seeing as it's Saturday, it's unlikely she'll be at the arboretum.

In her bed, Mack is still sleeping, her hair spread across her pillow. Leaving her, I shower, then after pulling on jeans and a hoodie, I go downstairs. The house is quiet and in the kitchen, I put the kettle on, gazing through the window at Kevin's garden. It's another cold morning, the grass sparkling where the sun reaches it, while the trees look like they've been dusted with icing sugar.

After making a cup of tea, I cup it in my hands. I'm still standing at the window when Luke comes in.

'Morning.' It's the first time I've seen him alone since we've got here.

'Hi.' He stifles a yawn. 'Thanks for looking after Mack. She'd have been pretty bored by now without you here.'

'I'm loving it,' I say honestly. 'Though she's been keeping me busy. Shopping, Brighton pier, ice skating...' We've been working our way through Mack's wish list.

'How did it go with your mother?' Luke asks.

'OK.' I pause. 'There was a change, though. A photo, of Olivia – on the wall. I'd never seen it before.'

'Sounds like progress?'

'Maybe.' I sigh. 'She still wouldn't talk about her, though.' Just then, the doorbell rings.

'Probably Rachel and Alex.' Luke gets up and goes to open it.

Rachel has dressed up for the day in a floaty pink dress and trainers. 'Did you hear me on the radio last night?' Pausing in the kitchen doorway, she looks as though she can't believe it. She turns to talk to Luke as Alex comes into the kitchen.

'Hi.' His eyes meet mine. Coming over, he stands next to me. 'Mum's beside herself after the interview.'

'She was great,' I say. 'Wasn't she?'

'There's going to be more tonight,' he says. 'Not about the band, but about helping people with dementia. I went to the arboretum the other day...'

As he mentions the arboretum, my ears prick up.

But he breaks off as Miles comes in. 'Hope you all listened last night. You won't believe how many calls we took. It was a great interview, Roxy.' He plants a smacker on her cheek. 'Coffee anyone?' He's clearly pleased with himself. 'Has anyone seen Kevin?'

Everyone has gathered in the kitchen by the time Kevin appears. Instead of his characteristic curtness, this morning he has an air of distractedness. 'Just had a rather strange call—' he says. 'A blast from the past, I suppose you'd call it.'

'Anything we should know about?' Luke asks.

'No.' Kevin looks perplexed. 'Absolutely not, in fact.'

'In that case, shall we get started?' Luke picks up the empty mugs and takes them over to the sink, Kevin remaining silent as everyone filters down to the cellar.

'What was that about?' Alex is frowning.

'No idea.' I pull out a chair and sit down.

Alex does the same. 'You are coming to the gig, I'm guessing?'

'Wouldn't miss it for anything – and I don't think Mack would forgive me if I did. She can't wait.'

Alex smiles. 'So when do you go back to Majorca?'

'Monday.' I frown. 'I can't believe you and Kevin came all that way to see Luke.'

'It was a strange coincidence of events that made it possible,' Alex says. 'I mean, Kevin being off work and my mother staying at her sister's... Otherwise, we wouldn't have been able to.'

'It was meant to be.' I'm silent for a moment.

'Maybe it was.' Alex smiles. 'Going back to the scene of the crime, so to speak, do you often go to the arboretum?'

'Let's just say not any more,' I say evasively.

'Oh?' He's clearly picked up there's more to it than I'm saying.

I sigh. 'I used to work there,' I admit, as I give him the abridged version. 'But I lost my job. Around the same time, I had to move out of my flat.' That I lost Phil too is suddenly insignificant. 'That's why I moved back to my mother's. After that, I went to find Luke.'

'Find?' Alex frowns. 'Sorry, there's a whole lot of this I don't get. I went to the arboretum recently. I got talking to someone, who said they'd just lost the girl who did their social media.'

'That was me,' I say. 'It's the reason I was fired. A ranty post about companies responsible for burning down the rainforests.'

'Good for you.' He looks impressed.

'Not exactly. One of their main investors is the chief exec of an oil giant.' I shrug. 'But so be it. If I hadn't left, I don't suppose I would have gone to Majorca.' I think how to condense the background of my life into a few succinct sentences. 'I should explain. You see, I've only recently discovered he's my father. My mother never told me. And there's no name on my birth certificate,' I explain. 'But when I moved back to my mother's, I found out.'

'Why didn't she tell you?' He looks astonished.

'She said the past was in the past,' I say. 'She's quite black and white about things, my mother. She doesn't really see things from anyone else's point of view.' Least of all her daughter's, but I leave that out.

'Did Luke know about you?'

I shake my head. 'He hadn't a clue. When I turned up...' I

break off, remembering. 'It wasn't the best way of doing it. But he's been nothing but welcoming.'

'Going back to the arboretum,' Luke says. 'Actually, there are two things about the arboretum.'

Going on, he tells me he thinks they're missing me.

My heart starts to race. 'I had a message from Geneva. She wants to speak to me – about some kind of business proposition.'

'That makes sense.' Going on, he tells me about Geneva's interest in dedicating a day a month to dementia sufferers.

'It's a brilliant idea,' I say quietly, wishing I could be a part of it. Because I know how glorious the grounds are, the feeling of peace that comes from the trees, the stunning views.

'Maybe that's partly what she wants to talk about.' Alex's eyes meet mine. 'She's offering a discount on the entrance price, but she said the main challenge is finding sponsorship, so that people who can't afford it aren't excluded.'

'Miles's radio station,' I say immediately.

Alex nods. 'His producer knows. I think Miles is going to be talking about it. I need to check with him.' He pauses. 'These last few days have gone quite quickly, haven't they?'

'I know. I'm looking forward to flying back.' I pause. 'Luke's asked me if I'd like to stay.'

Alex looks surprised. 'That's brilliant, isn't it?'

'Other than the small matter of sorting a visa, yes,' I say. 'It is. Completely brilliant.' I glance past Alex at Mack. Still in her pyjamas, she comes into the kitchen and climbs onto the chair next to me.

'They're rehearsing,' she says. 'Again.' Rolling her eyes. 'I opened the door to the cellar just now. It's really noisy down there.' She turns to me. 'Can I have breakfast?'

I forage in Kevin's immaculate cupboards for a plate and make her some toast.

'I have an idea,' Alex says. 'If the two of you aren't busy... How about we go for lunch at the arboretum?'

I stare at him. It's a brilliant idea.

'What's an arboretum?' Mack says.

'It's where I used to work.' I glance at Alex. 'They have rare and very wonderful trees there,' I tell her. 'And a coffee shop.'

'OK,' she says happily, picking up her toast to take with her as she slips off her chair. 'I'm going to get dressed.'

* * *

Half an hour later, we set off in Alex's car for the arboretum. It feels strange to think about going back, as though I'm not the same person who used to work there. On the way, I look up their Instagram feed. In the month since I left, there have been one or two posts, I'm guessing by Cindy, neither of which are at all inspiring, which won't exactly have drawn visitors to the place.

On the way, as Alex tells me about his research into climate change, his passion for preserving the natural world, it seems we have more in common than I'd realised.

'Until I worked at the arboretum, I didn't realise how important trees are,' I say. 'But they're the lungs of this planet.'

'And the beating heart,' Alex adds.

'My mum loved trees.' Mack's voice comes from the back. 'She said we wouldn't survive without them.'

There are fewer than a dozen cars in the car park when we arrive, in spite of the fact that it's Saturday, albeit a cold one, which should bring people flocking.

'What did you actually do here?' Mack says.

'I used to greet our visitors and work in reception. I also did our marketing and social media,' I tell her. 'All to try and get more people to come here. But judging from today, whatever they're doing now, it isn't working.'

But it's more complicated than I've realised. After Cindy greets me with an enormous hug, she explains that at the root of it, there's a dilemma.

'Plenty of people come here because it's a lovely place to walk. But lots of our visitors care about the environment. And it came out in the local press that our biggest sponsor works for an energy giant. The local radio picked it up. Just after you left,' she says.

'Oh dear. So what's happening about that?' I ask.

'Nothing.' Cindy's silent. 'What can we do?'

'Find another sponsor?' Alex suggests.

But it isn't that simple. 'If only there were a way to frame the sponsor more sympathetically,' I say. 'I mean, if he left his job, for instance, or publicly spoke up about change being needed.'

'Can you imagine him doing that? Because I can't.' Suddenly Cindy looks at Alex. 'You were looking for Bee, weren't you? When you came in before?'

'Pardon?' I look at Alex.

'Rumbled,' he says. 'I came here hoping to see you again. That's all.'

Mack's eyes are like saucers as she whispers to me, 'I think he likes you.'

'Is Geneva in?' I ask, on the off chance.

But Cindy shakes her head. 'Not till Monday.'

As we wander around the grounds, now and then my hand brushes against Alex's and a warm feeling comes over me, while I have a sense of coming home, of catching up with old friends as I gaze at the trees. From the way Alex looks at me, I think he gets it.

'They're special, Mack,' I try to explain to her. 'Some of them are very rare, and some are old. But every one of them is beautiful.' Leaning against one, I close my eyes for a moment, as that wonderful peacefulness comes back that I remember so well. 'I've missed this place.' I say it without thinking. My eyes spring open. 'I need to find Cindy.'

I know she's already sent me some stuff, but this building houses a treasure trove of information. It takes little persuasion for her to let me in to the staffroom, where the walls are lined with books and papers about everything to do with every tree you can think of. And while Alex takes Mack for tea and cake, I search for everything I can find on olive trees.

* * *

'It was amazing.' On my lap, I'm clutching an envelope of photocopies. 'I can't wait to show your dad, Mack.' I've come away freshly inspired to make Luke's olive grove profitable again. 'It's been neglected for years,' I explain to Alex. 'We want to start producing our own olive oil.' Crossing my fingers that I'll be there to make it happen.

Back at Kevin's, when he lets us in, he beckons us down to the cellar.

'We're just about done for today,' he says. 'But you're just in time to hear our last song.'

The three of us stand at the bottom of the stairs. Then, as I listen, I'm reminded of the first time I heard them, when Mack played their music in Majorca. Their sound is distinct, a little less polished perhaps. But Rachel is truly in her element, as though Roxy's her alter ego and when she sings, my skin prickles.

I glance at Alex. 'You did this.' There's wonder in my voice.

'There was a point I didn't think it was going to happen,' he admits. 'But they're good, aren't they?'

'The Ship is in for a treat,' I say, smiling at him.

After going upstairs, everyone's oddly quiet. But I suppose it's the fact that this is coming to an end. That after tomorrow, everyone will go back to their normal lives; maybe rarely, if ever, see each other again.

While Mack watches Kevin's enormous TV, Alex takes me to one side. 'Can I ask you a favour?'

He explains there's someone he has to pick up tomorrow night, before coming to the pub. 'If I drop my mother over here, would you mind driving her?'

'Wouldn't it make more sense for us to pick her up? I mean, we are all coming to Brighton.'

'You're sure?' He looks anxious. 'I probably need to go out just after five.'

'Fine. We can be at yours before then.' I pause. 'Who's the mystery guest?'

'His name's Leo. He used to be their roadie.' Alex hesitates. 'He isn't well. He doesn't want it broadcast but I may as well tell you. He has cancer. I'm really hoping he'll be up to joining us.'

As he talks, I get goosebumps. 'This is making a difference to so many people,' I say. 'You should be really proud.'

'It might yet go horribly wrong,' Alex says. 'She's been pretty good the last few days. But my mother can be completely random. Don't tell anyone, will you? About Leo?'

'Of course I won't.' As I speak the doorbell rings. When Kevin doesn't appear, I go to answer it.

There's a woman on the doorstep. Her dark hair is glossy, the collar of her fluffy coat pulled up round her neck, and as I look at her, there's something familiar about her.

'Hi.' She looks at me uncertainly. 'I was hoping to see Kevin.'

'Molly.' Kevin's voice comes from behind me as he walks towards us. 'I'll take it from here, Bee,' he says, clearly dismissing me. 'You should have told me you were coming,' I hear him say. 'Bloody chaos around here, I'm afraid. Come in. Can I offer you a drink?'

I leave them standing in the doorway, talking. But as I walk away, I have a light-bulb moment as I realise who she is. I hurry to find Alex. 'It's his ex-wife,' I whisper. 'I recognise her from the photo at the top of the stairs.'

* * *

The evening is a series of comings and goings. Alex takes Rachel home. Kevin takes his ex to the pub. Miles hurries off to do his radio show, which leaves Luke, Atlas, me and Mack.

We order a takeaway. Then when Luke takes Mack up to bed, I start telling Atlas about how I came to be here.

'Funny, you know,' he says thoughtfully. 'How things happen, I mean. A few months ago, you wouldn't have imagined any of this. You couldn't have, could you?'

'I'd never even heard of Luke,' I say. 'I had a job and a flat, and a sort of boyfriend.' Shaking my head, I think of Phil. 'When it all fell apart, it felt like the worst time in my life. And now...' Suddenly it comes to me. 'I can honestly say this is the best.' As I speak, I realise how true it is.

'You have to make way for the new to come into your life.' He speaks softly. 'And you've been brave, young lady.'

'I don't think so. I got myself into a bit of a hole,' I confess. 'I very nearly ended up working for my mother's friend and living with a stranger.'

'And if you had?' Atlas smiles quietly. 'It would have been another chapter – a kind of detour, if you like. It goes that way sometimes. We don't always take the shortest route. But I think ultimately, we end up where we're meant to be.'

In other words, events conspired to lead me to Luke. 'The trouble is, it isn't definite that I can stay.' I explain about needing a visa to live in Majorca.

'Keep the faith, young Bee. You were brave enough to go. And it was brave. You had no idea what was waiting for you. And now... Give the Universe a chance to work its magic for you.'

I stare at him. 'You believe that? Mack does too!'

He chuckles. 'She's a smart kid. But truthfully, how else do you account for all the miraculous things that go on in our lives?'

I'm silent for a moment. Until recently, I'd never met anyone who talked about the Universe like this. It's another way my life has changed. I look at Atlas. 'You run a hostel, don't you?'

'Indeed. I bought this big old house – nothing fancy, mind. It just didn't seem right not to share it. Too many folks have fallen on hard times – and often, it's just pure bad luck. You know for some, they're in the right place at the right time? Well, for these folks, it's the opposite. You listen to those politicians talk about how everyone has choices. But they don't know anything. Not everyone does. And sometimes, there's nothing they can do about that.' He pauses. 'Just makes me think, young Bee. When things are going your way, those are the good times. Hold on for the ride, that's what I say!'

Suddenly I remember the radio show. 'We should listen to Miles.' I switching on the radio and find the channel. Then as we listen, Miles goes up in my estimation, as he talks about the arboretum; about the healing power of nature for dementia sufferers.

Sitting there, I glance at Atlas, then at Luke as he comes back in, thinking how all of this started with Rachel's dementia, and

Alex wanting to help her. How bringing the band together has led to so much more; how everyone has played their part in this.

It's almost as though he reads my mind as Atlas glances at me. 'Pretty cool, hey?' He winks at me.

* * *

As I lie in bed that night, I can't sleep. So much has happened in such a short time. My perspective isn't the same, my priorities have been turned upside down. I haven't thought about clothes shopping, for instance. I haven't missed the boozy nights out. Instead, I'm focused on saving an olive grove.

The following morning, there is no hurry to get up. No houseful of people about to turn up here. After a lazy morning, I lose track of time. But early afternoon, the pace steps up.

'We need to be at Alex's,' I say to Mack. 'Shall we get changed?'

Mack wears her new dress with pink and orange sequins, with silver tights and pink trainers, while I help her curl her hair. Getting out the dress I picked up from my mother's, I stare at it. It's too dressy for a Brighton pub. But this is no ordinary night. It's a one-off. An important one.

Feeling a frisson of excitement at the thought of seeing Alex again, I slip on my silver shoes, realising how long it is since I dressed up.

'Wow.' Mack stares at me. 'You look really pretty, Bee.'

Bending down, I hug her. 'Thanks. So do you.' I pause. 'Are you ready?'

* * *

Mack chatters as we drive to Alex and Rachel's house, which by chance, turns out to be a couple of streets away from Saskia's flat. Christmas has come early to Brighton: the shops have sparkling window displays, roofs and doorways are decked out with fairy lights.

After parking, we get out. And as I breathe in the tang of salt in the air, it's as though I've never been away, until Mack slips her hand into mine.

'Which is their house?'

'Number seventy-six.' We start walking. 'Over there.'

Alex lets us in. He's wearing jeans and a dark shirt, his hair slightly untidy as though he's in a hurry. 'Hi. Mum's in the kitchen. She's making you breakfast.' He shakes his head as I glance at the clock. 'I know. But meals get a little out of sync around here.' He pauses. 'Can you make sure she turns the oven off? I usually persuade her not to cook, but she was most insistent.'

I glance towards the doorway where I can see Rachel in the kitchen. 'I'll go and check on her.'

'Thanks.' He lingers. 'You're sure you'll be OK?'

I nod. 'We'll be fine. Don't worry! We'll see you at The Ship.' I glance after Mack who's gone to find Rachel. 'I'd better make sure they're OK.'

Despite wide sash windows and high ceilings, the house feels cosy and character-filled. There's a large comfy-looking sofa in the sitting room and a wall that's covered floor to ceiling with bookshelves.

In the homely kitchen, Rachel is piling scrambled egg onto toast for Mack.

'Ah, glad you're here, Bee. Bacon or eggs?'

'Actually, I've just eaten,' I say. Then take in her outfit of a faded dress over leggings. 'Maybe you should think about getting ready?' I suggest.

She looks at me blankly. 'What for?'

'The gig,' I say uncertainly. 'With the band.'

She hesitates, then a look of horror washes over her face. 'I knew there was something. You girls carry on eating. I have to change.'

While she's gone, I turn off the oven and do the washing up. Twenty minutes later, Rachel reappears. And talk about a transformation. She's backcombed her hair, her dark eyeliner and matt lipstick giving her a sixties vibe. But it's the dress that takes my breath away. Beaded and tasselled it catches the light, perfectly paired with the metallic boots she's wearing.

'You look incredible,' I say.

'Not too bad for an old bird. Can you believe I used to wear this when I was a teenager?' Winking, she gives us a twirl. 'Well, I can hardly let the side down, can I?' She frowns. 'Where's my coat?'

I find it draped over the sofa and help her into it. There's a chill in the air as we make our way out to the car.

'Do you think it will snow?' Mack says hopefully.

'I do hope not,' Rachel says firmly. 'Dammed nuisance, snow. Very cold. And messy,' she adds, as Mack giggles.

As we drive, Rachel's quiet and I wonder if she's apprehensive about the gig.

'Are you looking forward to tonight?' I ask.

'I think so.' She fiddles with her hands. 'I suppose I am a bit nervous.'

'I think my dad is, too,' Mack pipes up from the back.

'You'll be great,' I say. 'You all will.'

There's a small private car park behind the pub. We get out and make our way inside. It's a large space and surprisingly full, but almost immediately, I see Kevin by the bar. When he sees us, he looks a little flustered.

'Ah. I'm waiting for someone. They haven't turned up yet.' Thankfully, he's ditched his dodgy-looking baseball cap. A waft of expensive aftershave comes my way as, fidgety, he glances at his watch. 'Can I get you all a drink?'

'Where's Dad?' Mack asks.

'Oh, yes. Backstage. Setting up.' Kevin glances towards the door again. 'Used to have someone to do it for us, back in the day. But needs must.'

'You mean Leo, don't you?' Rachel says.

'Right.' Kevin glances over our heads again, then back to us. 'Drinks?'

Leaving Kevin to wait for his mystery guest, we go backstage – which basically amounts to a little room off to one side, from which Luke and Atlas are setting their gear up.

'Hey!' Coming forward, Atlas smacks a kiss on Rachel's cheek. 'You've done Roxy proud!'

'Oh goodness.' She looks a little anxious. 'Do you think so? There's an awful lot of people out there.' Her face clears. 'Look. There's Miles.' She waves in his direction as he comes over.

'Sorry I'm late,' he says. 'Right. What needs doing?'

Mack and I drift away together. Not long after, I see Alex coming in, pushing a man in a wheelchair, who I'm guessing must be Leo. As they come closer, it's obvious Leo isn't well. But he manages a bright smile as Alex introduces us, then goes to get him a drink.

'Takes me right back, this does.' Leo looks wistful. 'It used to be me up there, setting everything up. Best days of my life, I reckon.'

'Didn't they help you?' Mack looks shocked.

'Not usually.' He chuckles. 'They didn't mean anything by it.

There were always people wanting to talk to them. Usually girls.' He raises his eyebrows. 'I just got on with it. It's how it was.'

Alex comes back and passes Leo a drink. 'Shall we go over there?' He nods towards a table near the front.

Over the next half-hour, people continue to come in off the street, until by 7 p.m., the place is crammed. Mack doesn't leave my side, just looks around, an expression of awe on her face as she takes it all in, while Leo doesn't speak. Just sits quietly, a thoughtful look on his face.

'I hope your mum is feeling OK,' I say to Alex.

'Me too.' He looks a little anxious. 'I wasn't expecting so many people to be here. I don't think any of us were.'

I try to reassure him. 'She must have been used to it once. You never know – maybe it will help her remember the good old days.'

At the sound of a single guitar, a hush comes over the room. Then Rachel walks out. She stands there for a moment; I try to imagine what must be going through her head. And then the music starts.

24

ALEX

My mother looks so frail and there's a lump in my throat as she starts to sing. It's seeing her up there, the fact that dementia has relinquished its grip on her, albeit only temporarily.

The mood around us is joyous as one song gives way to the next. I watch Kevin on the drums, imagine for a moment the much younger man he used to be. Lost in the music, Luke's aura of sadness is absent, while content to be in the background, playing away on his bass guitar, Atlas just smiles, at everyone.

Even Miles seems to have shifted into another gear, as suddenly I love the whole blinking lot of them. For being here, for doing this for my mother. Knowing it won't be perfect and not minding that.

But in a sense, it doesn't matter what happens tonight. It's knowing what this weekend has come to mean – not just to my mother, but to Luke in his grief, to Kevin's lonely life, and also, in his last chapter, to Leo.

But it's also boosted Miles's flagging radio show and brought out another side of Kevin. And I'm forgetting that this is a dream come true for me, too. In all the years I've wanted to know more about the band, I've never imagined I'd hear them playing live.

There is no new material tonight. Just a rehashing of old favourites. But no one minds. After they've been playing for an hour, Kevin comes forward and takes the microphone from my mother.

'Thank you all for coming tonight. I just wanted to say... To start with, we came together for Roxy, here.' Turning to my mother, he takes one of her hands and kisses it. 'Many of our lives are touched by dementia in some way and music can be a powerful way to bring memories back.'

Beside him, in a spontaneous gesture, my mother high-fives him as everyone cheers.

'But...' His eyes scan the crowd. 'I've learned a lot about myself these last weeks. I've let music go to some extent. In fact, I've let rather too many things go in recent years.' He pauses. 'Playing with this lot again...' He gestures towards the rest of the band. 'I've rediscovered my love of music, as well as how powerfully it can connect us to each other. That's what matters, isn't it? The people in our lives?' As his voice wavers slightly, you could hear a pin drop. 'But anyway, enough about me. There are collection boxes on the bar. And there are QR codes. Scan them to find out more about dementia and what any of us can do to help.'

'Wow,' Bee murmurs beside me. 'I didn't see that coming.'

'Nor did I.' As applause breaks out, I'm genuinely astonished by Kevin, that there really is a more sensitive side to him. I'm starting to wonder if his rudeness has become his defence against the world; if he wasn't always that way. My eyes turn to a woman I saw him talking to at the bar as things start falling into place. I nudge Bee, leaning towards her to make myself heard about the music. 'Didn't she come to the house?'

Bee's eyes widen. 'It's his ex-wife. Do you think...?' Her sentence goes unfinished as she looks past Kevin's ex, at someone who has just come into the bar.

I watch a look of shock wash over her face. 'What is it?' I ask.

She shakes her head in disbelief. 'It's my mother.'

The band finish to rapturous applause; to rowdy cries for *more*. Roxy takes the stage for one last song, accompanied only by Luke on the keyboard. A hush descends over the pub, before people start singing along with her.

At the end, time seems to stop for me as she stands there, a look of bewilderment on her face. Then Luke takes her hand and they walk away.

The music over, Bee squeezes through the crowd to go to find her mother, returning minutes later with her.

'Mum, this is Alex. This is Cassandra.' She frowns at her mother. 'I still don't know what you're doing here.'

'I heard about the gig.' Cassandra shrugs. 'I thought I'd come along. Be supportive.' Her face changes as she looks past us. 'Leo?'

He looks confused. 'Sorry. My memory isn't so good. The old brain isn't what it used to be.'

'It's Sandra, Leo,' Cassandra says. 'I used to hang out with you all. It was a long time ago – but it's really good to see you again.'

Things take an even stranger turn as Luke comes over, followed by Kevin. Both of them stare at Cassandra.

'Good God,' Kevin says eventually. 'What are you doing here?'

'I came to see Bethany.' She hesitates. 'Well, to see all of you, I suppose.' She turns to Luke. 'A bit like the old days, isn't it?'

'Hardly,' Kevin says crisply. 'Would you excuse me? There's

someone I need to talk to.' He heads off in the direction of his ex-wife.

'Always was a rude bugger,' my mother says.

Bee looks outraged. 'He's been so good, putting everyone up,' she says.

'No doubt there must have been something in it for him,' Cassandra mutters.

She makes no attempt to hide her antagonism towards him. But I'm frowning. It was the way Kevin and Luke had both stood there looking at her, the same expression on their faces.

'It's nice that you're here,' Luke says, adding, 'For Bee, I mean.'

'I wouldn't have missed it for the world.' Cassandra makes a clumsy attempt at being flirty that's excruciating.

Bee looks at me. There's desperation in her eyes and I feel for her. She's been looking forward to tonight, and her mother is ruining it.

'Can I get everyone a drink?' I say. 'Cassandra, would you mind helping me?'

Bee shoots me a grateful look, then as I lead her mother towards the bar, out of the corner of my eye see her talk to Luke.

'So you're Roxy's son,' Cassandra says. 'Is this all your doing?'

'I suppose I set things in motion.' Reaching the bar, I order some drinks before going on. 'But the rest of the band just swung into action. I can't believe so many people are here.' I pass her a glass of wine, curious. 'You must have known the band quite well – back in the day.'

'Some more than others,' she says cagily.

'Of course.' I pause, thinking of Luke. Then I follow my hunch. 'And Kevin?'

She stiffens. 'What about him?'

I hesitate. 'I just wondered.' I pass her a couple of glasses, then pick up the rest. 'Shall we take these back to the others?'

* * *

When I drive Leo home, there's a light in his eyes but he's clearly exhausted.

'Thanks for tonight,' he says. 'You were right. It was good to hear them again.'

'I'm glad you were there,' I say. 'Can I ask you something?'

'Ask what you like!' he chuckles before coughing uncontrollably.

I wait until he stops. 'Was there something between Sandra and Kevin?'

Leo doesn't speak. Then he shakes his head. 'Sandra was always hanging around the band. She had a thing going with Luke. But to be honest, I don't think she was fussy. It was no secret Kevin liked her. There was a rumour going around they had a bit of a fling. It kind of makes sense. When she and Luke started seeing each other, Kevin changed. She still flirted with him... Liked the attention, that one. But she almost broke the band up. Between you and me, Luke was lucky to get away.'

'I had no idea,' I say.

'Best keep it that way,' Leo says. 'It's history. Everyone's forgotten about it.'

'I suppose.' But my mind is racing. Maybe there's a reason Bee never knew who her father was. If she'd been seeing both Kevin and Luke, maybe Cassandra wasn't sure.

'Nice, though, that young Bee has met her dad at last. Look a bit alike, don't they?'

I frown. 'Do you think so?'

'Same eyes,' Leo says distantly. 'Surprised you haven't noticed. Here we are.'

Reaching Leo's house, I pull in and park outside. 'I'll help you in,' I say, getting out, then fetching his wheelchair out of the back.

'Time was when I would have argued the toss with you,' he says ruefully. 'But truth is, I can't do much for myself these days. Thanks,' he adds as I help him into the wheelchair. Then after closing the car door, I wheel him to the house.

Inside, Leo points towards a door. 'If you wouldn't mind taking me in there.'

I do as he asks. The room has a hospital bed on which his pyjamas are laid out.

'I normally have someone come in to change me,' he says cheerfully.

'I dragged you out tonight,' I joke. 'The least I can do is help you.' Crouching down, I slip off his shoes while he fumbles with his belt. Between us we get him into his pyjamas, then onto the bed.

'Thank you, young man.' Leo's chest is heaving from exertion. 'I didn't want to say anything earlier, but I've decided I'm moving to the hospice. Not sure how much longer I can go on like this.'

'I'll come and see you,' I say. 'If that's OK?'

'By all means.' He hesitates. 'Only if you have time, mind. But I'll look forward to it.'

* * *

I'm preoccupied as I drive back to Brighton. But at least in the hospice, not only will Leo have the care he needs, he'll have company, instead of spending most of his day on his own.

Back home, I glimpse my mother through the door into the kitchen. She's still in her rock star outfit, and I can hear her regaling Bee with fragments of stories. Passing Mack on the sofa, fast asleep, I pick up a blanket and drape it over her.

Seeing me, Bee smiles. 'Did Leo get home OK?'

I nod. 'He really enjoyed himself. It was a great night, wasn't it?'

'It was marvellous.' My mother claps her hands together. 'We simply must do it again.'

'Leo said something when I took him home.' I frown slightly, as I turn to Bee. 'It seems your mother had a bit of a thing with Kevin – way back.'

It's a throwaway comment. But Bee stares at me. 'Really?'

'Rubbish,' my mother says. 'I would have known. Where do you get these things from?'

'I should get Mack home.' Suddenly Bee seems distracted.

I put a hand on her arm. 'Did I say something wrong?'

She stares at me. Then shakes her head. 'No. You didn't. But Mack's tired. And we leave tomorrow.'

'Why don't you leave her – have a drink before you go?'

As Bee looks at me, there's angst in her eyes. 'I think it's best we go.' She goes through to the sitting room and gently wakes her. Stretching her arms, Mack yawns.

My heart sinks at the thought of them leaving. 'When's your flight?'

'Just after midday,' she says.

I help them both out to the car. 'We should stay in touch.' I stroke a strand of Bee's hair behind her ears. 'You're going to talk to Geneva, aren't you? I hope they put some work your way.'

'Thanks.' She looks at me. 'I hope you find a sponsor.' There's a reluctance about her as she stands there for a moment.

There's a distance between us that wasn't there before, which

I can't help thinking is to do with what I said about Kevin. I want to tell her not to leave like this; to stay. But just like that, she gets in her car and starts the engine.

I watch her drive away, then go back inside.

'Honestly, Alex.' My mother shakes her head.

'Honestly what?' I ask her.

'Letting that lovely girl go like that. I saw you looking at her. You like her, don't you?' She pauses. 'You have to seize moments, Alex. Haven't I taught you that?'

I say nothing. But there isn't really anything to say. If I had seized the moment, told Bee I wanted to see her again, with my mother to look after, with Bee flying back to Majorca, there's no point. 'It's getting late, Mum.'

'Midnight is not late,' she says waspishly.

* * *

As I lie in bed, my mind is restless with thoughts, of my mother on stage. Of the crowd who came to see the band play. Of Cassandra turning up, her coldness towards her daughter, and not for the first time, realising how lucky I am.

The question lingers in my mind. Does Bee have Luke's eyes, or are they Kevin's? But it doesn't matter. As I think of Bee flying back to Majorca in a few hours, I'm wide awake.

DEAR UNIVERSE

Today I don't really want to ask you anything. I want to say thank you. You did a good job. The gig was AMAZING!!

My dad looked happy. So did everyone. Except Bee's mum. But I don't think she knows how to be happy.

Actually, there is one thing I want to ask. It's about Bee. I know she wants to live with us, in Majorca. But I heard her say she has to get a visa and I think she's worried about it.

So this is my request. I don't mind not having a younger sister. I like the one I have.

Wonderful Universe, please do everything in your power so she can stay.

Thank you. Sending hearts and stars and unicorns.

Yours,

Mackenzie Friday

25

BEE

It's been a day of contrasts, of the unexpected. And it isn't over yet. When we get back to Kevin's, Luke opens the door. Scooping up a sleepy Mack, he carries her up to bed.

I go into the kitchen and pour myself a glass of wine just as Kevin comes in. Humming to himself, he looks the closest to happy I've ever seen. 'Can I ask you something?' I say tentatively.

'Ask away,' he says. 'Good. You found the wine. Might join you.' His good mood is bizarre.

'Did you have a thing with my mother?' I ask as he pours himself a glass of wine. 'Sandra?' The way he freezes gives him away. 'Fuck.' I stare at him. 'You did, didn't you?'

'Now just a moment.' Then he drops the bluster. Sitting down, he nods towards one of the chairs. 'Sit down a moment.'

I do as he says, silent as he goes on.

'It isn't what you're probably thinking,' he says. 'I thought your mother was the most exciting girl I'd ever met. She was beautiful – and full of life. I couldn't believe she was interested in me. Except she wasn't, of course. She liked Luke. From the start. I was just, er... I think I was a distraction. All a bit silly really. I should have seen through it. But as they say.' He pauses, adding more quietly. 'Love is blind.'

'You loved her?' I blink at him.

'Is it so surprising?' His eyes meet mine.

There's a question I have to ask. That I don't want to, but I have to know. 'Did you sleep with her?' I wait for him to deny it.

But his cheeks turn pink. 'Only once. I was the fallback.'

I get up. 'You had sex with my mother?' I say loudly. 'Does this happen to be around the same time she was sleeping with Luke?' I remember there was no mention of anyone else in her diary. But having found Luke's name, I'd stopped looking. 'You know what this means, don't you?' I say tearfully.

'What's going on?'

I turn to see Luke standing in the doorway.

Kevin stands up. 'I'll let Bee fill you in.' He looks deflated. 'I'm going to bed.'

Luke comes in and sits down, and I tell him what Alex said earlier, then what Kevin told me. 'Don't you see?' I gaze at Luke. 'I don't know which of you is my father.'

Luke shakes his head slowly. Then he picks up one of my hands. 'All I know is your eyes remind me of Mack's. I noticed it that first day.' He pauses, his eyes not leaving mine. 'But I've learned something over the years. It isn't so much about blood. It's about finding your tribe. And I know it was searching for answers that brought you into my life. But now you're here, whether I'm your father or not, I'd like it, very much, if you stayed.' Then he adds, 'Though, for the record, I'd also like to be your father.'

He gets up, comes over and envelops me in a hug.

'Even if you're not?' I say tearfully.

'Of course, it's up to you.' He's silent for a moment. 'But as far as I'm concerned, you are and always will be my daughter,' he says. Then he adds softly, 'I just wish Amanda could have met you.'

* * *

In bed, that night, I think back over the events of today. The gig and my mother turning up. Luke's affirmation that he wants me in his life; that from here on, Luke, Mack and I are our own little family.

I think of the time Alex and I have spent together. How nice he is. How bad the timing, meeting him now when I'm not staying.

Then I'm thinking of what Atlas said, about whatever happens along the way, we end up where we're meant to be. And that's my overriding feeling about what's going on right now. I just have to trust.

Suddenly I'm longing for Majorca's hills and clear sky. For the peace that's the opposite to the pace of life here. I close my eyes, thinking how in a few hours from now, we'll be on a plane taking us home, as I drift off to sleep.

I wake what feels like minutes later to Mack shaking my arm. 'Bee! Wake up! It's snowing!'

I get out of bed and go over to the window. Then hear myself gasp. The garden is covered in snow, as is the drive; large swirling flakes falling from the sky.

A strange feeling comes over me as I look at Mack. Wondering if she's thinking the same thing, that there's no way the airports will be open in this weather. That the Universe has conspired to prevent us leaving.

26

'Oh.' My mother sounds less than pleased.

Getting out of bed, I go to find her. 'Morning. Everything OK?'

'Not really.' Turning to look at me, there's a frown on her face. 'It's snowing.'

A strange feeling comes over me as I check the weather forecast on my phone. Then look at Gatwick flight arrivals and departures, my heart lifting as I read the airport is closed. I click onto the news, just to make sure and stare at the headline.

Heavy snowfall across the south-east of England has brought transportation to a standstill.

I look at my mother. 'You know what you said about seizing moments?' I pause. 'We need to get dressed.'

She looks at me. Then her eyes widen. 'Oh no,' she says.

But she isn't one to stand in the way of love, if that's what this is – or at least the tiniest, embryonic seeds of it.

'You're mad, Alex. You do know that, don't you? No one else is going out.'

After pulling on my clothes and boots, I pile blankets in the car, just in case we get stuck. And a shovel, because yes, it is that bad and there's a risk we might need it. But the car is four-wheel drive. I'm more than ready to put it to the test.

Of course, once we get going, the miles seem to become stretched out as I question the car, the weather, my sanity. The few cars that have braved the snow-covered roads are crawling at a snail-like pace, meaning what should take forty minutes takes three hours, my fear growing as we drive, that the weather will let up and the airport will open.

But it doesn't. Instead, we are blessed with the mother of all snowstorms. Never have a few miles felt so endless. When we at last turn into Kevin's drive, I breathe a sigh of relief.

'That wasn't very sensible,' my mother says. 'Oh look. There's Kevin.' Seeing him coming towards us, she gets out.

'What the devil are you doing here?' Kevin says. 'Didn't you look at the weather forecast before you set off?'

I nod. 'I did.' I notice Bee standing in the doorway. 'That's the only reason we came to be here.'

He looks at me as though I'm mad, which this morning, I probably am.

'Ridiculous,' my mother grumbles, Kevin-like, as she starts stomping towards the house, Kevin grabbing her arm in the nick of time as one of her feet go from under her.

Then suddenly Bee is standing next to the car. There are snowflakes in her hair and a wonderful light in her eyes as she smiles. Then I'm holding her, oblivious to the snow, the cold, to everyone standing in the doorway cheering us.

Pulling away, I gaze into her eyes. 'I couldn't let you go – without saying...'

Her eyes stare unblinking into mine. 'Saying what?'

I hesitate. 'I think I love you.' It comes out in a rush. 'I mean I don't think it. That sounds terrible. I do – love you, I mean. It's just that we've only known each other a short time. I didn't want you to think it's too much.' As I run out of words, I stand there feeling the biggest fool; waiting for her to laugh at me, or walk away.

But she doesn't. As a snowflake settles on her cheeks, I wipe it away. Then leaning towards me, she kisses me.

It's true. It doesn't matter how short a time we've known each other. That we haven't been on a handful of dates. That my life revolves around my mother's needs; that it's slightly bonkers and utterly unpredictable, because it's still staggeringly beautiful and I wouldn't have it any other way.

And sometimes, when you meet someone, you just know.

27

BEE

It's getting dark by the time Alex and I walk hand in hand to the pub. The snow has stopped falling and the temperature has dropped, the ground crunching underfoot as we walk; glistening under the street lamps.

Over a glass of mulled wine, we talk. Of course, I'm going back to Majorca when the airport opens, and Alex will stay in Brighton looking after his mother. In other words, we don't make plans. But we agree to stay in touch. To give us a chance. After all, when so much that's unexpected has happened in such a short time, who knows what life will bring our way.

Except Universe... If you're listening, I'd really like this man in my life.

'I can come and see you,' Alex suggests. 'If you think Luke won't mind.'

'I don't think he will.' I smile. 'I spoke to Kevin yesterday. He admitted he used to be in love with my mother. Quite sad really. I think she used him.' I pause. 'I talked to Luke about it. He said family is less about blood and more about finding your tribe.' I pause, thinking how Alex is part of my tribe. 'I really like that.'

'I'm sorry,' Alex says. 'I should never have said anything.'

'It's fine,' I say, smiling into his eyes. If I've learned anything over the last few weeks, it's to trust things will end up as they're meant to be.

* * *

'Is this what Christmas is like in England?' Mack is bouncing off the walls by the time we get back to Kevin's.

'No,' Alex says. 'It usually rains.'

'Kevin's making pizza,' Mack says excitedly. 'And while you were out, someone else turned up.'

I glance past her to see Kevin in the kitchen. Wearing an apron, he has an arm around none other than the mystery woman.

'They used to be married,' Mack whispers not too quietly.

I glance at Alex. So not such a secret any more.

'Where's your mum?' she asks. 'I nearly forgot. I've got something for her.'

'I think she's in the cellar – with your dad. She has this idea about writing a new song...'

'Wow.' A wondrous look crosses Mack's face as holding her notebook, she runs downstairs.

28

ALEX

A day later than planned, the airport opens again and Bee flies back to Majorca, with Luke and Mack.

'Has she gone?' my mother asks.

'Who, Bee?'

'Of course I mean Bee,' she says impatiently. 'I'd hardly be talking about anybody else.' She pauses, frowning. 'You know, it's a jolly good thing I had that fall,' she says.

I look at her. 'Why, exactly?'

'Well, if I hadn't, we'd never have bumped into Leo in the hospital. Or Kevin, come to that. Just think, Alex. We might never have got the band back together. And you wouldn't have met Bee.' She gives me an I-told-you-so kind of look.

I'm silent for a moment, considering that maybe she's right. It is in many ways, an extraordinary sequence of events that's unfolded. But more than anything, it's the timing that fell into place. If any one of us had been somewhere else, if it had happened three months earlier or later, we might never have been able to do this.

'So many coincidences,' she says.

'Maybe,' I say. But after what's happened, I'm not so sure about coincidences. It seems to me to be more about synchronicity. The way I see it, some of our paths are inter-twined long before we realise they are, only as our lives play out, bringing us together with those of us we are meant to share our journey with.

And with that, I put the kettle on.

'Cup of tea?' I ask my mother.

29

BEE

Back in Majorca, the next month passes in a whirl. The first sunny weekend, Mack and I go on our long-awaited camping trip – this time, with a tent and sleeping bags. And a torch. And a picnic. We spend a magical night gazing at the stars, talking about Amanda. So much so, it's as though she's there with us. Though I have a feeling, maybe she was.

Meanwhile, to further my education in olive production, I approach a couple of local farmers. They're a little reticent at first, but when they see the state of Luke's olive grove, soon realise we're years away from posing any serious competition. Taken under their wing, my knowledge grows almost exponentially.

Meanwhile, Augusta's friend's daughter offers me six months' work helping her promote her glamping site. I'm grateful, but the money still falls far short of the income required for my visa.

However, a few days after getting back, I speak to Geneva.

'Seems I rather shot myself in the foot when we lost you,' she says. 'I don't suppose you'd consider coming back? You'd have a pay rise. And the investor has gone. We were a mismatch. I can't believe I didn't see it before.'

I'm shocked. 'What will you do without him? The arboretum needed his money,' I remind her.

'It was hypocrisy,' she says briskly. 'Our philosophy stems from preserving the natural world, while his business is hell-bent on destroying it. We're talking with a new sponsor. It came out of a radio show, actually.' She sounds distracted. 'Most odd. A young man came to see me about starting a dedicated day for people with dementia. It was mentioned on the radio. Next thing, I had a phone call from a wealthy man whose sister has it. Believe it or not, he has a collection of rare trees. Anyway, the long and short of it is, he wants to support us. Quite extraordinary how things work out.'

I'm smiling to myself. It is... yet it isn't. It's simply the mysterious workings of the Universe. 'This young man you're talking about. That's Alex, isn't it?'

'How do you know that?' She pauses. Then she says, 'But of course you know. It was him who suggested I should call you. But that isn't the only reason. I was already going to. Will you think about the job, Bee?'

I think about it – for all of ten seconds, because I already know the answer. My heart is here, in Majorca, with Luke and Mack. 'Thank you, Geneva. I really appreciate it. I have other plans at the moment, but if anything changes, can I let you know?' I hesitate. 'Although... there may be something I can do to help you.'

We hash out a remote job for me, working online on marketing and social media for the arboretum. I can do it standing on my head – it isn't that different to my old job, other than me not working on reception there. But it's part time, and even combining my income streams, it still isn't enough to satisfy the visa requirements.

'So ridiculous,' Augusta says. 'You have family here. You're working to regenerate an important area of our landscape. There should be exceptions.'

I shake my head. 'There are strict rules on family.' I've searched exhaustively for a loophole. 'I'm too old, Augusta. I'm not a dependant.'

Luke refuses to give up hope. 'We'll worry about it in the New Year,' he says.

We're both aware, that by then, unless my income increases, my ninety days in Spain will be running out. But my first Christmas here is fast approaching and I allow myself to be drawn into Mack's whirlwind of excitement.

One afternoon, Luke comes home with a Christmas tree, albeit a slightly unconventional one.

'It's beautiful,' I say, taking in the robust, potted olive tree.

'I thought in the New Year, we could have a ceremonial planting,' he says proudly. 'To mark the regeneration of the olive grove.'

Mack gets out the family decorations and together, the three of us adorn it. It's a moment of bittersweetness; all of us thinking of Amanda; how this time last year, neither of them could have imagined she wouldn't be here.

Mack and I go Christmas shopping together in Palma. The shops windows are beautifully decorated, the streets lit. But as we search for presents, for the first year ever, the glitzy clothes and shoes have lost their allure. Well, except for a scarf my inner magpie can't resist, of softest pale grey through which a silver strand glimmers.

Then, out of the blue as these things sometimes are, something miraculous happens. I'm approached by an eco-tourism company, who offer me a part-time job. In addition to my other incomes, it pays just enough to meet the visa requirements.

Dazed, I go to tell Luke. For a moment he just stands there. Then a smile spreads across his face. 'This is great!' Embracing me in a hug, he's still hugging me as Mack comes in.

She stares at us. 'What is? What's happened?'

Suddenly I feel emotional. 'I'm staying, Mack. I can get a visa.'

Her eyes widen. 'Wow,' she breathes. Then her face lights up as she hurls herself into my arms. 'I knew it would happen. I asked the Universe. Didn't I tell you?'

'Don't you see? This changes everything. We can properly start on the olive grove. Maybe we should do up the rest of the house.' Luke sounds almost as excited as Mack. 'I'll ask my lawyer friend to help with the visa paperwork!' As he hugs me and Mack, it feels as though my heart will burst.

I become aware of the strangest sensation taking me over; the lifting of a weight I hadn't known was there. And as I let it go, a new feeling creeps over me. One of hope. Joy. And freedom. Taking Luke's hand, then Mack's in the other, the three of us dance madly around the Christmas olive tree, as I send a silent message from my heart out to the Universe.

Thank you.

* * *

The first person I share the good news with is Alex.

He's suitably over the moon for me. 'I'm thrilled, Bee. I know what this means to you.'

'It's changed my life,' I say more soberly. 'In the best way.' Then I say, 'I miss you.'

'I miss you, too,' he says. 'Sorry, I'm going to have to go. My mother's trying to put the kettle on.'

To anyone else, it's the lamest of excuses, but this is Rachel we're talking about. A shaky hand, a kettle of boiling water, potentially amount to a situation that doesn't bear thinking about. Not being able to see Alex casts the only shadow on my world. But I know I have so much to be grateful for. Pinning on a smile, I go to find Mack.

* * *

Christmas Eve dawns. A beautiful mild, blue-sky day. Getting out of bed, I pad into the kitchen in my pyjamas. To my surprise, Luke is up and about, which is just as well, because out of the blue, a delivery turns up. Not just a regular delivery. After manhandling an enormous box into the villa, assisted by Luke, it turns out to be an electronic keyboard.

Mack stares at it, goggle-eyed. 'This is so amazing.'

Luke looks perplexed. 'I didn't order a piano. I don't even need one. I have one downstairs.' He unfolds the delivery note, frowning as he reads it, before looking up, a slightly stunned expression on his face. 'Kevin sent it.'

As he goes outside to call Kevin, Mack stares at me. 'It's the Universe,' she says with awe in her voice. 'I remember now. I asked if I couldn't have a sister, if Dad could have a new piano.'

'It was Kevin. He said he thought I could use something more portable.' Luke still looks dazed when he comes back in. Then he glances at his watch. 'I have to go out. A bit of last-minute shopping. Should have done it before, shouldn't I?'

He kisses my forehead – a gesture that's unfamiliar. Then he goes to the sofa where Mack is sprawled and does the same to her. As I make a cup of coffee, I hear his car drive away and I turn to Mack.

'Enough of this lying around,' I say sternly, before winking at her. 'You and I have a feast to prepare.'

But she doesn't move. 'I've been thinking,' she says slowly.

'Uh-oh.' I'm starting to learn the way her mind works. 'What about?'

'Well, we have all this space here.' Sitting up, she looks thoughtful. 'I mean, there's the olive grove and all the land... And now Dad has this new keyboard... Remember that idea I had? It was ages ago – about organising a festival.' She watches me, as if gauging my response.

'Actually, I do,' I say cautiously, already guessing what's coming.

'I have it all planned, Bee. Seriously. We could decorate the trees. And we'll have a stage and fairy lights, and Dad's band can play the music!' Suddenly looking excited, she leaps to her feet. 'It would be so cool!' she says, gazing at me. 'I know Dad will probably say it's impossible.' She rolls her eyes. 'But I can see it. In here.' She points at her head. 'We have to make him realise we can do it, don't we?'

And for a moment, I can picture it, too. But a festival takes some organising. 'I love the idea, but I think we should talk to your – our – dad.' I still can't get used to Luke being my dad, too.

Mack chatters on about her plans – it seems she's thought it all out. No doubt she's already asked the Universe, in which case, I wouldn't mind betting it will happen. But right now, it's Christmas Eve and we have a meal to prepare. There are four of us tomorrow – Augusta is joining us. And there will be spare roast potatoes for Cato, as Mack insists there should be. But in fact, there's enough food for twice as many people, which as it turns out is just as well, because there's one more surprise in store. When Luke returns, he isn't alone.

Alex is with him.

* * *

And so, it turns out to be the most perfect Christmas ever. Of course, there are quiet moments; Amanda is on everyone's minds. But even so, it feels like a proper family Christmas, with the woman who saved me that day I arrived at the airport with nowhere to go; with the little half-sister I love with all my heart. My estranged father who isn't estranged any more. And with the man I have a feeling is going to be the next important person in my life. It turns out Rachel is spending a few days with her sister, Lorna, meaning Alex was free to come here.

My mother calls briefly.

'Merry Christmas, Bethany.' She pauses. 'I've sent some money to your bank account. I thought it might come in useful.'

'Thanks, Mum. That's really kind. Merry Christmas.'

Usually she sends me a modest ten or twenty pounds. But it turns out it's quite a lot of money – five hundred pounds to be precise, which with my dwindling funds, will indeed be useful.

That evening, I sit with Alex on the terrace, gazing at a sky that's glittering with stars. 'I didn't know that Christmas could be like this.' I lean my head against his shoulder.

'It's been the best day,' he says softly. 'Did you know that Kevin made a massive donation to the arboretum? A Christmas present, was how he put it. To cover the dementia days.'

'No.' I'm astonished. But it gets more surprising.

'He and his ex-wife are back together again. She heard Miles's interview with my mother, and then... after hearing

Kevin talking at the gig too, it seems being in the band again brought back the Kevin she fell in love with.'

Life is astonishing. And it changes. Goes on changing. But if it didn't, we'd all stay the same. We'd miss out on so much. And I've learned, too, that after the darkest, most challenging times, there can be magical days, just like this one.

It seems Alex feels the same. Turning towards me, he pulls me close. As he kisses me, I have this feeling deep inside I've never had before.

I'm exactly where I'm meant to be.

Nine Months Later

As I embrace my new life, in a flow of what feel like unstoppable synchronicities, one things leads to another.

And OK. So it isn't a festival as such...

'We don't need caterers, Mack. It's just a party. There aren't going to be many people here,' Luke says.

She gives him a look that suggests he hasn't thought this through. 'Dad, you don't know that.'

'I do,' he says firmly. 'It's just the band coming over – and a few friends from the village. That's all.' He glances at his watch. 'They should be getting on the plane around now. I just hope Rachel copes with the journey.'

He's talking about the band. 'Alex has plenty of help,' I remind him. And it's true. Kevin and his no-longer ex-wife, Atlas and Miles are all booked on the same flight, as is Rachel's sister, Lorna. As well, the airline has been notified. In short, we've done all we can to make it easier for her and Alex.

'She will be fine,' Mack says knowingly, from which I take to mean she's already asked the Universe to keep an eye on her.

And as it happens, it's one of Rachel's good days and she takes the journey in her stride, arriving at the villa calm and unruffled, almost as though she's popped next door for a cup of coffee.

'Goodness,' she says, looking around. 'Rather lovely, isn't it?'

* * *

We spend a leisurely couple of days in the grounds of the villa.

'Where's the pool?' Rachel keeps asking, each time Alex gently reminding her it isn't finished yet.

Our feet have barely touched the ground this year. As well as starting work on the pool, there have been other changes – in the nurturing of the olive trees, to the house which now has five freshly decorated, comfortable bedrooms. But as the day of the party arrives, it's all hands on deck again and suddenly Luke goes into panic mode.

'There isn't enough food.' He looks flustered. 'And it's too late to do anything about it.'

'I know.' Augusta's voice comes from behind us. 'Which is exactly why Nico is here.' She nods towards the man standing beside her. 'He's a chef. You don't have to worry about a thing.'

Luke shakes his head. 'You don't understand. There isn't the food here to cook.'

Augusta raises her eyes towards the sky briefly. 'You can't honestly imagine I wouldn't have thought of that?' Behind her, someone's carrying boxes into the kitchen. 'By the way, there's a mobile bar on its way, too.'

Luke frowns. 'But I'm doing the bar.'

'You're hosting. I imagine you're also in charge of the music.' Augusta is matter-of-fact. 'Really, Luke. You can't do everything.'

With Rachel in the care of her sister and Kevin's ex-wife, Alex helps me put up the last of the lights, then arrange blankets and cushions under one of the trees for people to sit on, while on the stage, Luke's new keyboard is set up in anticipation.

'Leo would have loved this.' Alex is silent for a moment.

'He would, wouldn't he?' I think of the last time I saw Leo, at the gig in Brighton, of how happy he'd been seeing everyone together again, before six weeks later, he passed, peacefully, in his sleep.

'A year ago, I couldn't have imagined anything like this.' He stands there looking around as if he can't take it in. 'Everyone's been so helpful. They've changed Mum's life.' He pauses. 'They've changed mine, too.' Turning to me, he takes my hands and pulls me close. 'Especially you, Bee.'

A warm feeling fills me as I gaze into his eyes. He asks for so little, deserves so much, this lovely, selfless man. 'Ditto,' I say softly.

* * *

The sun is sinking lower, music drifting through the olive trees by the time people start arriving. Then in a true example of how community works around here, they're followed by more people, drawn by knowing what Luke and Mack have been through, by Rachel's story, by the knowledge that time is precious. That sometimes moments come along for all of us to treasure.

It's a night I will never forget – that I don't think any of us will. As the stars come out, the garden is lit by hundreds of fairy lights.

Mack comes over, a look I haven't seen before on her face. 'Hey, are you OK?' I ask.

Her eyes are wide as she nods. 'Look.' She points towards Luke. He's with a woman with long dark hair, eyes that sparkle as he says something to her. 'Do you think he likes her?'

'Maybe.' I put my arm around my little half-sister. 'Is it OK if he does?'

She looks up at me. 'I've been asking the Universe.' She pauses. 'I think this might be her.' She looks anxious for a moment. 'I just don't want him to get hurt again.'

'Don't worry, Mack,' I say gently. 'You need to stop worrying about him. Dad's doing OK.' I break off, realising what I've said.

Mack's eyes widen. 'You called him Dad,' she says.

'I did, didn't I?' A smile spreads across my face, as, leaning down, I kiss her cheek. 'Anyway, whatever this is...' I glance at Luke again. 'You know don't you? It will turn out the way it's meant to.'

The band starts to play and Mack runs off to find one of her friends. Gazing up at the sky, I wonder if somewhere out there, Amanda is looking down on us. I hope she is.

Beside me, Alex takes my hand. 'Shall we dance?'

I walk with him; soak up every detail. The grass under my bare feet. The soft, pine-scented Majorcan air. The moon rising above the trees, as we join everyone gathering in front of the stage, such as it is.

Then standing there, I take a moment. To remind myself how special this place is. But so are the people, while tonight the magic around us is tangible in a way it never has been before. But the magic is always there. It always was. It's just taken me till now to actually notice it.

* * *

MORE FROM DEBBIE HOWELLS

Another book from Debbie Howells, *The Making of Us*, is available to order now here:
https://mybook.to/MakingOfUsBackAd

ACKNOWLEDGEMENTS

I'd like to say a huge thank you to the brilliant team at Boldwood Books, in particular my editor, Isobel Akenhead, also to Nia, Claire, Niamh, Issy, Marcela, Wendy; to Sandra Ferguson for copyediting. You are all so wonderful to work with and thank you so much for everything you do, on the road to publication as well as after.

Huge gratitude as always, to my wonderful agent, Juliet Mushens and the Mushens Entertainment team. Thank you so much, for everything.

When I started writing this book, I had an idea about two people with very different lives whose paths kept crossing. This story is also about the joy music brings into our lives. It's about being brave. Risking leaving the familiar behind and taking a chance.

This book was also inspired by trying to portray the impact dementia has on so many people – both those who suffer from it and those who care for them. It's something that touches so many of our lives. For a while, I cared for a much-loved member of my family who had dementia. There were many challenges – not least because I was still trying to keep to a writing routine of sorts. It was also devastatingly sad, but I have an overwhelming feeling of gratitude that I was able to be there, and for what I learned throughout this time. And I learned so much... The way the most routine actions can become challenging, while dementia can change how people think, and perceive the world around them.

It makes it no less real, as I've tried to portray in this book. And this is the thing – because to them, it's their reality. But in a less extreme way, each of us sees the world the way we see it, unless we challenge ourselves to view it through someone else's eyes.

The characters I've written about are fictitious. But a note about The Rhythm Sheds, the band in the story, who were real, by the way! They were a vibrant, well-loved group who played in Sussex in the eighties. Chris Philps, their charismatic singer, sadly passed during the writing of this book.

Huge thanks also to my sisters and my family. I am so lucky to have you – and you know what this book means. Thanks also to my wonderful, supportive friends. To Dayzi for inspiring the gorgeous and sassy character of Mack! To Georgie and Tom – I love you to the moon and back. To Martin, ditto. Thank you for being there, and for being my rock.

And to you, my readers. Thank you from the bottom of my heart for reading my books. For loving them and sharing them. It means everything and I wouldn't be doing this without you. I hope you enjoy this one. xx

ABOUT THE AUTHOR

Debbie Howells is a *Sunday Times* bestseller, who is now fulfilling her dream of writing women's fiction with Boldwood. She has perviously worked as cabin crew, a flying instructor, and a wedding florist! Now living in the countryside with her partner and Bean the rescued cat, Debbie spends her time writing.

Sign up to Debbie Howells' mailing list for news, competitions and updates on future books.

Visit Debbie's website: www.debbiehowells.co.uk

Follow Debbie on social media:

facebook.com/debbie.howells.37
x.com/debbie__howells
instagram.com/_debbiehowells
bookbub.com/authors/debbie-howells
goodreads.com/debbiehowells

ALSO BY DEBBIE HOWELLS

The Life You Left Behind

The Girl I Used To Be

The Shape of Your Heart

It All Started With You

The Impossible Search for the Perfect Man

Time to Take a Chance

The Last Days of You and Me

The Making of Us

This Thing Called Love

Boldwood

Boldwood Books is an award-winning fiction publishing company seeking out the best stories from around the world.

Find out more at www.boldwoodbooks.com

Join our reader community for brilliant books, competitions and offers!

Follow us
@BoldwoodBooks
@TheBoldBookClub

Sign up to our weekly deals newsletter

https://bit.ly/BoldwoodBNewsletter